PRAISE *for* DAVID ANNANDALE

"Truly the stuff of legend – both fun and unnerving."

Forbes

"Annandale has a real talent for the cinematic and the strange."

Starburst

"Exhilarating, terrifying, and heart-wrenching. Annandale marries campfire horror with grimdark military sci-fi to yield a blood-curdling tale of consummate terror."

Grimdark Magazine

"An epic and grim story of destruction and the grinding engines of war."

Heresy Online

"Huge scope and scale, packed with fun, exciting action, heroes you can root for, and an emotional and inspiring climax."

Pop Culture Vulture

"Annandale's mastery of atmosphere and descriptive prose only ever seems to grow with each story he writes."

The Sci-]

CURSE
of HONOR

David Annandale

First published by Aconyte Books in 2020

ISBN 978 1 83908 017 3

Ebook ISBN 978 1 83908 018 0

Cover art by Nathan Elmer

Rokugan map by Francesca Baerald

Distributed in North America by Simon & Schuster Inc, New York, USA

Printed in the United States of America

9 8 7 6 5 4 3 2 1

ACONYTE BOOKS

An imprint of Asmodee Entertainment Ltd

Mercury House, Shipstones Business Centre

North Gate, Nottingham NG7 7FN, UK

aconytebooks.com // twitter.com/aconytebooks

For Margaux, always, and with joy.

Kaiu

Crab
Lands

Kuni

Hida

HIDA CASTLE

The Shadowlands

Earthquake Fish
Bay

Yasuki

Rokugan

CHAPTER 1

Above the mountain peaks, he saw winter closing in on them, and he knew that this day would be added to the litany of his failures.

Hida no Kakeguchi Haru had looked back north to check on the progress of the merchant caravan. The slope of the path he had chosen through the Twilight Mountains was steep here, and the train of wagons was stretching out more than he would like as the horses struggled to pull their laden wagons uphill. At first, he was merely irritated. Everything about this journey was taking longer than he had planned, and every day that passed drew his return to Striking Dawn Castle shamefully further from what he had promised.

Then he saw the clouds. Heavy, shimmering silver-gray with threat, they were a wave breaking over the mountains. Haru had never seen the dividing line of the seasons before, yet he knew that was what he was witnessing now. Those clouds were drawing a barrier between the earth and the sky. When it passed over his head, it would seal away the light and warmth of the sun. And white ruin would fall through the air. Already, the wind from the north was blowing colder. It pried at the seams of Haru's armor. He could feel it at the back of his neck, gnawing. Soon it would be numbing.

A mass of cloud billowed slowly forward, the prow of a ship spreading the wake of cold. It was the shape of inevitability. It was the announcement of his failure.

The caravan had left the Summerlands over a week ago. There was still the best part of a day's march to Striking Dawn. A day's march in clement weather. And it was already the hour of the horse.

"Will we reach Striking Dawn before the storm arrives, Lieutenant Haru?" Chen, the head merchant, had seen the clouds too. Sitting on his wagon, his fingers tight around the reins, the gray-haired man was looking at Haru with that expression the merchant thought was properly reserved, but radiated fear and need. The man disgusted Haru. It was a constant effort to keep his contempt submerged. The mere sound of Chen's voice, rough as if he perpetually needed to clear his throat, and with a timbre stopping a hair's breadth from being a whine, was exhausting.

"We will arrive safely at Striking Dawn," Haru said. He disliked speaking to someone of so low a station. To address Chen was to stoop, and there had been too much stooping in Haru's life. Yet reassuring Chen was a necessary evil. The man was nervous. Unchecked, the anxiety of the caravan's leader would spread. What Haru needed more than anything else was for everyone to focus on making the best speed possible. "You should have no doubt about the successful outcome of this journey," he said.

Chen's eyes widened as he realized the insult he had unintentionally given. "I am sure you are correct, Lieutenant Haru," he said. "Please excuse the clumsiness of my question. I did not mean to imply doubt."

Haru gave the other man a long stare, then turned away. He had made his point. Now Chen would be more scared of him than of the approaching winter. For a while, at any rate. That would contain the possibility of panic.

As long as everyone else faced forward and did not look at what was coming.

Ishiko rode up beside him. She was the most veteran guard in the escort squad Haru commanded. Her armor was less burnished than his. It showed the tolls of the road more clearly. Haru's armor gleamed because of the care he gave it upon rising every morning. He had fought in almost as many battles as Ishiko. Yet the ease with which she wore her armor, as if it were a second skin, as did Fujiki, Hino and Ekei, the other bushi in the squad, had the effect of heightening Haru's insecurity. Ishiko was never insubordinate. She had never challenged his orders. And still, how often he had read judgment just beneath her neutral gaze, whether it was present or not.

"You saw, then?" Ishiko asked. She gave her head a subtle jerk in the direction of the clouds.

"I did," said Haru.

"The snow will hit us."

"I know. So we will march through the snow to Striking Dawn." He spoke, he thought, with the right degree of calm certainty. His anxiety diminished. Delay would be less significant than the achievement of bringing the last caravan home, not before the coming of winter, but *through* it. He pictured the arrival, and the sense of accomplishment he would feel. This was good. This was something he needed, and for more than his sense of self-worth. It would, he thought, improve his standing in his mother's eyes. As heir to Daimyō Akemi, he needed to do better to show he deserved to be. Perhaps then Barako might also look at him with favor. Maybe.

If he was honest, he wasn't sure which he hoped for more.

"We are approaching dangerous terrain," said Ishiko. "Crossing it in a snowstorm will be more than difficult."

Haru thought about what was ahead. Ishiko was right. The ridge they would soon reach was completely exposed. The hope of glory turned slippery in his grasp. He sighed. "This voyage has been cursed by ill luck," he said. Days of bad rain had sent torrents and rockfalls across the path of the caravan again and again. "One less flash flood, and we would already be at Striking Dawn. One less wall of debris."

"We have had our share of obstacles," Ishiko said.

What does that mean? Do you agree with me? Or is it that all of these events were predictable and I should have allowed for more time? Maybe I should have taken a different route? Too many possibilities. Maybe all were true. Or maybe Ishiko meant nothing more than what she said, and he was hearing the voices of his own doubts. He heard them often. They were loud enough at the best of times.

The rains were not my fault. We could not have gone faster. The storm is not my fault. It is the risk that attends the final caravan. This could have happened to anyone. It could have happened to Ochiba.

Only it had not happened to the commander of Striking Dawn's forces. It was happening to him. *What matters is what I do now.*

"We could take shelter here," Ishiko suggested. They were in a wide pass. The mountainside to the right was only a few hundred yards away, and there were numerous overhangs. They would provide protection from the snow, and some relief from the wind.

"Nothing big enough for the whole caravan,' said Haru. "We'll be very spread out." He shook his head. "I don't want to be trapped here."

"You think there will be enough snow to block the pass?"

"Not this one. There are much narrower ones ahead. And we have no way of knowing how long the storm will last."

"We have supplies aplenty, if it comes to that. We have enough for many days."

The thought of a prolonged siege by the storm was not a comforting one. "For food, yes," Haru said. "But for heat? For how long?" There were so many ways a snowstorm at these altitudes could be lethal. Cold was the first of them. "I will not risk it. We push on."

This caravan is all that my mother will entrust to me. She has made me a bodyguard to merchants, and how can I blame her? I deserve no better. If I cannot even complete this task?

What would Barako think if she saw us now? The thought of Striking Dawn's other lieutenant of the Kakeguchi was too piercingly painful. He pushed it away.

I will not fail. I must not.

"Where do you plan to stop for the night?" Ishiko asked.

Haru's original intention for the day had been to keep going as long as possible. He had hoped to reach Striking Dawn without having to spend another night in the mountains. He had known that would mean continuing to travel after sunset. He had hoped to make up enough time that it would not be necessary to travel long in the dark.

You hoped. Did you really think it was possible?

I didn't think. Not the way I should have. And here we are.

Where do we stop for the night? He had no good answer. He could not even guess how long they had before snow made further travel impossible. "We keep going," he said, conscious that he was repeating himself. He looked straight ahead as he spoke, as if he could already see their goal. "We keep going for as long as we can. The further we can get, the better." The words sounded meaningless even to him. It did not matter how firmly he spoke. His confidence was a hollow shell.

Ishiko said nothing. She nodded. He had issued his commands, and that was an end to it.

Haru almost asked her what she would do instead. Pride stopped him.

They rode on in silence.

As the hour of the goat began, the caravan reached the top of the pass and started across a long ridge. It rose gradually and then descended, tracing an arc a few miles long before the route entered another pass. The ridge was wide enough for three to ride abreast with confidence in clement weather. Haru ordered a single file. The wind was growing stronger, and the slope to both sides of the ridgeline was steep.

Overhead, the clouds had arrived. They hid the sky behind a shield of heavy gray. Haru glared at them, silently commanding them to hold off, demanding that winter delay one more day.

In answer, the clouds mocked him. Half an hour after the last pack horse had left the comparative shelter of the pass, the first snowflakes fell.

They were few at first, innocuous in their gentle fall, tiny and light, dancing on the wind, uninterested in ever touching the ground. They landed one at a time on Haru's arm, lingering a bit, then melting away. They posed no threat. They were barely visible.

The escalation happened gradually. The flakes became more numerous and more insistent. The wind picked up. Its gusts turned into blows. Haru fought against them to remain steady in the saddle as the buffeting increased. The snow no longer danced on the wind. It flew against Haru's armor with a purpose. Though the wind was from the north, mercifully blowing against the back of the caravan, errant gusts hurled the snow into his face with stinging force. Flakes caught in his eyelashes. He wiped them away brusquely, cursing under his breath as they blurred his vision.

"It's snowing," said Chen.

"Merchant," Haru snapped, "if you have nothing to say except to point out the obvious, you will be silent."

Chen shrank from the reprimand. He huddled in on himself, wrapped in a cloak. He looked as if he hoped he could disappear behind Ishiko.

The rocky ground began to change from gray to white.

Midway across the ridge, there was enough snow for the horses and wagons to leave prints.

Haru glanced back at Ishiko. She was concentrating on the road ahead, checking behind at the caravan periodically.

"We will manage this," he said, though she had asked nothing.

"We are," she agreed.

For now, Haru thought. *That's what you're thinking, isn't it?*

The wind picked up again. What seemed like a gust hit, and kept hitting. Haru looked back in time to see one of the merchants leading a pack horse slip and fall. Ekei was close by, and rode up, staying close until the man had regained his footing.

"The visibility will be a problem before long," Ishiko said.

"I know." The pass they had left behind was a blurry vagueness in the distance. The peaks ahead were the same. To the left and right, the vista was disappearing into limbo. It would take the best part of an hour at least, if the snow did not descend much harder, before the caravan could reach the next pass.

If the snowfall did not grow worse. If it did, and it became impossible to see where they were walking, they would be trapped in the open.

"We should go faster," Haru said.

"I do not think we can. It has been a long march without a rest already. The heimin on foot could not go faster even if it were not snowing."

Haru almost insisted on driving the merchants harder. *They will be worse off if we do not go faster.* The hope of reaching Striking Dawn was fading with every heartbeat. There were no good outcomes to the day now. Being caught on the ridge was the worst of the bad ones, though.

Whose fault is that? You could have stopped when Ishiko suggested finding shelter.

Too late for that. We must go on, and we must get out of the open. There are no choices. It is that or death.

"No faster," Haru agreed, "but no slower. No pausing. Not until we are off this ridge."

Despite his words, he urged his horse forward. If he could only coax a little bit more speed out of the merchants. Not enough to be dangerous, just enough to get to the next pass. Chen would make sure he kept up if he saw Haru pulling ahead, and the other merchants would do the same.

And then? If we reach the pass, what then?

He had no answer. He pushed the question from his mind. The snow forced him to concentrate on the present moment. He had enough to think about to make sure he, and everyone in his charge, stayed on the disappearing trail.

The light began to fail. The storm declared its intentions, and sank its claws into the mountains. The clouds descended, obscuring the mountaintops. The wind howled. The wind shrieked. The snow came down in blankets. The pass seemed to recede further and further from view. There was less and less of the world around Haru. There was only gray instead, streaked with the implacable white and inhabited by vague, shadowy masses that might not be real any longer. He could still see where he was going, though he had to squint against the driving flakes. He could barely make out the rear of the caravan, though.

"We will have to stop soon," Ishiko said, "or we will walk off into air."

"If we stop here, we die," said Haru. *Faster. Still a bit faster. We must be almost there.*

Haru tried to make out the pass. The curtains of snow hid it from him. And then someone cried out.

He whirled. Fifty yards back, a pack horse had slipped and fallen. It whinnied in panic, its legs flailing. It began to slide down the slope. The merchant guiding it was tangled in the lead rope and fell too. The animal dragged him with it towards the drop.

Eikei and Hino were close. They leapt off their horses and ran to help. Hino grabbed the merchant and hauled back, digging her heels into the deepening snow. Eikei grabbed for the reins, seeking to free the man's legs.

The ridge was too narrow to ride past the wagons, so Haru and Ishiko leapt from their mounts and ran hard. Already, the snow was deep enough to slow them down. Haru was wary of his footing, horribly conscious of how long it would take to reach the position of the accident.

The horse kicked wildly. A hoof struck Eikei in his chest plate. He fell. He and the horse slid further down, dragging the merchant with them. Hino could not hold him. She began to slip too.

CHAPTER 2

Grimacing into the wind, Haru sprinted. The merchant, Eikei and Hino were moments away from plunging off the ridgeback. Haru saw the scale of his failure expand. He could not deliver the caravan to Striking Dawn on time. He could not reach the castle before winter. His charges were not in shelter, and the storm was upon them. And now to lose fellow bushi…

Not like this. Not like this. Not like this.

He tore down the slope, heedless now of the danger to himself. Eikei was unconscious. The horse was whinnying in terror. Hino cried out from the pain of the effort to slow their descent, but she held on.

Haru drew his katana, and launched himself over the last few yards. With one hand, he grabbed Eikei's left arm by the leather plating of his ashigaru armor. With his other hand, he cut the reins.

The horse disappeared over the edge, screaming. Eikei's momentum pulled him forward. Haru dug his heels into the slope. Snow built up against his boots. He stabbed his blade into the ground, a desperate anchor. He finally came to a stop.

Eikei's legs dangled over the precipice. The weight was pulling Haru's arm from its socket. He couldn't move. If he tried, he would lose his grip, or he would fall with Eikei. His grip was uncertain. His fingers began to cramp.

Then Ishiko and Hino scrambled to his side and took hold of Eikei. Together, they pulled him back up. They carried Eikei to the front of the caravan and placed him in Chen's wagon.

The winds were blowing even stronger. All trace of the mountains and the pass ahead had vanished. From this end of the caravan, Haru could not see the rear.

"What is going to happen to us?" Chen asked. "What will we do? What will we do?" Fear was making him disrespectful.

Murmurs and sobs came from the wagon behind. The wind was too loud to hear much else. Haru did not have to. The mood of the caravan was clear.

Hino turned to him, waiting for his orders before heading back down the line.

"Stop your sniveling!" Haru snapped at Chen. "Do you have no honor at all?"

"It is so cold. We can't see."

"This is snow. It is a snowstorm. It is not the coming of darkness from the Shadowlands."

"But what do we do?"

"We do what we have been doing. We move forward. Would you prefer to stay? You can stay and die, if you like. That would rid me of you, at least."

Chen shook his head. "Please forgive me, Lieutenant Haru," he said, remembering his place.

Haru ignored him. To Hino, he said, "Tell Fujiki we keep going." The last of Haru's bushi was bringing up the rear of the caravan. "We should be less than a mile from the pass."

The caravan moved on. Though the pass had disappeared behind the curtain of falling snow, Haru could still see the ridge for several yards ahead. The way forward was clear, though it seemed to be a way forward into nothingness. The wind hammered at his back. Snow drove against his armor. It fell almost horizontally. Gusts hurled it into spiral dances. The day darkened to twilight.

The pace of the caravan slowed to a crawl as the horses struggled to pull the carts through the deepening snow. Haru lost track of time. Every moment was the same, just his horse plodding on in the endless whiteness, nothing to see except the same narrow stretch of ground. The whiteness grew stronger and stronger. Wind and snow were one and the same, smothering light and hope. The perpetual strain of marching forward was hypnotic. The whiteness, a whiteness that brought darkness with it, closed in, a fist, a curse, a mockery.

I am winter, the wind seemed to howl. *You and your dreams of a restored reputation are less than nothing. I will show you. I bring nothing, and to nothing I will cast you.*

The cold gnawed at him, a dog with a bone. It pried open the seams of his armor. It sank through his skin. It congealed his blood. It nestled into his core and made itself a den. It would never leave. He shrank in on himself, huddling tighter for a warmth that was no longer there.

"We have to stop," said Ishiko.

Haru blinked, startled out of his trance of effort. He brought his horse to a halt. The creaking of the wheels behind him had ceased.

"It's too dangerous," said Ishiko.

Haru's attention had so narrowed, he had been focused only on the next few feet of snow before him. He had not realized that was now all he could see. He suppressed a shudder. Ishiko was right about the danger. It would be easy now to wander off the ridge, and then fall down the slope into the abyss. Why was he still riding? What was he thinking?

He dismounted and peered through the whiteness, searching for some hint of landscape, the slightest phantom of a mountain. There was nothing. The world had deserted him. There was only the presence of the void. The terrible drop waited, hungry, for Haru and his charges. The ground on which he stood was suddenly a tiny island, and a step in any direction would be fatal. He struggled against vertigo and the pull of the fall.

Lead them to me. Embrace the end. You can do nothing else.

Haru shook his head, hard, pushing away the fancies of despair. Yes, Ishiko was right. They had to stop. Only they must not.

"We cannot stay here," he said. "That is certain death."

"So is walking this ridge blind."

"I agree. So we must counter the risk of our march." He saw what he had to do. A wave of giddiness passed through him. He bit his tongue to hold back mad laughter, and the sensation of being *glad* that death hovered close to the caravan, because he knew how to save everyone. He did not know how to reach Striking Dawn safely. He did not even know how to survive the day. But he saw the way out of the present moment.

That sufficed for him. It would be a victory, and he would show that he was capable of leadership. It would be a spark of light in the darkness of failure, and it would warm him.

"Gather rope," Haru said to Ishiko. "If there is not enough rope, tie cloths together. Anything to make tethers so that every member of the caravan is fastened to another. We will move forward as one, carefully, one step at a time. I will lead. If any one of us steps wrong and falls, the others will hold fast.

And then what?

That was the question Ishiko did not ask. She accepted his command and went to work.

And then what?

The words were Haru's curse upon himself. He hurried to put his plan into effect, trying to outrun the question.

Fingers clumsy with cold, it took more than an hour to finish tying the carts together. No one rode now, and the merchants fastened one wrist to the animal or wagon they trudged beside. It would work, Haru thought. The caravan had the strength of unity now. A single person could make a mistake. They would be safe, and the caravan would be alerted to the danger.

By the time they were ready to move again, the cold was ferocious. When he faced into the wind, Haru experienced the tempest as a pure, sharp pain. His skin turned numb, but the pain did not diminish. The snow was knee-deep, turning every step into a heroic effort.

"We follow in your footsteps, Lieutenant Haru," Ishiko said.

Haru grunted, this time sure he perceived her other meaning: *Do not walk us off a cliff.* He started forward. *Lead them. Lead them well. They are following in your footsteps. Show them that you deserve their faith.*

The progress was agonizingly slow. Haru thought carefully before each step. Behind him, a trail formed, growing more certain and easier to walk as his followers marched through it, packing down the snow. For him, though, there was only the white. The blinding white, the stinging white, the mesmerizing white that erased the difference between ground and air. He had no way of knowing, before he set a foot down, if he was still going in the right direction. All he had was hope, and precious little of it.

He struggled on. Ishiko was not much more than a periodic tug on the rope around his waist. When he looked back, the blast of the wind and the sting of the snow were so strong, he could barely see her. And Chen was a vague, stumbling shape. The rest of the caravan was a mere shadow, vanishing in the whiteness.

He would have to order torches to be lit very soon. He hoped they would reach the pass while there was still light enough to walk without them. Without shelter, the storm would smother any open fire. He was not sure there were enough lanterns on hand to show the way for the entire caravan.

Show the way! Show what way?

Onward, slowly, onward into numbness and cold and blindness and the end of day. Haru was alone on the ridge, alone in the howling and the white, the white, the white. And he was glad he was alone. He wanted to be alone. The closer the ultimate failure of death loomed, the more he wished to seal himself away from the caravan. But even with his charges reduced to less than the traces of ghosts, he felt the weight of silent judgment. It came from Ishiko, and Hino, and Fujiki. It came from Chen and his people, though they had no right to judge him. No one had said a word, and there were no faces for him to see. It did not matter. He could feel the judgment. It sat heavily on his shoulders. It forced his feet deeper into the snow, and made it that much harder to lift his legs to take another step.

Soon the day would end. Soon the darkness would come, and they would not be able to move at all. Death would come, and when it did, it would strip away more than the last of his reputation. It would destroy his last chance to be the warrior and the succor he should be for his family. He would journey to Meido with nothing to show for his life but shame. He held his rank of lieutenant only because he was heir to the daimyō. His performance on the battlefield was mediocre at best. Shameful at worst. He was his own harshest judge in that regard. No one had accused him of being responsible for the death of his father ten years earlier, when the Kakeguchi had repelled an assault on the Wall. But he knew. His strategy had been poor, his position had been overwhelmed by goblins, and his father, Genichi, had overstretched his own forces in rushing to his aid.

No, no one had blamed him. But in every engagement

since, his contingent was either in reserve, or acting in support of an action led by Ochiba, the captain of the guard at Striking Dawn, or by Lieutenant Barako. It was as if Akemi had ordered them to act as his battlefield nursemaids for the rest of his life.

The worst part of it was that he was grateful.

The light became more and more dim. Once, twice, three times, and then four, he wandered off the ridge in spite of his care and deliberate pace. The snow gave way beneath him, and he started to slide. Ishiko caught him, and when, once, she started to slip too, the solid mass of Chen's wagon held her back. Haru was able to scramble back up to safety, the wisdom of his plan justified, yet his dignity even further eroded.

He had wrapped a scarf around his helmet, but it did not prevent ice from building up on his eyelashes, threatening to freeze his eyes shut. He kept having to rub his face to break the ice, and then the cold would make his eyes water, and the process would start over again. He was trapped in an eternal cycle of repetitive, painful, pointless effort. Perhaps he had already died. Perhaps this was what had been awaiting him in Meido.

The sound of the wind changed. The snow eddies ahead became more violent. He squinted, struggling to see through the billowing, bellowing curtains of the storm, and he saw it. A mountain face was close on the left. And so was another on the right.

They had reached the pass.

"We are there!" He had to shout for Ishiko to hear. He wanted to laugh in the giddiness of victory. He had to remind himself this was no victory. They were still miles and miles from Striking Dawn. The caravan had escaped the exposure of the ridge. That was all.

Even so, he grinned with fierce relief. He claimed victory over the danger of a single moment. It was satisfying enough.

Were those grateful shouts he heard? Or just his imagination shaping the sound of the wind into what he wanted to hear. He decided there were shouts. He would not be the only one to seize onto the mirage of safety.

He walked more quickly, struggling at first against the pull of the rope until, slowly, the rest of his samurai and the merchants walked faster too, freed from the immediate terror of falling off a cliff.

"To the right," he called to Ishiko. The pass was in a sharp cleft between the mountains. The bottom of the pass was a treacherous gorge, but the path was on a wide platform of even ground extending out of the mountain on the west. To Haru's left, though he could not see it, he knew there was the sharp drop into the gorge. But to the right, the ground was level, and then encountered a vertical cliff wall. With the mountain at their side they would have a faithful guide through the pass.

And then what?

He had a few minutes before he had to think about that question again. He banished it from his thoughts.

In the pass, the wind blew stronger, screaming as if at the prey that had escaped it on the open ridge. The snow was deeper too, already forming drifts closer to the rock face. The greater effort seemed a small price as the high, black wall came clearly into view. Haru approached until he could reach out and touch the granite. He still could not see forward more than a couple of yards, but there was no risk of disaster for the time being.

He would leave the ropes attached, though. If anyone fell too far behind the rest of the caravan, or wandered off at all from the path, they could easily be lost. If the snowfall became much worse, the danger would be a certainty.

"What are your orders, Lieutenant Haru?" Ishiko asked.

And then what? She was forcing him to think about more than the next footstep. He resented that, but she was right. She almost always was, and that was fortunate for him.

"Forward. Always forward." *For now.*

"I am grateful for your leadership," she said, her tone fully respectful and devoid of any trace of irony. "We are fortunate that you have a plan in place to deal with the exposed regions that lie ahead."

Of course, there were more ridges to come. He knew there were. He knew very well. But the need for a victory, for any kind of victory, had narrowed his attention to the present moment. It was as if he could no longer think clearly about the future. And he had to, or everyone would die. There was another ridge between here and Striking Dawn that was even longer than the one they had just left behind. By the time the caravan reached it, night would have fallen. It would be impossible to cross.

Haru realized he was still imagining returning to the castle without stopping. The fear of what seeking shelter for the night might mean had made him refuse to countenance the possibility.

Think this through. You must, or you fail in your duty.
I know. I know. We go no further. That is the truth.

"We must seek shelter here," Haru said. "We will wait for the morning, and hope the storm has abated enough for us to move on then." *And hope that the snow is not ten feet deep and trapping us in the pass.*

There was no shelter here. The cliff was sheer, unbroken. As he started forward again, Haru racked his memory about what lay ahead, trying to remember the precise shape of the mountain face. *You must know it. You've gone through this pass often enough.* His memory refused to give up the detail he had never had reason to notice before. He couldn't picture the cliffs any more than he could see them.

He almost asked Ishiko if she knew what was coming. He stopped himself. The question would be an admission that he did not know what he was doing, and her answer would make no difference. The wind was shrieking through the pass, seeking vengeance for the caravan's escape from the ridge. There was no choice but to go on. They had to keep moving until they found refuge, or they died.

Onward, and the drifts were deeper yet. Onward, and the light was failing, close to death. Haru tried to move faster, but the wagons kept getting stuck in the snow. Everyone was in the grip of exhaustion and cold. Haru was barely able to lift his legs. The wind carried the moans and weeping of the merchants to him, the chorus of his failure.

A deeper note entered the refrain, a low, long, sharp cracking. Then a rumble, a thunder that did not pass but only grew louder.

"Avalanche!" Haru shouted. "Hurry!"

The merchants took up his cry and repeated it down the length of the caravan.

It was impossible to tell where the avalanche was coming from. In the pass, the shouts of the mountains bounced off one another until directions were meaningless. The thunder rumbled from everywhere at once. If the snow was coming down on the caravan's position, everyone was doomed.

Haru plunged through the snow, praying that in another ten feet, or another ten feet, or another ten feet, he would find any kind of shelter. All he asked for was an overhang. Anything other than the vertical cliff.

The thunder of the avalanche built in a fearsome crescendo. The mountains roared their anger. They bellowed their announcement of his absolute failure. There was no shelter. And there was no hope.

Then the thunder faded. The wind shrieked to new heights, assaulted by the passage, swift and violent, of the snow. Where the avalanche fell, Haru could not see. All that mattered was that it did not fall here.

He pushed on. The caravan had been granted more time. He had another chance to save his charges. He struggled forward another ten feet, and then another ten feet, the wall of rock mercilessly featureless ahead of him, but visible for so short a distance that there was always the chance, just a bit further, just a little bit further, that they would find refuge.

There. *There.* Was that something different he saw? Did the rock turn in? Was that the dark line of cleft?

For just a moment, he was able to see almost a hundred

yards ahead before the veil of snow concealed the vision from him. It might have been an illusion.

It might not be, though.

Haru plowed through snow three feet deep. There *was* shelter there. There had to be. He willed it.

The cracking thunder came again, and the roar that followed, the snarl of a terrible beast. The clamor of echoes overwhelmed the song of the wind.

Haru did not have to see the avalanche to know that this time, there would be no mercy. "I see shelter!" he called. It did not matter if he really did or not. If he was right, they had hope. If he was wrong, no one would live to condemn his lie.

The roar, the roar, louder, louder. The onrush of white death.

He ran, hauling on the rope as if he could yank the entire caravan after him. His lungs were full of stones. Breathing was such agony he could not speak. The pains of fear and hope worse yet. He felt the tug of Ishiko racing too. There was no need to shout a warning. The entire caravan knew that chance had become the enemy. The merchants and their horses would be panicking. There was nowhere to run except for the dream of shelter, the dream that had vanished as soon as he had seen it.

Nowhere to run, but nothing to do except run.

Haru ran. He ran through the white darkness, until the roar descended on them all.

CHAPTER 3

The cries of the merchants filled the smothering dark. The lamentations were close by, but in the pitch black, Haru could not see the merchants. They were as invisible to him as he was to them. For a few moments, he could wrap himself in oblivion and not confront the cost and the scale of his failure. For a few moments, though it shamed him to admit this to himself, he could rest in the illusion of irresponsibility. In this void, there was nothing he had to do any longer.

"I am here, Lieutenant Haru," said Ishiko.

He had been named. The illusion was over. He was summoned to resume his duties.

"I am here," said Hino. "I have Ekei with me."

Silence from Fujiki.

"Give us some light," Haru commanded.

After much fumbling, Chen managed to get a lantern lit. From its glow, others spread as the surviving merchants found their lanterns, and the surroundings came into view.

The caravan was inside a deep cave. The entrance,

blocked by the avalanche, was about fifteen feet wide and high. Past the entrance, the ceiling went higher as the cave bored into the mountainside, until the cavern became a high split in the rock, as if struck by a monstrous ax. After the first fifty feet, the cave narrowed until it was a fissure no more than five feet wide that vanished into the heart of the mountain.

Haru took a breath and with his bushi began to take stock and to count the cost.

"A bit more than half the caravan remains," Ishiko summarized when they were done.

He nodded. The rest of the merchants were gone. So was Fujiki. No one said they were fortunate that the losses were not worse. The shame of what had been lost was too great.

Haru picked up a lantern and strode through the merchants to the entrance. He looked up at a solid wall of snow.

"We will not be leaving again in a hurry," said Ishiko.

"There is no need to," Haru answered. "We are safe from the storm here. We have food enough, and we can make all the water we need." They could survive in this cave almost indefinitely. "We will dig our way out, however long it takes. If the storm is done, we move on. If it is not, we wait it out. Divide these laborers into digging teams. One hour each. That will give them something to focus on." He turned and looked at the merchants. "We are safe," he said again, more loudly. "The danger is past. We will prepare a way out for when it is time for us to resume our journey." He chose his words carefully, making the snow seem like a useful tool instead of an impenetrable wall trapping them inside.

Haru and his bushi led the digging shifts. He wanted to set the example of industry, of the calm determination that would re-emphasize the lesson that there was nothing to fear.

This was what he told himself.

And it worked. It *was* the right decision. Haru took the first shift, using one of the spades in the caravan's supplies. He scarred the snow with the first cuts himself. The unblemished whiteness was an ominous sight. It was too final. He dug into the wall, and turned it back into mere snow. What lay ahead was a long, arduous task, not an impossibility. The merchants on his shift attacked the barrier with a will.

The wails that had come with the darkness ceased entirely. The merchants no longer mourned the lost. They were grateful to be among the survivors. And they were grateful also to their savior.

"Lieutenant Haru," said Chen as he dug into the snow and added to the pile behind him, "we are in your debt forever. Your foresight has preserved us."

Haru grunted. He kept working. He clenched his jaw shut to keep himself from lashing out at the merchant's sycophancy. *I do not deserve your thanks.*

"Lieutenant Haru…" Chen began again.

Be silent! "Save your breath for work," Haru said, coldly, but keeping his temper.

Chen's thanks grated. They shattered the wall of mindlessness that Haru sought to create through heavy labor.

Foresight. What a bitter joke that was. If Chen were not such a spineless creature, Haru would have suspected him of satire. It would be a pleasant thing, a *joyous* thing, to say that he had known the cave would be here, that this had been his goal all along. Instead, he had only luck or fate to thank. Both shamed him. He wasn't sure which made him more uneasy.

Chen kept quiet now, but it was too late. Haru attacked the snow as if it were his guilt given form. He sweated with effort. His muscles began to ache as he punished himself with the heaviest load he could take with each spadeful. Nothing he did let his mind rest.

He kept seeing Barako's face. She did not look on him, as he so often wished she would, with tenderness. She looked at him instead with judgment in her eyes. In reality though, he had never seen her do that, either. There had never been anything other than a respectful neutrality in her gaze.

Haru had no illusions about himself and Barako. He would, in due course, be wed to the woman of his mother's choosing, selected for political advantage and the extension of the lineage. Barako was a warrior, not a courtier. She served under Ochiba, the captain of Striking Dawn's guard.

Her political unsuitability was only one obstacle, though. There was also Haru's incompetence. He had yet to perform on the battlefield in a way that would measure up to Barako. He had never done anything that would earn her respect, let alone her admiration. That neutral, disinterested gaze hurt. He would move mountains to see some other emotion directed his way.

I've done that now, haven't I? I've brought one down on us.

No, he had no illusions about Barako. But he had his dreams. He had been thinking of those dreams when he had pushed the caravan onto the ridge and away from certain shelter. He imagined how she would look him when he finally did reach Striking Dawn, with half a caravan or less. The condemnation he pictured was another dream. It was a nightmare. It was no more real than the tenderness he was used to conjuring for himself. Barako was the model of honor. She would no more show her disappointment in him than she would a forbidden love.

That means nothing. She would not show what she does not feel.

He dug even harder at the snow. *Be silent,* he shouted silently, at himself now instead of Chen. *Put this aside. It doesn't matter. It will never matter. Those dreams were foolish. Now they're dust. Get back with what you can. That's all that's left.*

Haru threw himself into the work. He would have been grateful for total exhaustion. The more Barako and thoughts of shame haunted him, the more ferociously he worked to put them aside. The dig turned into a backbreaking rhythm. He worked until the cavern felt like a furnace. The cold of winter was far from him. He only felt it now and then on the back of his neck, a single point of cold. It scratched at his mind. The chill cut through the sweat to make his skin prickle.

Just before his first shift ended, when despite all his efforts, Barako and who she was loomed in his mind's eye, he heard the whisper. Close and far, a breath in his ear and an echo lost in the stars. When he stopped moving, the whisper was gone.

That was her voice.

No, it wasn't. You didn't hear it properly. You didn't even hear what it said. You must have misheard.

When his shift was over, Haru moved back in the cavern, away from the merchants and the other bushi, putting some distance between himself and the din of the work. Taking up his watch duty, he listened for the whisper.

He did not hear it again. He did discover why he had felt cold on his neck. A draft blew in from the depths of the cave. It was sporadic, and so gentle it would have been unnoticeable except that it was so cold. It came after long intervals, a slow sigh of the mountain.

Haru looked into the darkness of the narrowing cave. He wondered how far the fissure went.

Ishiko was leading this shift of excavators. Haru watched her as he waited for the next touch of the cold, and still listened for the whisper. He began to lose track of time. Ishiko jerked at one point and looked around, startled, then resumed her digging.

Haru had heard nothing. He looked at the other bushi. Ekei was unconscious, and too badly injured to be of use. Hino was asleep, resting before her turn digging and keeping watch. Haru waited until the hourglass he had taken from a wagon marked the end of the shift. It was, as near as he could guess, the hour of the ox.

Ishiko woke Hino and then came to Haru to relieve his watch and let him rest.

"What did you hear?" Haru asked.

Ishiko hesitated. But he had not given her the option to say she had heard nothing. "A whisper, I thought," she said.

"What did it say?"

"I don't know. I must have been mistaken."

"I don't think you were," Haru said.

She nodded in understanding of his implication.

He felt the exhalation of the mountain against the back of his neck again. "What do you make of that draft?" he asked.

"I'm not sure. It might come from another entrance."

"That is my thought as well." He wanted to keep the whisper separate in his mind from the draft. There were other possibilities. Neither Haru nor Ishiko wanted to articulate them just yet. "We need to see how far this cave goes," Haru said. "And where it goes."

Ishiko nodded.

They spoke briefly to Hino. Then Ishiko took one of the lanterns and they started deeper into the gloom. As the cave narrowed, it became a tunnel. The ceiling was invisible. Ishiko held up the lantern. The fissure above them never closed. The crack seemed to run all the way to the peak of the mountain.

Soon the passage was no more than five feet wide. It turned sharply, but always straightened, going ever further into the mountainside. It kept heading west. The sounds of the digging became muffled very quickly. Soon they were inaudible. Haru and Ishiko were alone, two ants tunneling through a hairline crack in stone.

The cold draft came at sporadic intervals.

"Is it stronger now?" Haru asked.

"I think it is," said Ishiko.

Haru kept listening for the whisper. He wanted to hear it again, to learn what it was. He hoped he would not hear it, so he could dismiss it as an illusion that he and Ishiko had somehow shared at different moments.

The air in the deep mountain was still. It was oppressive. It was heavy with waiting.

After half an hour, the relentless westward direction of the passage began to worry Haru. It was also sloping downward. It had been almost since Haru and Ishiko had left the caravan, and the descent had been much steeper in the last while.

Ishiko must have had the same thought. "If we keep going this way…" she began.

"I know." They were deep now into the last of the mountain chain before the Kaiu Kabe, the Carpenter Wall against the Shadowlands, the region of darkness where all that was evil dwelled, all the hungry dead and the demonic oni that fell under the dominion of the fallen kami Fu Leng. "We still have a long way to go," Haru said.

He tried to picture the caravan's precise position. Striking Dawn was south of the Castle of the Forgotten, midway between it and Hida Castle. With most of a day's march still ahead of the caravan, Haru knew that, relative to the Wall, the caravan was at a considerable distance to the north and south from one of the twelve Kaiu Towers. They were parallel with one of the sections of curtain wall. It was impossible to patrol every part of that huge length at all times. These were the regions of the Kaiu Kabe most vulnerable to attacks from the monsters from the Shadowlands.

Even so, if the tunnel ran all the way through the mountain, which Haru still wanted to believe was unlikely, then they would still emerge with the Wall before them. He was facing enough current disasters without imagining new ones.

The descent worried him, though. He could not stop himself from picturing this crack going down and down and down, below the roots of the mountains, and passing underneath the Wall.

Is it possible? It isn't likely. But it isn't impossible.

What if it's true? To find such a break in the defenses would be extraordinary.

It would be a way back from the disgrace of failure. It would mark a return in triumph. A return, also, to the respect and reputation he deserved. He would have found something critical to the survival of the Kakeguchi, and perhaps of the Wall itself.

Too much imagining. Set this aside. Concentrate.

That was enough fantasizing. Indulging in fantastic hopes was not the least of his flaws. He lived too much for what he hoped. That had been his downfall on the battlefield more than once. Disaster for the Kakeguchi family had been averted by Ochiba and Barako. And by his father. It was his hopes of restoring himself in the eyes of his mother, and most of all Barako, that had made him lose half the caravan. What was he hoping for now? Something terrible and vast? Anything he found that was as important as he wanted would also be something that two samurai could not possibly defeat.

Not two samurai led by me, at any rate. So stay focused. Think about real consequences.

Consequences. If this passage somehow led all the way to the Shadowlands, then the cavern was not a refuge for the caravan at all. But he did not know this. It was still entirely possible that he and Ishiko would simply find another crack in the mountainside, perhaps one they could use, perhaps not, and nothing more extraordinary than that.

The breeze blew again. It was stronger. Haru was certain. There was more than a frozen touch on his cheek. The breeze pushed against him. As it did, he heard the whisper.

Haru jerked to a halt, hand on the hilt of his katana. "Did you hear it?" he asked Ishiko. "The whisper?"

"No. Could you make it out?"

Haru shook his head. That was almost a lie. Though the breeze made no sound, the syllables of the whisper hid beneath it, wrapped in its cold, their presence discernible but not their shape. Yet there had been two syllables.

A sigh like hunger. *Aaaaaaaaaaa.*

A cunning moan. *Oooooooooo.*

That was not my name. I did not hear my name. I'm just looking for a pattern.

Aaaaaaaaa… oooooooooo…

Not my name. Not my name.

No point in saying anything to Ishiko until he was sure. Better that she listened unbiased.

It was a little while before the breeze came again. When it did, it was stronger than ever. Colder. And it lasted longer.

Ishiko gasped.

Haru paused and turned to her. "You did not hear your name," he said.

Ishiko stared back at him. "How did you…"

"Because earlier, it was not my name that I heard."

She nodded slowly.

"This is the first time you've heard the whisper since we left the caravan?" Haru asked.

"It is. You heard nothing just now?"

He shook his head.

"Perhaps it is not our names," Ishiko said, expressing less a concession than a hope.

"But it is real," Haru admitted.

"You think we should go on, Lieutenant Haru?"

"I think we need to know the nature of the threat. *If* there is one. We are presuming the worst. We might be wrong to do so."

"You believe, then, that it would be a greater risk to the caravan not to go forward?"

"I do." *I am aware of my responsibilities. I am thinking of the consequences.* This felt like the right decision.

They moved on, still heading west, still descending. The breeze soon became a wind. It blew with increasing frequency, until it became a continuous blast. The breaths Haru had felt before now revealed themselves to have been the gusts, so powerful that not all the twists and turns of the passage could block them completely.

"We must be nearing a way out," said Haru. He had to raise his voice. The wind keened in shrill pain.

Snow began to appear. The wind hurled flakes with stinging force down the tunnel. There were no more whispers. The howl of the wind sometimes sounded like voices.

The further Haru and Ishiko went, the fiercer the wind became. Haru had to lean into it. The wind strained against him, a physical barrier that sought to halt his advance. The cold pulled his lips back in a frozen grimace. It bit into his nose and cheeks, its teeth sharp and painful. Then it gnawed until he was numb.

The tunnel narrowed again. There was barely enough room for Haru to pass. His shoulders brushed against the frost-covered walls. The wind screamed. His breath hissed with the effort to move forward.

Haru followed the bend as the tunnel curved to the left, and suddenly the exit was before him. The wind screamed at him once more, the snow blinding him. He could just make out that he was not coming to a cliff, that there was stone stretching out in front of him. He took another few steps forward, and then he was outside.

No longer funneled into the passageway, the wind lost its strength. It fell back, defeated.

Haru wiped the snow from his eyes.

Ishiko stopped beside him. "What…" she began, staring at what lay before them.

"I don't know," Haru whispered. His throat had gone dry, and the words came out in a croak.

CHAPTER 4

The snow still fell, but the moon shone through a break in the clouds. It cast light as cold as bone over a huge bowl within the mountain chain. Haru and Ishiko were at the top of a slope that led down to a ridge, thin as a spine. Spears of granite pointed up at jagged angles from the ridge. It looked like the skeleton of a huge, fallen beast. The drops on either side of it were precipitous, and the bottom of this bowl inside the greater mountain chain was invisible. The spine switchbacked across the bowl until it reached the gates of a city. The guard tower rose as if it had burst from within the rock and hurled it aside, creating granite formations like leather wings.

Beyond the gates, the city was shapes made of shadow and pallid light. In their center was a huge tower that gazed down on the landscape like a jealous and baleful lord.

It was not snowing as hard as it had been in the pass. Wide flakes dropped steadily, gently, and landed with the faint sound of breaking glass. The flakes shattered into tiny puffs of powdered crystal on impact. Haru flinched when a flake landed on his face, expecting it to draw blood. But what touched him was merely snow, and then merely water, trickling down his cheek like a mockery.

Haru rubbed his eyes, trying to clear them. He was having trouble looking at the city. Snow hung over the roofs and walls in strange positions. It was like a shroud, and it also seemed on the verge of flowing like a liquid. It distorted shapes and confused the gaze. The shapes of the buildings were wrong. Their contours were difficult to make out. What Haru could see made him think of the distorted reflections in a rippling pond. Lines wavered when they should have been straight. Even the guard tower, which he could see more clearly, defied his stare. It made his eyes water. When he rubbed them clear, his vision still felt blurred. Was it darkness that half-obscured a window? Or was the aperture in two places at once, its selves overlapping and slightly beside each other?

He shook his head, trying to banish the illusion.

"This is a dark place," said Ishiko.

"Yes." Everything Haru saw made him uneasy. Yet he resisted the impulse to beat an immediate retreat. "We have not crossed into the Shadowlands," he said. "The Wall is still to our south, beyond those peaks."

"True. We did not travel nearly far enough." She did not sound relieved. "I do not know where we are, though."

"Nor do I. I have never heard of this city." *This is a discovery.* Excitement bubbled up through his unease. The promise of redemption rose like the sun. What he had lost would seem like a trivial sacrifice compared to what he had discovered. If this was an outpost of the Shadowlands to the north of the Wall, then this was the most important night of his life. Even if the city was not something that deadly, the discovery would hardly be less important.

The mountains surrounded the city, clutching it like the fingers of a clawed hand. The only way in that Haru could see was across the spine of rock. "This could have been hidden for centuries," he said. "We only entered that cavern by chance. Without doing that, no one could find this."

If Ishiko felt any excitement in the discovery, she was hiding it well. "We may not be in the Shadowlands," she said, "but I feel their touch here. This is a dangerous valley."

The architecture swam in Haru's gaze. It was like looking at objects in a dream at the moment of waking, or at the moment of plunging into a deeper sleep. Ishiko was right to be wary. *He* was wary. "We will be careful," he said.

"As we do what, Lieutenant Haru?"

"We will go as far as the guard houses. No further, for now."

"What is our purpose there?" Ishiko's voice was very quiet with the effort of keeping the question respectful.

"We must tell the Castle of the Striking Dawn what we have found. We will bring back an artifact of some kind. You and I do not know what this place is, but someone else might. We must give them the means of identifying this city if we are to know what it is and what the Kakeguchi family should do."

He would find something, *anything*, to take back, as long as he could do so without endangering his charges further, or bringing undue risk to Striking Dawn Castle. He would show what was here, and that it was important that *he* return.

Blades drawn, Haru and Ishiko made their way down the slope to the ridge. The top of it was uneven, broken, slippery. Though the wind had dropped, its gusts snapped at Haru's balance. Between the spines, he was exposed. If he leaned too heavily into a gust, it would be easy to fall when the air went still for a moment. The drop below was as profound as fate. Haru walked with care. He made each step deliberate, watching for ice.

Halfway along the ridge, at one of its jagged turns, they negotiated a tiny, curving ledge around an outcrop. The wind whistled and tugged at them, whispering of falls. The chasm below was on three sides of Haru as he worked his way around the corner. The chasm was hungry. The wind plucked at him with curiosity. He was a simple slip away from embracing the great black of absence. The void would swallow him, and its hunger would not be sated. It would never be.

At last, Haru and Ishiko rounded the final turn of the ridge, and the gated wall came back into sight. It was large now, concealing the city beyond. It remained dreamlike. Haru felt as if he were approaching a mirage that, this time, would not dissipate, and would be there for him to touch. He reached out for the gate, expecting his hand to pass through it. He touched cold iron instead.

The two halves of the gate were not completely closed. There was a gap, just large enough for Haru, if he wanted to squeeze through. He looked past the opening, at the waiting city, at the gray shapes, veiled and unveiled by the snow. He looked at what he should not see at all. The city revealed itself, and concealed itself, as if the night were a fog, descending clouds of darkness torn by the spectral rooftops.

It would be a simple matter to cross the threshold and enter the city.

A simple matter to give in to temptation. An easy step to another mistake and another defeat. Do not cross this without a company of samurai.

He waited, daring the wind to carry the whisper that was not his name to him, daring the city to call.

There was nothing behind the wind except silence. The fall to temptation would be his doing alone.

He stepped back from the brink. He looked away from the city and turned to the guard tower on the left. Strangely, the twenty-foot-high tower had a small doorway on the outside of the gate, like an invitation. Haru walked up to it, struggling to keep it in focus. Now he made out the details of the engravings marked on the door, coiling around the frame, and squirming across the brickwork. It turned his stomach. He touched his throat, feeling the reassuring shape of the finger of jade he wore as protection against the taint of the Shadowlands. He and Ishiko were on unclean land now. Mastering his revulsion, determined to best the enemy engraving, he did not look away, and saw, at last, why he kept seeing double. The motif was intricate, and deceptive. It misled the eye and hurt the mind. It was sinuous, and there was a suggestion of scales, but what he saw was no serpent. The intertwining layers were too fine and too lithe, and when he looked more closely, what he had thought were scales seemed more like teeth.

"Do you know this design?" he asked Ishiko.

"I do not. I see no good in it."

"No. Nor do I."

He tried the door. It opened. Inside, the rooms on the ground floor were empty. They climbed the steps of the tower. On the upper level, they did not find much more. In the interior rooms, there were a few cushions and a low table. The wooden floor was marked with the sinuous pattern. The design kept varying. Haru had yet to see it repeat itself, even though its identity was strong from piece to piece, from wall to wall.

"There is something false here," said Ishiko.

"What do you mean?"

"Can you feel it, Lieutenant Haru? It is as if we are being lied to."

"Yes," Haru said after a moment. "I feel it too."

They were at a guard station looking back over the bridge. Haru brushed his gauntlet over the stonework. The edges were worn from wind and rain. The wood of the parapet was heavily weathered. The tower had been standing here a long time. Yet there was also an air of pretense about the tower, as if everything Haru was seeing was for show. There was also the problem of its abandonment. It felt deeply empty, as though its guards had left it so long ago, they were not even memories. Or perhaps there had never been any at all. And though the tower showed signs of age, and of the elements having eaten away at it, the tower also seemed strong. It was not a ruin. It would stand here forever.

The design of the engravings kept working on Haru's perceptions. At least, he thought it was the design. Unless he looked fixedly at what was before him, the tower would start to double again, as if he were cross-eyed. Even with him standing inside the tower, it tried to be two specters at once.

"Is this an illusion?"

"It can't be, Lieutenant Haru," said Ishiko.

Haru hadn't realized he'd spoken aloud. "Yes," he said. "This is real. The idea that it is an illusion is a lie. This is *real.*" He struck a wall with his fist. The rap was clear and sharp, and oddly loud. It echoed across the city.

Ishiko and Haru froze. They looked at each other. They had not been trying to be quiet while they explored the tower. Their sound had felt muffled, contained by the gusts of wind and falling snow. The knock of his fist had sounded too much like the summons of a bell.

"We should not be here, Lieutenant Haru," Ishiko said.

"We should not," he agreed.

Wisdom, not cowardice, urged the retreat. Yet he still had not found what he was looking for.

"One circuit," he said. "We'll finish walking around the tower, and then we leave."

And if you don't find what you're looking for? Do you search the other tower as well?

I'll decide when I have to.

On the opposite side of the tower, he paused to look at the city in its clouds of night. The darkness seemed to move like mist through the streets. Perhaps he was wrong. Perhaps he was just seeing the falling of snow. Perhaps. Perhaps. The impossible city wavered in his vision, and the snowflakes dropped, and dropped, like ash, and broke with the sound of glass.

You have to go. You have to go.

Yes.

He was ready to leave now. If he stayed much longer, he did not know if he would be able to resist the temptation to go deeper into the city. That would be folly.

We are but two. We will come back. If no one believes me, Ishiko will bear witness.

His throat went dry.

What if something happens to her?

Something easily could. So much else had gone wrong. What if the sole other witness died before they reached Striking Dawn? Then who would believe him?

We have to go.

Whatever this city was, a thing of the Shadowlands or not, it was dangerous.

What is better? Being disbelieved or knowing you were foolish again?

Better to seem foolish than to be a fool.

"Let us return," he said. He turned for the stairs.

"What is that?" Ishiko pointed.

A pale talisman on a chain dangled from a corner of the roof.

How did I miss that? He was sure it hadn't been there a moment ago. It turned in the wind, clicking and tinkling as snowflakes broke against it. Haru approached the corner of the parapet. The talisman hung from a hook attached to the eaves. It was out of arm's reach. He tried with his katana and managed to put the tip through the loop of the chain. He unhooked the talisman, and it slid down the shaft to him. He examined his prize.

It was a finger of white jade. A simplified version of the spiral design of the city had been carved onto one side. It drew the eye, but it did not repel the soul in the same way as the other carvings. Haru held it up for Ishiko to see.

"White jade?" she asked.

"Yes." He handled the talisman carefully, but the material gave him confidence. This would be a ward against evil. A powerful one. "Perhaps this is the design before the city was corrupted," he said.

"Left behind by the last warrior to fall," Ishiko speculated.

"Are we agreed to bring this back for Junji to examine?" The monk would know what the carving meant, or at least would know how to discover its meaning.

Ishiko looked at it closely for another long moment, then nodded. "White jade," she said again. "It is right to remove the sacred from this place."

"Precisely," said Haru. "I don't believe we have a choice. What we have found cannot be ignored. We'll leave now, but we *must* return. Even if the secrets here invite our scrutiny, even if they are a trap. They must be confronted especially if they are a trap."

He faced the huge tower in the center of the city once more. It stared back at him, imperious, challenging. It commanded him to besiege its secrets.

Haru had the means, now, to make sure he returned in force.

I will defeat you. This is my vow.

They left. They descended the tower and headed off onto the ridge once more. The wind picked up again, pushing harder at their backs, a vicious last gesture from the valley of cold light and flowing darkness. The cold burned, sharp as flame. The snow struck their helm and armor. As Haru and Ishiko followed the turns of the spiny ridge, the broken glass flakes whipped past his cheeks, stung, and drew blood.

The wind's wrath grew. When they reached an exposed corner, it tried to lift Haru off his feet and hurl him down the mountainside. He resisted, teeth bared in a grimace of effort, and a grin of triumph. Once they put the ridge behind them, and started up the slope heading back to the passage through the mountain, the wind's howl shook the valley with its rage.

We are escaping. You are not pleased.

At the entrance to the tunnel, the howl became a piercing, deafening shriek. Haru could no longer hear the crunch of his footsteps on the snow. Blood ran freely down his face and into his eyes. Half-blind, he stumbled into the passageway, feeling his way forward while Ishiko struggled to relight the lantern.

The wind was the voice of the city, he thought, wrathful at their defiance.

We are beyond your reach. Rage all you like now. Your displeasure will be as nothing compared to when I return.

After the first bend in the tunnel, the wind dropped, defeated. Soon, it was only a sporadic breath again. The cold diminished.

Haru clutched the finger of white jade tightly as he walked slowly eastward and up through the mountain, back towards the caravan. Its importance made it seem heavier than it was. He had discovered something that had to be confronted, and a possible clue to how the city should be faced. It had been too long since he had done something of true worth for the family.

Surely this night was no accident. It was fated. This is my destiny. It has finally arrived. This is how I will become what I must be.

This was how he would prove himself worthy of one day being the daimyō of Striking Dawn.

The breath of the wind, when it came, seemed feeble, almost warm. And when Haru set foot again in the cavern where the merchants huddled, he was sweating. The work at the entrance had progressed much faster than he had hoped. The caravan would be free soon. He was certain of that. The storm would be abating, and at dawn, he would lead the way forward again.

All was certain. There was no doubt about any of this. It was fated.

The sooner the caravan left, the sooner he would return.

CHAPTER 5

"Are you watching for him?" Ochiba asked.

Barako kept a straight face. "I'm watching to see which one of us was right."

Ochiba had just joined her in the north-east tower of Striking Dawn Castle's gate. The first storm of winter had expended its wrath, but another was marshaling its forces. The snow had stopped falling for the moment. The clouds were low, and heavy as iron. The wind had dropped. It no longer hurled drifts against the wall and turned the landscape into a phantom world of gray and white. During her patrol shift the day before, the peaks surrounding Striking Dawn were not even shadows in the storm. They were the ghosts of mountains, faint, shifting traces that appeared and vanished from moment to moment. Their slopes were solid enough now, though their heights vanished into the encroaching clouds.

The stone walls of Striking Dawn surmounted a lower peak. From its position, the castle controlled the trails snaking through narrow passes to north and south, toward the Castle of the Forgotten and Hida Castle, and to the west, toward the Wall. A path branched off from the intersection of the trails to make its way back and forth up the steep rise to the gate. The other three sides of the castle's outermost wall looked down on the grim faces the mountain presented to any who would seek to climb it.

Striking Dawn's position was strong. It was not unassailable. The guards of the Kakeguchi family patrolled its walls, their vigilance unwavering, and even more determined now that winter had come with its obscuring snow and the long nights.

"Half a caravan or less," said Ochiba. "Such faith in the daimyō's heir."

Barako smiled. Ochiba was speaking softly, their banter for each other's ears alone. She leaned a bit closer to the wiry captain and lowered her voice too. "A full caravan?" she asked. "You stand by that prediction? Your faith is astonishing." Their experience with Haru on the battlefield was as extensive as it was unfortunate. Barako still could not decide if Haru was cursed by incompetence or evil fortune. Perhaps both.

"I have faith in Ishiko," Ochiba said. She gave Barako a reassuring tap on the shoulder. "She is a steadying hand."

"She is a *steady* one," Barako amended. "I have no doubts about her ability. We could have no one better at Haru's right side. What I question is whether she is able to make him *listen* to her."

Ochiba sighed. "I agree. That is the question."

"Yet you stand by your prediction."

"I choose to be hopeful on behalf of Ishiko."

Barako nodded. "Your trust in her does you credit."

"And so we stand by our choices."

"As ever, I temper your hope with my pessimism, captain."

Ochiba rolled her eyes. "We owe our lives to that tempering, Barako."

Barako bowed slightly. Their exchange had moved to the edge of formality, but was gilded by humor and comradeship. They were both conscious of and grateful for the precious balance they achieved between themselves and the victories it led to in war.

The two women leaned together against the wall, the top of Ochiba's head barely reaching Barako's shoulder. The day felt warmer to Barako, its problems softer.

"The daimyō is worried," Ochiba said, growing serious. "This was a bad storm."

"Is she more pessimistic than we are? Does she imagine the entire caravan might be lost? We should have supplies enough for the winter, if we are careful, and if the spring does not come too late."

"She is much more worried than that."

"She thinks Haru might not have survived at all?" Barako asked.

"I don't know that she thinks it is probable. She is concerned it might be. She has to be."

"Of course." Akemi had no other children. Haru was her sole direct heir. If he fell, her hold on Striking Dawn would be weakened in ways that went beyond the question of succession. Barako thought for a moment. "I believe he has survived."

"I hope you're right."

"Now you're the doubtful one."

"It's as you said. The storm was bad. His judgment is variable. The worst could have happened."

"His judgment is variable but not invariably bad," Barako said. "He can be foolish, but he is not a fool. He does know how to survive, even if sometimes he seems to forget." She gave Ochiba a crooked smile. "I have little faith in him, but I have faith he will return to us."

"And so we will not lose the heir of the Kakeguchi family in Striking Dawn Castle," Ochiba said dryly.

Barako took a deep, steadying breath. "I am glad the health of the daimyō is good," she said. "Our duty would be much more arduous without her."

"The day will come when we must shoulder a greater burden."

"Then we will shoulder it together." As the Kakeguchi family did, and as the Crab Clan did. She and Ochiba served a whole more important than any individual, and that whole was the source of true pride.

Ochiba clasped Barako's upper arm with thanks. She looked out at the path from the north. "Whatever choices he made," she said, "he would not be here before now."

The tension in her voice made Barako wonder how precarious the daimyō's position was becoming. "Does Lieutenant Doreni believe his moment has come?"

"I am not sure. I suspect that neither is he. I do believe he is asking himself the same question, though."

The Kakeguchi family did not garrison Striking Dawn on its own. Hiruma Doreni led a contingent of his family's soldiers to complement Akemi's forces. The arrangement was meant to be cooperative, and driven by pragmatic concerns. Striking Dawn needed large garrisons, to protect itself and to send reinforcements to the Hida on Wall. Only the history of the castle was not simple. No history ever was. Though the Kakeguchi had held Striking Dawn for more than a century, it had not always been theirs. The Hiruma family had a claim on it too. Akemi had the strongest claim as long as Haru was her heir, and there was a prospect of that line continuing. If she had no direct heirs, then Doreni's claim would be at least as strong as that of any Kakeguchi. Both families were vassals of Hida, and the greater power had imposed the cooperation of the lesser ones.

"I have never known Doreni to act underhandedly," said Barako.

"He has no faith in Haru," Ochiba said. "He will not rest easy with Haru as daimyō."

"You fear he may confuse his ambition with his concern for Striking Dawn."

"It would be, for him, a tempting mistake."

"True. If Haru does not return, the temptation would be even stronger. He will return, though."

"Naturally he will," said Ochiba, a playful note coming back into her voice again. "He's not yet had his fill of gazing at you longingly."

Barako sighed. She gritted her teeth when she saw the smile lurking at the edge of Ochiba's blank expression. She tried to look serious. "He appears to be impervious to indifference."

The grin spread. "Indifference?"

Barako laughed. She could not do otherwise when Ochiba smiled. "I will not explicitly express contempt for my daimyō's heir."

"That is probably for the best."

"It would be pointless to do otherwise. Haru will not see what he does not wish to see."

Ochiba shook her head. "There you are unjust. I have the advantage of being able to observe how he looks at you, and to see his expression when you refuse to look at him. He feels your… let us call it *indifference*. He feels it acutely. Many of his mistakes occur as he tries to be worthy of your favor."

"My favor," Barako muttered. The words tasted like spoiled meat. "If he feels things as acutely as you say, then his persistence in dreaming of something else is a sign of madness."

"Not at all," said Ochiba. "You wound him continuously by existing. You are what he cannot have, and what he cannot be."

"So are you."

"He expects me to be his captain once he becomes daimyō. Also, my circumstances are too well known."

Barako nodded. She avoided looking at Ochiba directly. *You are what he cannot have.* The words echoed and re-echoed in Barako's head, and in her heart.

Ochiba's immediate family had intended her to become a courtier. From birth, a prospective husband had been selected for her. Every step of her political path had been preordained.

It had not, though, been her choice. She had chosen the way of the sword. From her earliest memories onward, she had always known that she was destined to be a bushi, not a courtier.

Ochiba had set herself against her parents' will, though not outwardly, at first. Her determination had been absolute. She had practiced with her blade in secret, and then timed the full bloom of her rebellion with the same strategic brilliance that would later define her command. She proved herself in a border dispute skirmish with the Crane Clan. She showed she was a far more brilliant warrior than she would ever be a courtier. In the lands of the Crab Clan, such skill mattered. Her family had to capitulate, but her refusal of marriage had required a sacrifice. To avoid bringing disgrace upon her family, she had forsworn any other union. If the sword was to be her path, then she had to commit herself to that path to the exclusion of all else in her life.

This she had done, and continued to do.

Barako would never try to make her deviate from her vow. She would never ask Ochiba to court shame. And she would do anything to prevent Ochiba from ever suspecting that Barako had to hold herself to these resolutions.

"Then I must resign myself to fate," Barako said.

"Union with Haru?" Ochiba asked mischievously.

Barako glared playful daggers at her. "His pointless attention," she said. Barako looked up at the sky again. The clouds were growing darker, and getting lower. "The storm will not be long in coming," she said.

"Yes. If Haru is going to reach us today, it will have to be soon."

They fell silent then, consumed by their vigil. With the sky closing in, Barako no longer felt even the cynical amusement with which she and Ochiba had been keeping their concerns at bay.

If you have lost your caravan, Haru. If you have failed your daimyō so completely that you shatter her hold on Striking Dawn, then you are no better than a traitor, and I will curse your memory. Do not be heroic. Be competent. That really is not too much to ask.

"I think I see him," said Ochiba.

Barako saw it too – movement in the distance, small, darker shapes in the deepening gray of the day. Soon she could make out the silhouettes of people, horses and carts. Ochiba called out to the guards in the other tower to send word to Akemi that the caravan was approaching.

Barako watched the procession as it reached the slopes of Striking Dawn's peak and began the slow climb toward the gates. "Less than half," she said.

Ochiba pursed her lips in displeasure, not for having lost the wager, Barako knew, but for Haru's poor showing. "This will not look well," she said. "This will strengthen Doreni's position."

"And look at him," Barako said. She glared at the mounted figure leading the caravan. "You can feel the pride from here. He sits on his horse as if he were a returning conqueror."

"That is odd," said Ochiba. "Arrogance is not like him. He usually has the decency to know when he should feel shame."

"Then he has something to be proud of. Or there is

something he is proud of, whether he should be or not."

The two samurai looked at each other. Barako had always found Haru a cause for concern on the battlefield. But so, she knew, did he. Now he came to Striking Dawn with only a portion of the caravan but an air of victory.

The back of her neck prickled with premonition.

They had all been there to meet him at the gates. His mother, standing solemnly at the head of the crowd. Doreni, as was his right as the perpetual honored guest, at her side, just half a step behind. He had made a good show of barely holding back a frown of disapproval, though Haru had known he must have been pleased to see yet another failure on the part of the daimyō's son. And standing behind Akemi, Ochiba and Barako, their faces impassive, their eyes forever alert for a threat.

They had all looked at him at the moment of his arrival as a failure. But then they must have seen the solemn expression on Ishiko's face, and realized that the state of the caravan was not the most important news that had come to the castle gate.

"Daimyō Akemi," Haru had said, "I must speak with you. The matter is an urgent one."

And so, as the caravan entered the gate and the merchants began the process of bringing the supplies to the massive larder on the east side of the keep, Haru had crossed the courtyard with Akemi and her commanders and entered the main doors of the keep. The hall beyond turned left to open into the main hall. A fire crackled in a large sunken hearth in the center of the room. A gilded folding chair stood on a raised platform against the western wall. There, his mother had seated herself, and gestured for him to speak.

Haru had kept Ishiko with him. It was diminishing to feel the need to have a witness to what he would unfold. It was also realistic.

He knew how others saw him. It was the same way he did.

He had held his gaze on his mother as he spoke, telling her what he had found, revealing a wonder, and calmly yet forcefully, showing through his discovery that he had an important role to play in the destiny of Striking Dawn.

Now he had finished. He looked around at the council before him, waiting for a response. One day, a day he dreaded because he would never be good enough to meet its demands, he would command them all. On this day, they were his judges. Before the discovery of the spectral city, he had been dreading this moment too, dreading the gaze of the people who, no matter their rank, were his superiors. Since leaving the cavern, though, he had been looking forward to this. For once, he had no fear of shame. He expected some, perhaps all, of them would not believe him. That didn't matter. He almost hoped he would be disbelieved. He had proof. The taste of vindication would be sweet.

Akemi leaned forward, looking at Haru carefully. His mother seemed older than she was. Her hair was gray, and her face was weathered by wind, by war, and by care. Her eyes disappeared behind creases. They were dull glints, wise and careful, giving nothing away. Thirty years ago, during a defense of the Wall, she had been badly wounded in the left leg. She walked with a cane, a shaft of carved, polished bamboo. She was hardly less lethal than she had been before. Her movements were still precise and strong. Time had eroded the stones of her being, and had tempered her steel. It was very sharp. Its edge cut deeply.

Ochiba and Barako were on Haru's left, where he stood facing Akemi. Physically, they were stark contrasts, yet to anyone who knew them on the battlefield, it was as if they were a single being. Ochiba was short and lithe. Barako was tall, taller than anyone else in the room, and broad-shouldered, as if born of the Kaiu Kabe itself. Ochiba's long, dark, braided hair whipped around with her quick, sharp movements. Barako kept her shorter hair in a tight bun, always ready to don her helm. Like Ochiba's, her physical presence mirrored her approach to combat. Ochiba was the lightning that struck the enemy. Barako was the thunder that came after and crushed them. Ochiba used the katana, Barako the hammer. Ochiba's leadership was daring. Barako was more cautious. Between them, Ochiba took the needed, calculated risks, and Barako ensured they were successful. They were the speed and the power of the Kakeguchi.

They were looking at him as fixedly as was the daimyō. Barako's features were long, sharp, the slope of her nose straight as a sword edge. She was as unreadable as ever. Ochiba's rounder, mercurial face, quick to frown or laugh, was as neutral as Barako's. Haru had no idea if either of the bushi believed him or not.

He had no doubts about Doreni, to his right, standing

at the base of the dais. The Hiruma bushi was frowning at him, his high forehead creased with displeasure. His face was almost as sharp as Barako's, accentuated by the hard angle of the beard on the end of his chin. When he was still, as he was now, he looked like he had been carved from a branch of oak, slim and strong, and was twice as hard and beyond entreaty.

A few steps away from Doreni, as if he needed the space to separate himself from the political currents of Striking Dawn Castle, was Junji. The squat, shaven-headed monk was the only one present, apart from Ishiko, who appeared to have no difficulty believing Haru. Junji was frowning too, but he was looking past Haru, his eyes focused on something beyond the walls, and beyond the present moment.

There was a knock on a side door to the right. Akemi sat back in her chair, looked over at the guard and nodded. The bushi opened the door, and a Hiruma warrior marched in briskly, the heels of his boots knocking against the wooden planks of the floor. He bowed to Akemi, whispered to Doreni, who grunted, and then withdrew.

Doreni turned to Akemi. "I have had an accounting of our stores done, daimyō," he said. "The situation is as I feared. With the losses sustained by the caravan, we must hope the winter is not a long one."

"We have enough," Akemi said. She kept her eyes on Haru.

"Perhaps. With rationing." Doreni turned his attention back to Haru. "But barely."

"Your concern is noted, Lieutenant Doreni. We will deal with that matter in due course, and it is not the first time we have had to do so."

"We should not have had to."

The note of challenge in his voice made Ochiba stir.

"Be content, Captain Ochiba," Akemi said. "Our discussions today must be frank. It would seem there is much at stake."

"More at stake than there should be," said Doreni.

"We understand you perfectly well," Akemi told him. "We also understand, I believe, that the question of what the nature of this city is more immediately pressing than the long-term situation of the stores."

"Then allow me to go further, daimyō," Doreni said. "We have only Kakeguchi Haru's observations upon which to decide what must be done. Past experience in the battlefield leaves one doubtful about the accuracy of his descriptions."

"Are you saying that he hallucinated an entire city?" Barako asked, anger in her voice.

She defended me! Haru felt dizzy, giddy.

"No," Doreni answered, wrong-footed. "That is not what I meant."

"What he told you is what we saw, Lieutenant Doreni," Ishiko broke in.

"You are an honorable bushi," said Doreni. "You stand by your commander. But loyalty can be misguided, and when it is, it can lead us to grave errors. Can any of us say that this is not so?" He paused. When no one spoke, he went on, "Then with respect, and with apologies, these observations are not enough."

"Of course, of course," Junji said, sounding impatient. He was barely paying attention to the tensions in the chamber.

"But for now, let us hear more of what Lieutenant Haru has to say."

"Lieutenant Doreni's doubts are natural," Haru said. He smiled, and saw a flicker of unease pass over the Hiruma's face. Doreni was not prepared for his confidence. "I am well aware of my failures in the past. That is why I have brought this back from the city." He pulled the talisman from his pouch. Holding the chain, he held the symbol out to the council. It gleamed dully, reflecting the fire in the sunken hearth.

The members of the council stared at the finger of jade. Junji took a step forward, stopped, then took another tentative one. He was reluctant to go any further. "Where did you find this?" he asked.

"In a guard tower." He was relying on Junji to confirm the importance of what he had found. The problem was how rarely Junji committed himself to confirming anything.

"Yes, but where?" said the monk.

"It was hanging from the roof."

"Just like that? In the open?"

"Yes. It had no reason to be where it was. And yet."

"Do you recognize it?" Akemi said to Junji.

"No, daimyō. I do not." He came closer, and put out a tentative hand. "May I?" he asked Haru.

"Please." Haru lowered the talisman into Junji's palm.

The monk jerked slightly at its touch, as if he had expected it to burn, and felt it slither instead. He looked down at it. With the finger of his right hand, he began to trace the spirals of the design. "Teeth," he muttered, shaking his head in disgust.

Akemi rose and approached with the others. They crowded around Junji.

"The design is unpleasant," said Barako.

"Yet it fascinates," Ochiba murmured.

"Yes."

"It is of the same nature as the designs I saw everywhere," said Haru. "They do not repeat, but they… they coil. Like this." He did his best to speak with authority. "I believe this is the symbol of the city, perhaps of what it used to be."

"What is it?" Akemi insisted.

"It's white jade, isn't it?" Haru's stomach twisted with sudden uncertainty.

"I don't know," said Junji. "I don't know."

"We have to know more," said Akemi. She sounded very worried.

"Yes!" Haru said. "Yes! We must." His heart beat with triumph. This was everything he had hoped. At long last, he had done something important for Striking Dawn. Do not let this moment slip away from you. "Now that we know it is there, we cannot ignore it. There is no time to waste. Winter is upon us, and if we delay, it won't be long before it will be too late. We don't dare wait until spring."

"What are you proposing?" said Ochiba.

"We must return at once. In force. Daimyō, I am ready to lead the expedition."

Akemi shook her head. "No one is going."

"But…"

She raised a hand. "No one is going *right now*. I agree. The city must be investigated. It is potentially an extremely grave threat. But I will send no one there, *no one*, until we have done what we can to learn more. To begin with, there are rites to be performed."

Haru bowed his head. "Of course." Everyone from the caravan would also have to be examined for any bruise, wound or other physical sign of possible taint. He and Ishiko especially. Striking Dawn Castle was not notable enough to have a permanent Kuni shugenja in residence, and it had been some time since one had last visited their castle, so it fell to Junji to lead the examinations.

To Junji, Akemi said, "I leave the talisman with you. Is there any chance of learning what city this is? This cannot be the only time it has ever been seen."

Junji nodded. "I don't believe that is possible either. I will see what I can find." He was still looking at the talisman. "I do not think this is white jade," he said. "It resembles it closely, but there is something wrong. We must increase all precautions against the works of the Shadowlands."

"We shall." Akemi took her cane and began to walk away from the dais, signaling the council was at an end. "Double the watch," she ordered. "Let all be vigilant. It may be that this talisman is not the only thing to come to Striking Dawn from the city."

Ochiba, Barako and Doreni bowed their heads in quick, firm acknowledgment. Haru savored the look on Doreni's face. His facile triumph was gone. He was still frowning, but not with the theatrical disapproval of before.

Barako defended me!

Haru turned to thank her, but she was marching out behind Ochiba, and she did not look back at him.

CHAPTER 6

Junji entered the library of Striking Dawn. He took a deep breath, releasing the pent-up tension in his chest. He rocked his head back and forth, easing his sore neck. It was a relief to be away from the main hall and its political undercurrents. He did all he could to hold himself above the power struggles between the Kakeguchi family and the Hiruma contingent. More and more often, though, he had the sense of clutching on for dear life to the rock of neutrality while the rapids tried to tear him away. He had repeatedly made his position clear to Akemi and Doreni. He was a Kakeguchi by birth, but a monk by vocation. He refused to play their games. All that mattered was that the redoubt of Striking Dawn stood firm against the Shadowlands.

Yet they kept pulling at him. And the news that Haru brought was not going to calm things down at all. He could see that daimyō and the lieutenant each imagined the discovery might help their cause, either by proving Haru's worth as an heir, or discrediting him once and for all.

Junji took another deep, deliberate breath. He closed his eyes, and exhaled slowly, centering himself, purging thoughts of power struggles. That was not why he was here. He was here to consult his beloved scrolls. He was here to journey back through the history of Rokugan. Haru had made one discovery. It was up to Junji to make the next.

He opened his eyes. He was ready now.

The chamber that held Striking Dawn's archives was a large one, with shelves extending to the high ceiling. Ladders provided access to the alcoves where the oldest scrolls resided. There were many corners in the upper reaches that had not been visited in a long time, and where organization had gone awry many decades past.

Junji climbed a ladder. Up here, in the high altitudes of the past, that was where he needed to begin. It disturbed him that he had no idea what city this was that Haru had stumbled upon. The talisman disturbed him even more. If he could find a name, and even the roughest fragments of a history, perhaps he would feel better. The unknown was dangerous. He disliked it.

As he began to comb through scrolls, focusing on maps and historical chronicles, the image of the talisman kept surfacing in his mind. It taunted him. He had placed it on a table in the center of the library inside a small, sanctified chest of green jade, thus sealing it off. The more he examined it, the less he trusted it. With it in the chest, he would also not have to see it except when necessary. But he could not banish its image. In his imagination, the spiral really did move. It turned and turned with a sickening sinuousness, as if it would draw light and souls into its center.

Whatever he found would be dark. There could be no doubt of that. He could only hope that he *would* find something, and that what he found could be used.

Evening was falling and the storm had started up again, and when Barako entered the library, she found Junji seated at the long table that took up most of the chamber's central aisle. He was surrounded by stacks of scrolls, both open and rolled. Papers were laid out before him, overlapping each other with little discernible order. Lanterns hanging from the ceiling cast pools of light over the table. Junji had his head down over a scroll, his brows furrowed in concentration. He was in his element, doing what he loved more than anything else in the world.

You're enjoying this, aren't you?

Barako chastised herself for the ungenerous thought. Junji had been visibly alarmed when Haru had produced the talisman. He would not be taking any possible danger from the Shadowlands lightly. He would, though, also relish the chance to vanish into his precious archives. If his duty required he retreat once more from the political front lines, then so much the better.

Junji's neutrality frustrated Barako. She had tried, several times, to convince him that by failing to show full support to Akemi, he was helping ensure the very struggles he despised so much would continue.

That isn't why you are here now, though.

No. She was here to help. Junji frustrated her, yes, but she also admired his scholarship.

She scuffed her boot heel against the floor, making a bit

more noise so she wouldn't startle Junji when she reached the table. He jerked slightly and looked up. His smile was tired, and a little cautious.

"Are you here to help or to lecture me again?" Junji asked.

"To help," said Barako.

"Good. I could use your eyes here too."

Barako pulled out a chair opposite Junji and sat down. They had spent many days here together in silent study. Barako used the library more than any of the other warriors in Striking Dawn. She used every chance she could find to learn more about the enemies of the Kakeguchi, whoever and whatever they might be. The knowledge she gathered was one of the weapons she brought to the battlefields, and Ochiba, grateful for her lieutenant's research, put the knowledge to good use.

"Here," said Junji. He leaned forward and pushed a heap of scrolls over to Barako. "Start with these. Chronicles of voyages through the mountains. There might be some mention of the city in them."

The first scroll that Barako picked up was brittle with age. It shed dust as she unrolled it carefully. The calligraphy was faded, the black ink turning gray. "An old chronicle," she said.

"They all are. If the city had been written about recently, we would know about it."

"Do you think it has been written about at all?"

"We must hope it has," Junji said quietly.

Barako started reading. She went through the scrolls as carefully but as quickly as she could, scanning them for the characters for *ruins* and *city*. She soon lost track of time. Like Junji, she disappeared into the documents, her world shrinking down to become nothing more than the calligraphy before her. The only sounds in the library were the rustling of papers. She and Junji barely moved except to place one scroll aside and unroll the next one.

She did not know how many hours she had been there when Junji grunted. Barako looked up. "Something?" she asked.

Junji nodded. "A reference to it, I think. It is a passing one, recorded at third hand. This traveler has heard of an ancient city somewhere in the mountains south of the Castle of the Forgotten."

"Is there a name?"

"Yes. The City of Night's Hunger."

Barako took this in. Her jaw tightened. *Haru, what have you done?* "That sounds ominous," she said.

"It is," Junji agreed.

"Is there more?"

"No. Just that reference."

"That is a beginning, at least."

They resumed their search, now with greater focus. Barako felt they had the scent of their prey. They had a name to look for. She did not rush through the documents where she did not find it right away, though. There might be other references, ones that used a different name, or none at all.

They worked until dawn. By then, they had found a few more, precious scraps of knowledge about the city.

Barako stretched, working out the kinks in her shoulders that the hours of hunched sitting had turned into painful knots. "We should show Akemi what we have managed to find," she said.

"I will leave that to you," said Junji. "I will keep looking."

"Do you think there is more to find?" Barako eyed the piles of scrolls they had already gone through.

"There could be. We are a long way from having exhausted the possibilities in this library." Junji was quiet for a moment. "Still," he went on, "to have so little to show for our efforts so far has me thinking dark thoughts."

"In what way?"

He waved his hand at the few documents they had collected that bore even the slightest hint of the City of Night's Hunger. "So few fragments," he said. "Where there is a mention of it, the author is too brief, especially for a city of the size and nature that Haru describes. Why do they not remark upon it? And why are there no direct witnesses? Only vague memories of someone else's vague memories of someone else's stories. It is as if the city were concealing itself, not just from our eyes, but from our thoughts."

This is worse and worse. "If that is so, what do you think we should do?"

"That is not for me to decide." Junji was firm. "I will find all I can. The course of action to take will be up to Lady Akemi."

"Your wisdom could be vital."

"I have none to give. Not on this matter."

"When do you find there are matters where you do have wisdom to share?"

Junji did not reply.

"The time may come when you will have to take a stand," Barako told him, and rose to depart.

• • •

Haru paced back and forth in his mother's quarters, his face illuminated by the flickering of the lamps. Barako had left several minutes ago. Her words, however, still hung in the air. *The City of Night's Hunger*. Akemi had said nothing since the samurai had left. She kneeled on the mat, sipped her tea, musing, and ignoring Haru as he passed in front of her.

Finally, Haru could wait no longer. He kneeled in front of Akemi. "Well?" he demanded.

Akemi raised her eyes slowly. The look she gave him was infinitely patient, which only made him even more frustrated. "You are going to tell me what you think I should do, aren't you?" She drummed her fingers slowly on the head of her cane.

"No… I…" Haru stammered. She was right. That was what he had been about to do. The presumption would be offensive, and lose him whatever respect she might have for him. "My actions are yours to command," he said. "They always will be. I would never suggest the opposite."

"Good."

"Please, though. Please tell me what you think about what Barako told us."

"The name of the city is a dark one," said Akemi.

"I agree."

"Go on," Akemi said. "You will be lord of Striking Dawn in times to come." She spoke with more certainty than Haru felt. "Tell me what you would do."

"The city is dangerous. We do not know in what way. And we cannot afford to ignore it."

"True," Akemi put in. "Now that it has been found, the

city may be as aware of us as we are of it. Or what lurks there might be. One of us has entered it and left. Who is to say that what lies within might not leave the city too, following the path that has been left to it?"

Haru winced at the rebuke. *Should I have ignored what I found? Should I have ignored what Ishiko and I experienced in the cavern? What would you have done differently? What makes you think we would be safe if we had never found the city? What makes you think that danger would not emerge from it, sooner or later? How could we prepare if we did not even know the city was there?* He swallowed the defensive responses. They would do him no good. Better to accept what Akemi said with dignity. Perhaps that would make her more receptive to what he had to say. "If there is danger, it must be destroyed before it threatens us. If there are amends to be made, I must make them."

"What do you propose?"

"What I have been saying from the start. We must return to the City of Night's Hunger. If this is an extrusion from the Shadowlands, it must be eradicated."

"The destruction of a city is no small matter."

"I know. It will take time to raze it. First, though, if there is something there, it must be defeated. Let me take a company. I will defeat the enemy that I have discovered."

Akemi looked at him for a long time. Her face softened. When she spoke, she looked away from him. She looked past him, as if she did not want to see his eyes. "No," she said. "I cannot grant you this request."

"Why not?"

Now she did look at him, with disappointed sorrow. "You

know why. You are right to say that we must take action. You have discovered something of terrible importance. Whatever the circumstances of that discovery, it matters. It matters a great deal. Be proud of that."

"Please," Haru said, despising himself for begging, and wishing his mother did not have good reasons to refuse what he asked. "Do not ask me to remain here."

"And if you return to the city, and are lost to me, what of the Kakeguchi of Striking Dawn then?"

"What will that do for my standing if I stay behind? Will anyone consent to be led by a coward?"

Akemi pressed her lips together. She tilted her head, very slightly, as if conceding his point. "Very well," she said. "You will return."

"I will leave at dawn."

"In this storm? And die before you even reach the city?"

"When the storm passes, then. Though we cannot wait indefinitely. Past a certain point, I believe we must risk the journey. The risks in not doing so would be even graver." He paused, waiting for Akemi to answer. When she did not respond, he found himself pleading again. "I must go. I cannot remain on the sidelines. If I did, I would lose any chance of ever having the authority necessary to be lord of this castle. Better I should die in the preservation of this castle. The result for your legacy would be no worse."

Another silence. At length, with a sigh, Akemi said, "Perhaps you are right. You will go, then."

"Thank you. You will not regret—"

Akemi raised a hand, cutting him off. "You will go with a company led by Ochiba. She will be in command."

"No…" Haru struggled to find words. The hurt and anger were a ball in his throat. He could barely breathe. "Why? Why would you do this to me? Do you not see how I will be diminished in the eyes of all the samurai in Striking Dawn?" This was almost worse than being left behind.

"I must do, in the end, what is right for this castle. As you must, when your time comes. And this is not the first time you have served under Ochiba's command."

"When have I not? But this is different. This is *my* discovery."

"Yes. You were the one to discover it on our family's behalf. On the Crab Clan's behalf. Now do your duty and serve Striking Dawn in the way that I deem best."

There was no point in arguing. Akemi had decided. She would not be swayed. Haru bowed. "I will bring honor to the Kakeguchi," he promised, and left the room.

He would be true to his vow. No matter what Akemi ordered.

Haru strode quickly down the corridor. He had preparations to make.

CHAPTER 7

"I can confirm that the City of Night's Hunger is ancient," Junji told the assembled council. "The few references we have found suggest that it was known of, if only by a few, before the construction of the Wall. Beyond that, there is little else I can say without engaging in mere guesswork."

"Was it built by mortals?" Akemi asked.

Junji spread his hands. "I cannot tell."

"We are not much better off than we were before," Doreni said, voicing everyone's frustration.

"The name is significant," said Barako.

"Indeed." Junji nodded. "And I will say this about the words we *have* found written about Night's Hunger. They are whispers."

Junji was not fanciful. Barako knew how much he despised and avoided drama. What he said was not intended to sound portentous. It was how he had truly experienced those documents. Barako agreed with him. She too, had heard the whisper of fear when she read those few, furtive words. "He is right," Barako said.

"So," said Akemi. "There is little doubt now that the city is a danger. But we do not know in what ways, or how to ward off the danger."

"That is so," said Junji. "Apart from what we do to confront anything tainted by the Shadowlands."

"What would more knowledge really change?" Haru asked. "What we must do is as clear today as it was yesterday. We return with enough strength to deal with anything we might find there. The Crab Clan's duty, and its privilege, is to fight against the Shadowlands. So let us do what we know we must do."

Barako had been keeping a surreptitious eye on Haru since the council had gathered. He was quivering with impatience. Haru looked younger than he was. His restless energy was one reason for that. So were his insecurity and his bravado instead of confidence. His face was unlined, his lips ragged from an unconscious habit of biting them. Barako suspected he would always look youthful and untested, even in old age. Right now, the air around him was almost thrumming with his need to rush back to Night's Hunger. He made her uneasy. He was not wrong in what he was saying. No one in the main hall would disagree with him. It was the way he was saying it that was dangerous. He could barely stand still. He was primed to make bad decisions and take worse actions.

"We will go," Akemi said. "You will go. Captain Ochiba will lead a company to the City of Night's Hunger. It will depart at the first dawn after the storm." She turned to Doreni. "The defense of Striking Dawn will remain in your hands."

Doreni bowed his head, but did not look happy. He glanced quickly at Haru, then said, "Are you entirely satisfied that this is the wisest deployment available to us?"

"The castle needs you here," Akemi said, gazing at him steadily.

Doreni bowed again. "As you command." He did not sound mollified.

Barako's jaw tightened. The undercurrent of Doreni and Akemi's exchange was clear to her, though she thought it might not be to Haru. Doreni did not like the idea of Haru, especially in his reckless state, going back to the city. Perhaps he resented being left behind as well. Barako approved of Akemi's decision, though. As much as she dreaded Haru's incompetence, this was the least worst choice to be made. And Akemi had blocked Doreni's political aspirations again. He could do nothing but serve her and the castle faithfully without casting away any shred of respect.

Haru showed no sign of being aware of Akemi's careful strategies that took in more than the City of Night's Hunger. All he heard was the announcement of delay. "It could be weeks before the storm exhausts itself," he protested. "We should leave at once."

Akemi raised an eyebrow. "I do not see how casting out a company to become lost in the storm and then freeze to death can be seen as acting expediently."

"I just think we must find a way there sooner."

"If you think of a practical solution, I will consider it."

Haru frowned. "We are wasting time," he insisted.

Barako frowned. If he had not been Akemi's son, she would have spoken against this show of disrespect. Stay calm, she told herself. There is nothing to be gained in trying to discipline a rabbit.

"Night's Hunger has been near us for centuries," said Ochiba. "It can wait a few more days for our presence."

"Can it?" Haru asked. "Can we?"

"What is your concern?" said Doreni. "Are you worried something followed you back?"

The samurai's tone was serious. This was not a taunt. Haru reacted as if it were. "No," he snapped. "No, I'm not. Do you think I would not have noticed us being followed?"

"We do not know what is in that city," Ochiba said calmly. "It is quite possible that no one would know that something walked behind them. It may be that subtle."

"We were careful," said Haru, as if those words had meaning.

Barako turned to Junji. "What do you think?"

Junji thought for a moment. Barako wondered whether it was evidence he was weighing, or whether his opinion would be viewed as political at all. Then he said, "I believe there is greater urgency of action." He gave Haru an apologetic look. "You have discovered something that must be countered, Lieutenant Haru, and you have provided valuable information. But I am afraid that in so doing, you have also increased the danger. The talisman you brought back allowed me to identify the city, but it is not white jade."

"What is it, then?" Haru asked.

"I believe it is a congealed piece of the city itself. I have sealed it away. It can do no harm itself now. But its journey here could have drawn the attention of whatever lies in Night's Hunger."

Haru closed his eyes in a wince of emotional pain.

"Then it is decided," Akemi said. She stood, signaling the end of discussions before Haru could say anymore. "Captain Ochiba, prepare for the first clear dawn."

"We will be ready, Lady Akemi."

Akemi left, trailed by Ochiba and a frowning Doreni. Barako touched Haru on the shoulder and he stopped as suddenly as if she had grabbed him. He looked flustered before she had even spoken.

"I need to ask you something," she said.

"Of course."

"You are clear about your duty? You understand what you must do?" In another clan, so direct a challenge to the heir would have been unthinkable, even if, for now, Haru held the same rank as she did in the castle guard. But the Crab Clan did not have the luxury of elaborate etiquette. Directness was a means of survival.

"I do understand," Haru said. "Of that, you may be sure."

Barako watched him go. She was not sure at all.

Light was failing when Haru found Ishiko in the barracks. He had waited for most of the day after the council before speaking to her. By then, Ochiba had already addressed the company that would be heading to Night's Hunger. Preparations were underway, and it was easy to draw Ishiko aside unobtrusively. He led her outside, where the snow was falling hard, and the wind roared, biting at the nose and cheeks.

"We have a special duty," Haru said. "We might have to leave before the others."

"Why is that?"

"The situation is a serious one. The City of Night's Hunger is a threat from the Shadowlands. There is no time to waste. We must find what is there and destroy it. But the storm is stymieing us. Every hour it holds us here is an hour the threat grows. So there will have to be risks, and it is our duty to take the biggest risk, because we found Night's Hunger and we know the way."

"And what is the risk?"

"We march as soon as the wind drops. We do not wait for a dawn."

Ishiko looked around, squinting into the driving snow. The roofs of the castle were dim gray shapes. The outer wall was invisible. Ishiko did not look happy. Haru wiped the ice from his cheeks. He kept his expression firm and calm. He couldn't hope that she believed him. He did not think she would challenge him, though. He wished she would believe. He wanted her to understand. *I'm telling you the truth. We have to act. We have to act now.* Was wounded pride spurring him on? Of course it was. And he was thankful for it. The need to do what was most important for the family as a whole was why he was willing to defy Akemi. He was answerable to a greater duty. If it came to a choice between obeying his mother and saving the castle, then there was no choice at all. Was there? No. There was not.

"The march will be difficult," Haru said.

"As soon as the wind drops," Ishiko repeated his earlier words, as if testing them for madness. "The pause might be a short one."

"Yes. Exactly. That is the risk. But there is no choice."

"And we go even at night?"

"Yes. I know what we are undertaking. So do you. Sometimes, necessity and folly cannot be distinguished. This is one of those times."

Ishiko said nothing.

"The victory our mission promises is as great as its risks," Haru went on. "Because of the risk, the entire company cannot share in the glory. When we go, it must be done quickly and silently. For the sake of morale."

More silence from Ishiko.

She doesn't believe a word I'm saying.

Why should she? he realized. He was babbling, piling up falsehoods and rationalizations. He should have stopped speaking when he ran out of truth. All that mattered was that Ishiko did as he ordered. The more he tried to convince her, the worse her doubts would become, because she would hear his unspoken doubts too. He hated being forced into this position. He hated having to disobey Akemi. *I do this for the sake of the castle and the glory of the family. I swear I do.*

Haru cleared his throat. Enough. They had been standing out here too long already. No one could see them. No one could see anything. He just wanted this conversation to be over. Only the developing frostbite was preventing his face from burning in a shame he did not wish to acknowledge. "You understand what I need you to do?" he asked.

After a short hesitation, Ishiko nodded.

"Good." He left her. He felt her eyes on him long after he would have been hidden from her by the snow.

Haru trudged through thigh-deep drifts. He made slow

Legend of the Five Rings

progress across the courtyard, lost white emptiness. He could see neither the castle nor the wall. If he kept straight, sooner or later he would reach the wall, and that was good enough. He needed to be active, expending energy in the struggle to move forward instead of chasing his own thoughts.

The effort did him no good. A gust hammered into him so hard it almost knocked him off his feet. The cold stole his breath.

You want to lead your troops into this?

No. I will wait for a break in the weather.

Even if that means leaving with Ochiba?

Yes, if that's when the storm abates. All that matters is getting there as soon as possible.

"That's all that matters," he muttered. The wind ripped his words away. It didn't believe them any more than he did.

A high, long shadow appeared ahead of him. It gathered substance, and gradually coalesced into the wall. When he reached it, he found he had traveled far to the right of where he had thought he was heading, and was disoriented for a moment.

The thought of doing the same thing in the mountain passes made him queasy. He grimaced, and forced himself to go on. This is what needs to be done. You know it is.

Haru worked his way along the wall until he reached the gate. He dragged open the door to the north-east tower and went inside. He climbed to the top, stomping on the stairs to shake off the snow sticking in clumps to his legs and boots.

The guards on duty bowed smartly when he appeared.

"There will be an expedition to the City of Night's Hunger," he said. He brushed snow from his shoulders.

"Yes, Lieutenant Haru," said one. The other two nodded. They had heard, then.

"I have come to let you know the mission may begin at night. If the wind drops, I will be leading the first contingent out. The first hint of clearing is your warning to be ready. I expect the gate to open at my approach."

"Yes, lieutenant."

"Good."

Haru faced north. There was nothing to see. The wind screamed at him, pushing him back from the parapet. The cold sank venomous fangs into his cheeks and forehead. The snow drove hard, spun in vortices and hurled itself into the tower. All there was to see was violent, turbulent white. No mountains, no sky, not even the ground. The world had vanished. There was no hint of clearing. The storm besieged the Striking Dawn Castle, determined to last forever.

"Are you taking over Junji's duties?" Ochiba asked.

Barako looked up from the papers laid out before her on the library table. "Looking. Like he is. Looking for anything at all." She rubbed her eyes. She had been here since completing the preparations with her contingent. She should rest, but it seemed unlikely the storm would blow itself out before a few days had passed, at the very least. If there was even the smallest chance of finding something useful about the City of Night's Hunger, she had to look. Junji had been doing the same all day, and had gone for a short rest when full dark came during the hour of the rooster. Barako had decided to work through at least the hour of the dog. "Has something happened?" she asked. She was pleased to see Ochiba, but the captain was not a frequent visitor to the library.

"That's what I wanted to ask you," Ochiba said. "You spoke to Haru after the council."

"Yes. I wanted to remind him of his duties."

"He needed reminding?"

"I think so, yes."

Ochiba sat down beside Barako. "You sound worried," she said softly. She put a hand on Barako's.

"I am. I'm worried about his need to prove himself." She wanted to take Ochiba's hand in hers, but kept her palm on the table.

"Haru will always be trying show his worth," said Ochiba.

"The need is much more intense than before. I'm certain it is. He discovered Night's Hunger…"

"…and now he's forbidden from leading the return," Ochiba finished.

"Yes. We cannot rely on him."

Ochiba snorted. "We never have."

"He'll be worse this time. He has too much at stake."

"Why? Does he plan to reside there? To make Night's Hunger another Kakeguchi fortress?"

"I don't think he knows," said Barako. "All that matters is that the accomplishment, whatever that turns out to be, is his. We will have to watch him carefully."

Ochiba squeezed Barako's hand. "As we do. As we always have. We know how to deal with him." She squeezed. "We've had enough practice."

The warmth of Ochiba's touch ran through Barako's blood. "We must not be overconfident," she said. She looked into Ochiba's eyes, and let her see all the worry that was in her heart. "He will be prone to more than the mistakes of incompetence. He will be reckless."

"You're worried he will endanger all of us."

"Yes."

"He has before. He will again. How is it different this time?"

"In the scale of the danger that will come from him. He will aim high. His failure, if it comes..."

"You mean *when* it comes," Ochiba interrupted.

"...will be catastrophic," Barako finished.

Ochiba squeezed her hand again. "Understood. We will be careful. We will take nothing for granted. We will watch him. You know I would."

"I just needed to hear you say it."

Barako should have felt relieved. It worried her that she did not.

CHAPTER 8

Haru had given orders that he be woken at the start of each hour during the night. It took an effort to fall asleep at all, but he had to have some rest. He could not afford to be exhausted before he even began his march. Nor did he dare miss the opportunity to make the first start. The storm seemed like it could last until spring. But it might end without warning.

It was the silence that woke him at the hour of the ox. Dawn was still some time away, but light streamed in through the window of his quarters. He jumped up from his sleeping mat and ran to look outside, blinking away the smear of sleep.

The wind had not stopped entirely. It rattled the shutters and moaned to itself. It was so much weaker than it had been, though, that it was as if Striking Dawn Castle had fallen into a deep well of stillness. The snowflakes were gentle and sparse. The moon shone through a break in the clouds. The ground glinted with a million crystalline reflections.

Haru had lain down fully clothed. Now he threw on his armor as quickly and silently as he could, and grabbed his katana and his finger of jade. He slid open the door to his chamber just as Bushi Hachi was coming to wake him. "I know," he said. He did not whisper. He must not appear as if there were anything wrong. He walked as quickly and as quietly as he could with Hachi to the west barracks, where his squads were quartered. When he arrived, he found that Ishiko already had the warriors awake and ready, awaiting his command. When he saw that she had obeyed his orders so completely, he was almost dizzy with gratitude.

"Duty summons us," he told his troops. "Glory awaits us." No time to say more, and too risky. He could not order silence. He could only hope the noise of departure would not raise any alarms.

He left the barracks and trudged through the snow toward the gate. The journey across the courtyard seemed endless. These were the worst moments. If word reached Akemi before he could get through the gate and down the trail, his shame would be fatal. He would never recover from it. Akemi would never be able to leave Striking Dawn in his hands.

The one good thing about the deep snow and the fact that it was going to force the journey to be a foot march was that he would be leaving with much less noise than if his contingent were mounted.

Haru looked straight ahead. He kept his eyes on the gate. Perhaps, if he did not look back at the castle, no one there would think to look at him.

The guards in the towers did see him and his thirty samurai. They reacted as he had commanded, and the gate was already open by the time he reached it. He nodded crisply at the guards, letting them know he was pleased, and then he was through.

And then he was heading down the steep slope.

And so were his samurai.

And then the gate closed behind them.

The moon shone brightly through its hole in the clouds. It illuminated the path down the slope to the road leading north. Haru led a fast march. He saw the hand of fate in the moonlight, in the cessation of the storm, and in the moment these elements had combined. His decision had been the right one. This was his moment of destiny, and he had seized it with both hands.

They reached the bottom of Striking Dawn's mount and headed north. Only a little while now, over the top of the next rise, and Haru's troops would be out of sight of the castle. He grinned. He looked at Ishiko, marching at his side. She had to be feeling the same sense of destiny. She had discovered the City of Night's Hunger along with him. She had heard the whispers too. Her expression was impassive, her gaze focused straight ahead on the path up between the mountainsides, the snow bright in the moonlight, a ribbon of white showing the way to glory. That squint-inducing glare was another sign, Haru thought. He was surrounded by good omens.

"The ancestors smile on our venture," he said to Ishiko.

"What do you mean?" she asked.

Haru snorted. How could she not see what he did? He

waved an arm, taking in the calm night. "We could not ask for better conditions."

"We could have asked that the storm end in the morning," said Ishiko.

Haru cursed himself. He should have kept still. If Ishiko harbored doubts about whether Akemi had authorized this particular march, his words would have done nothing to allay them. "True. A day march would have been preferable," he lied. "But sooner is better too." And that was no lie. "Now that we know what is there, and we have seen what we have seen, every hour of delay is dangerous. Don't you agree?"

"The city must be dealt with," she said.

That sounds like an equivocation. Haru did not press her. If he did, he might push her into a place where she was being forced to choose between him and the daimyō. For the moment, she could still, he hoped, allow herself to believe that he was acting according to Akemi's orders.

Haru marched in silence now. He tried to maintain a rapid pace, but the snow was past his knees. He kept trying. The moonlight might not last.

It didn't. They had covered perhaps a mile from the base of Striking Dawn's mount when the ribbon ahead faded from white to gray as the clouds covered the moon again. The gray of the path and of the mountains blended together. The road lost definition. Then it dropped into darkness.

Haru ordered lanterns lit, and his contingent moved on, more slowly now. He could see no further than the circle of light from the lanterns.

It began to snow.

"Not again," Ishiko muttered. She gave Haru a significant glance.

He shook his head. "We don't turn back," he said.

"There are exposed ridges between here and the City of Night's Hunger."

"We will deal with them as we did before. Glory calls us forward."

Ishiko opened her mouth to speak. She hesitated. "And if there is another avalanche?"

"That risk would exist at night or day, under snow or clear skies," Haru said. "But I believe in destiny. How can I believe that it was pure chance that brought us to Night's Hunger? We were guided there. We shall be again, to do what must be done."

Ishiko did not respond to his triumphal affirmation. At least she did not disagree vocally. Haru set his face into the snow and marched with renewed determination. *She'll see. She'll see that I'm right.*

The wind grew stronger. The snow fell more heavily, but not enough to kill all visibility. Haru could see at least ten feet ahead. That would do.

He looked back once. There was a faint glow in the sky where the clouds shrouded the moon. There was just enough light to give him the impression that it was snowing much harder in the direction of Striking Dawn.

Barako was up and pulling on her armor before she was even aware of being awake.

Something is wrong.

The instinct was acute, the conviction iron. She raced

from the upper level of the east barracks, where her chamber was, to the sleeping quarters below. Her troops were asleep. All was well here.

She grabbed a lantern and ran outside into driving snow. The storm was as strong as it had been when she retired.

Something's different. But what?

It was hard to see. The torches on the outer wall were faint embers, winking in and out of existence as the snow pelted down. Barako could make out almost nothing within a few feet of where she stood.

It's Haru. You know it is. Find him.

She started though the drifts toward the west barracks. As she neared the doors, she saw the trail left by marching feet. A wide swath of snow had been beaten down. Its shape had softened, partially filled in by the new fall.

Barako moved onto the trail and ran to the gate tower. A guard stepped forward to greet her. "Lieutenant," he said. "Are you leaving too?"

Too? Oh no.

"When did Lieutenant Haru and his contingent depart?"

"An hour ago."

"In the storm?"

"It abated for a short while."

Just long enough for Haru to act on his pride and invite disaster.

"Thank you," Barako said to the guard. She kept her anger from her tone. *Don't make things worse.* If Akemi chose to condemn Haru for disobedience, that was her decision to make.

She headed back toward the castle. She had to wake

Akemi. And there was precious little else she could do. *That fool is trying to kill us all.* She seethed at the thought of the consequences of Haru's actions. The storm was as strong as it had ever been. He was leading a third of a company to almost certain death. Rescue was impossible.

You prideful, pathetic little man. I could wish what is coming on you, if that didn't mean condemning your warriors too.

She almost wished he had acted out of malice. At least then, she might at least trust his instincts for self-preservation.

He's going to kill himself for the sake of his pride.

She feared how many samurai he would take with him.

CHAPTER 9

Day broke with sullen reluctance. Darkness bled away to a dark gray. Haru could not see much further than he had during the night. The lanterns were useless now, and the snow shrouded the mountains. But the storm was not as intense as it had been on the journey to Striking Dawn. He was able to keep the march going, and do so with confidence. During the exposed crossings, he was able to see enough to keep away from the edges. He did not have to slow down. Walking through the accumulated snow was drudgery. It was miserable. It was also safe. It was impossible to go fast enough to run any risks.

In an effort to temper exhaustion, he had his warriors rotate the order in which they walked, and he reluctantly made himself take his turn as well at the back of the line, where the snow was tramped down and the going was easier. He wanted to be the first to enter the cave that led to the City of Night's Hunger. He wanted to be in the lead when they reached the cave.

Be patient. Don't concern yourself with the trivial. The

discovery has already been made.

He worried too that he might not recognize the cave. So much snow had fallen that the landscape, what little he could see of it, had changed.

What if there has been another avalanche? What if the cave mouth is covered?

"Do you think you'll know when we're near the cave?" he asked Ishiko when his anxiety overcame his pride.

"I think so," she said, after a pause that Haru wasn't sure how to interpret. "We saw it clearly enough when we left it."

"We can't see anything clearly now."

"We know the route well enough," she said.

"True." He hung on to her reassurance.

When he was at the rear of the march, it took all of his will to prevent himself from looking back. He must not appear to be worried about pursuit. He wouldn't be able to see one until it was too late, anyway.

They aren't following. They can't. Not if the storm was building up behind us like it seemed to be. They would have had to stop us right away, or not at all.

That he was worrying about who might follow bothered him. That he even thought the word *pursuit* made his gorge rise in shame.

I did the right thing. We'll be there soon. It might have been months if I had waited. It might be too late. Mother will understand. When I present her with victory, all will be forgiven. We are the Crab Clan. We do what must be done. And this must be done.

They stopped for frequent short rests. They had to or be spent before they reached the cave. The progress was slow, it was frustrating, and it was real. And when the gray began to shade towards night again, and Haru was about to order the lanterns be lit once more, he saw the cave.

It was that simple. They were in the pass that he *thought* was the right one. He was near the center of the formation at that point. He looked to the left, hoping he hadn't been mistaken, and there it was. It was uncovered, open, a deeper black in the snow-driven twilight. It would have been easy to miss if he hadn't been looking. But he *had* looked, as if he had always been meant to.

As if this was his destiny.

It is. It is. And now I'm sure.

Ishiko saw the cave a moment after he did. They both slowed. The other samurai were marching on, aware of little else than the sheer, miserable effort of walking through the storm.

"Halt," Haru called out. "We have reached our goal."

Now what?

The voice was little, wheedling, recognizable through long and hated familiarity. It was the voice of his self-doubt returning. It had been quiet since he had left Night's Hunger in the triumph that came with carrying vital news. But he had come back. He had come back with a purpose. The doubts seized onto that purpose, as they always did. They knew what he was worth when it came to successfully prosecuting a campaign.

Now what? Here we are, returning in strength. But now what? How do we fight the city? Is there even anything there to fight?

Now what? Now what?

"Go away," he muttered.

"What was that?" Ishiko asked.

Haru winced. He hadn't realized he'd spoken aloud. "Nothing," he said. He started across the narrow stretch of unbroken snow that separated the troops from the cave. The drifts closer to the mountain wall were several feet deep. With each step, his legs plunged all the way down to his groin, and he had to lean forward, flailing his arms, to seize enough momentum to lurch another step. His progress was slow and frustrating, and strenuous enough to force the inner voice down again. Now what? It didn't matter. This was not the moment to ask. That time would come when they were in the city. And then he would know. This was his destiny. Fate would not abandon him.

"This way!" he called unnecessarily. Every one of his samurai was following his example. As one, they forced their way through the snow to the cave.

Haru was the first one inside. Ishiko followed right behind. The order pleased him. The good omens were multiplying. He advanced into the shelter of the cave, leaving the storm behind, and as soon as he was out of reach of the wind, he felt the cold breath of that other wind, the one that blew through the city and traveled through the mountain to become that chill, luring touch. Haru held his breath, listening for the whisper. He heard nothing.

No need to call me now, is there?

Or perhaps the City of Night's Hunger did not want him to come. Maybe it knew it had erred in revealing itself to him.

Too late to change your mind. I have come, and I will conquer you.

"Any whispers?" he asked Ishiko, softly enough that no one else would hear them as the warriors tromped into the cave.

Ishiko shook her head.

"An excellent sign, wouldn't you say?"

Ishiko shrugged. "I do not hear it at this moment. I might in the next."

"If you do, or if I do, so be it. We can answer it this time." He moved forward to the back of the cave, where it narrowed into the tunnel. He paused there, waiting for the full complement of samurai to be inside. Hachi and Hino caught up to him and Ishiko. Haru smiled at them. "And so we are gathered here again."

"I did not expect to be back here so soon," Hino joked.

"Are you disappointed?"

"We are honored," said Hachi.

"We are," said Hino. "It has been a burden to think that we were not able to be at your side when you beheld the City of Night's Hunger for the first time."

"You were doing what was needed. Your duty was here, in the cave, digging our way out. Now I give thanks that I have returned to the city with all of you. This is all as things should be." He raised his voice. "Onward!" he cried to the assembled warriors.

He plunged into the tunnel.

It was such a relief to be able to walk without struggling that the journey through the mountain seemed much shorter than Haru remembered. The breath of the wind grew stronger again. The darkness tried to press in too, but there were too many lanterns this time, and they held it at bay. This time, too, he knew what was on the other side. There was no mystery to the passage. It was nothing more than the final obstacle before he saw the city again.

When he reached the exit, he pushed his way through the final blast of wind with a furious grin. It had failed to stop him before. Its efforts were worse than futile now. It was night again when he stepped out onto the slope, and as before, the storm was weaker here, as if the City of Night's Hunger refused to be concealed by darkness and snow. And as the flakes landed, and Haru heard the sounds of breaking glass again, he realized that the snow was falling here in precisely the same way that it had been when he first set eyes on the city. The weather was unchanged. The wind had the same strength.

Ishiko noticed too. "Nothing has changed," she said. "Time stands still here."

"Yes," said Haru. Then, "No. No. That is not quite it." If time had stopped, the wind would not blow. The snow would not descend. "It is as if time does not matter here. It is irrelevant."

Time was frozen.

Then he wondered if even that was true. The city skewed perceptions. He could not trust what he saw. He had doubts about what he heard. He had to be cautious about everything.

Do not draw conclusions.

That seemed very important. He promised himself he would be careful.

The samurai gathered behind Haru. They stared in silence at the city, and the great central tower that looked back at them, dripping with malformed snow, its shape both massive and blurry to the eye.

"There is our goal, and our opponent," Haru said, looking back at his troops. "That is what we will conquer for the glory of Striking Dawn Castle and the Kakeguchi family."

He hadn't actually expected a cheer, but the ripple of unease that ran through the samurai was disappointing. He would never accuse any of these bushi of being cowards, but he had hoped for more excitement.

It doesn't matter. They have come with you, and you're here. That is what you wanted. Now do what you came to the city to do.

He moved down the slope, towards the narrow, twisting, spiked ridge that led to the gate. The snow was no deeper than it had been before. Of course it wasn't. Though his and Ishiko's footsteps had vanished. There was no trace anyone had been here, whether days or centuries ago.

Haru believed he knew his way forward well enough. He had crossed the ridge twice. Its terrain was not strange to him anymore. Even so, he resisted the temptation to rush, and he congratulated himself on his restraint. For a moment, he wished that Ochiba and Barako were here to see his thoughtful leadership. They would see that he had changed, that he could be trusted.

Oh, so that's what Ochiba and Barako are thinking right now, are they? Do you believe they're favorably impressed to discover you are gone from Striking Dawn?

He snorted, and pushed the thought away. He rebuked

himself to keep his focus.

And he did. He kept track of his contingent. He never rushed. And they all crossed the ridge safely. Even when they were close to the gate, and the temptation was there to run forward, he held back. He advanced steadily, carefully. No one slipped. No one fell. And at last he stood before the gates to the City of Night's Hunger. With him was every single samurai who had left Striking Dawn.

The gates were open. Not by a lot. There was not even enough space between them for a single warrior to squeeze through. But they were not barred. All that was needed was a push.

Haru touched the iron of the left-hand gate. "Was this open before?" he asked Ishiko.

"I don't think so." She grimaced. "I'm struggling to remember. Did we look closely enough?"

"I can't remember either." Some of the details of the first encounter with Night's Hunger were blurred as if infected by the architecture. The city was hurting his eyes again. Even the dark iron of the gate had the intricate engravings, and swam in the corners of his eyes. Bile rose in his throat, but he pushed it down.

"An open invitation?" said Ishiko.

"Or a challenge."

"Either makes me wary."

"Rightly so. But we were wary before. This changes nothing. If the City of Night's Hunger wishes to challenge us, that is why we have come."

Perhaps he spoke with too much fierce joy. Ishiko gave him a sharp look. "We have come with caution, as well as determination, I hope," she said.

"We have," Haru told her. He did his best not to sound impatient. "We have." He gripped the gate with both hands. He leaned against it experimentally. It was heavy. "Together!" he called to his samurai.

On the verge of shouting something about glory, he stopped himself. Now was the time for sober command.

Half a dozen warriors pushed the gates, and they swung open, the dark grind of the metal ringing across the city like a cry. Haru drew his katana and marched in. He said nothing, but in his mind, he laid claim to the city in the name of the Kakeguchi family.

Beyond the gates, a narrow road wound between the ruins. And the structures *were* ruins, Haru now saw, or at least many of them were. Their construction was strange, as deceptive to the eye as the sinuous engravings that coiled across every stone. Twisted pagodas leaned at dangerous angles. Some looked as if they were melting. Others had walls so broken that the roofs appeared to float in mid-air. Then there were structures that resembled huge shrines, but the sweep and angle of their gables was too great, too pronounced, turning them into wings and grins. Across all of the buildings, the drifts of snow hung and entwined with the engravings, creating a suggestion of movement in stone and wood that writhed at the edges of Haru's vision.

Looming over everything was the central tower. It was so much higher than anything else that Haru lost sight of it only for brief moments, when a ruin was close before him and blocking his path.

Even the road was tainted. There was no grid to the city,

though the paths did seem to lead, like an infection, to the great tower. The road twisted like a worm. Other avenues – none wider, many smaller – branched off it. At first Haru stayed on the first road, but soon its path writhed back on itself, curling away from the great tower. He began to take branches. If the tower had not been there, its massiveness looking down on the Kakeguchis, its presence a mountain and a buzzard, Haru would have been lost in the tangle of streets almost immediately. The other landmarks were too uncertain. A ruin that presented one appearance from a distance looked completely different close up, and different again as it receded from view behind other deceptive shells.

And then there were the snowdrifts. Haru was sure the sense of their crawling movement was more than could be explained by the scudding of clouds across the face of Lord Moon. When he looked directly at any of them, as cold and deep as mourning, they were still. They could be congealed pools of the moonlight itself. When he looked away, they thawed and ran, trickling over walls, rushing down the sides of the street, lingering like tongues in the frames of windows and doors.

"The drifts," Ishiko said softly, her blade at the ready. "I do not think they have been formed by the falling snow."

"What do you mean?" Haru asked, reluctant to receive an answer.

Ishiko nodded forward, looking up at the crown of the central tower. "They come from there."

Haru's mouth dried. He had been trying to dismiss the impression that the currents of snow always flowed away from the tower. He exchanged a glance with Ishiko, then looked back at his troops. Even the nearest of the samurai was a shrouded figure, faces close to invisible inside their helms, the colors of their armor faded to the gray of deep twilight. The troops marched steadily. There were no tremors of cowardice. But Haru caught some glimpses of faces. He saw their grim cast. He saw the eyes that were already wounded from seeing so much that was unnatural.

He faced forward. He glared at the tower, ignoring the taunting shift of shadows around him. "Then that is where we must go," he said. "It is the center of all things here. In every way. You agree?"

"I do," said Ishiko.

Haru walked a bit more quickly. They had been making for the tower from the start. Now he felt a stronger sense of purpose. He had an enemy. He was not exploring a hostile terrain. He was leading a charge.

He was looking at the tower when its horn sounded. The blast reverberated in his skull. It thrummed down his spine. He felt it in the depths of his gut. The ground vibrated in terror, as if the sound were about to tear the mountains up from their roots. The horn was long and low and pitiless. It was howl and thunder, warning and summons.

The blast ended, and the echoes answered. They came from all directions, the contorted angles of the City of Night's Hunger twisted into shouts and whispers and cries and laughter. The echoes slid over each other like ripples in flesh. Haru was suddenly cold. His arms and the back of his neck crawled. When the sounds finally stopped, it was with the scuttling withdrawal of insects.

Haru found he was standing still. So was Ishiko, and everyone else.

This is unworthy of you. Get moving.

He swallowed. He took a step forward. The breaking-glass crack of the snow under his boot was almost comforting.

"It's darker," said Ishiko.

She was right. The shadows were thicker on the ruins. The moonlight was colder, a stark shine of ice and bone that caressed the snow in the center of the road, turning it into a lure for the darkness. It glanced off the corners of walls, silvered the edges of empty shells, making the shadows deeper. And the drifts crept in, barely bothering to hide their movement, the tide of white night lapping closer and closer to the samurai. Haru thought of corrupt kansen pushing the snow forward. And he thought of a tide of hungry ghosts.

"To the tower!" Haru snarled and raised his katana. He started forward, but Ishiko caught his arm. "What?" he snapped. He needed the momentum of a charge. If he didn't get everyone moving, the terror might catch up to him.

"Listen," Ishiko hissed.

He didn't want to. He didn't want to hear the wind whisper his name. He had been able to pretend that was not what he had heard that first time in the tunnel. He wasn't sure he would be able to convince himself he had heard an illusion again.

The wind moaned. It mourned. It whirled around the peaks of towers and blew with sorrow and anger down the narrow street. It did not whisper. Instead, a rattling rode the wind. Subtle at first, distant perhaps, then growing louder, closer.

The rattle came from the corpse-windows of the towers, from the other side of the blind doors, from behind the walls, from the darkness of the streets. As it closed in, Haru began to hear other sounds. There was the clank of armor. There was the tread of boots.

"We're surrounded," said Ishiko.

Haru turned around slowly, looking for the enemy, looking for his strategy, looking for the hope. What was coming was still veiled by the shadows. Haru was standing at an intersection. He peered down the streets, and into the vacant blackness of the buildings beside him. He could not see the foe. He could not see what he must do.

He could not see the hope.

And then the doors in the ruin closest to him opened. Wood dragged over stone thresholds. Hinges screeched with drawn-out pain.

The rattling was close.

It was close in the streets, and close on the other side of the solitary wall that leaned into the street.

It was closest on the other side of the doors.

Haru looked up. He saw what had come for them.

The tower's horn thundered again, and Haru heard what he had not the first time it sounded. He heard the hunger.

It was the hunger before the feast.

CHAPTER 10

It was the third dawn since Haru had left. Barako was on the wall, looking north, standing in the gate's east guard tower. She had taken as many watches there as she could. Hours of night, staring into empty blackness. Hours of day, watching the shrieking white of the snow. There had been no break in the weather since the storm had closed in again. The wind had raged against Striking Dawn Castle with such fury, it seemed intent on hurling down the walls.

Barako had stood the watches, staring back at the storm without flinching. Let it do what it would. Let it conceal what it would. It would do nothing against Striking Dawn and the Kakeguchi family while she stood.

Ochiba entered the guard post. She had been on the ramparts, and was caked in blown snow. In the slight shelter of the tower, she wiped away the ice from her lashes and hair. "Still here," she said to Barako.

"My watch ends at the hour of the dragon."

Ochiba squinted into the driving snow. "It's a wonder we even know what hour we are in. We have day and we have night. That is all." She joined Barako against the back wall, away from the worst of the gusts. "You are taking too many watches," she said gently.

"I'm doing what I must."

"What are you accomplishing except courting exhaustion?"

"Your patrols have been frequent."

"Yes, but I'm resting too. Are you?"

"I'm resting enough." That was the truth. Tired, she would be prone to error. She was not about to jeopardize her ability to perform her duties to the castle, to the family, and to the daimyō.

"I still think you are imposing a penance on yourself."

Barako shrugged.

"Lady Akemi does not blame you."

"I know. She is kind. But I was asleep when Haru left. I saw that he was on the verge of doing something reckless, and I failed to stop him."

"We all did."

"But I knew," Barako insisted. "I think I even knew what he was going to do."

"Did you know the storm was going to give him the opportunity?"

"No," Barako admitted. She sighed.

Ochiba touched her arm. "What should you have done? Watched him every moment, whether he slept or woke, until the storm ended? Do you enjoy his company that much?"

"No." Through her long watches, Barako had cursed Haru. He had been an irritant before. He had become a threat to Striking Dawn. For Akemi's sake, and for the sake of the political stability at the castle, she prayed to their ancestors for his safe return. For her own sake, she would have cheerfully decapitated him for his idiocy. She sighed. "I have to blame someone," she said, rueful. "Since Haru is not here, I will have to do."

"Then share the blame," said Ochiba. "There is enough to go around, if we want it. But it really belongs to Haru. All of it."

Barako circled the post, slowly, glancing through the door to the staircase to make sure there were no guards coming who might overhear. Then she went to stand close to Ochiba again. "Set aside the City of Night's Hunger," she said. "If Haru returns, I wonder if that is still the best thing for Lady Akemi or not."

"It's what she wants."

"Of course it is. He's her son."

"What are you saying?" Ochiba asked.

"I'm not sure that I know," said Barako. "But Haru has done enormous harm to himself and the daimyō."

"Agreed."

"Do you think the damage can be undone?"

Ochiba was quiet for a moment, pensive. "I can't guess," she said. "You're worried that Doreni will use what has happened to his advantage."

Barako snorted. "He would be a fool not to. If I were a Hiruma, I would think he was the Striking Dawn Castle's best hope."

"We are not Hiruma. We are Kakeguchi. But all of us are Crab Clan."

"And it is Striking Dawn that matters more than the family that governs it."

Barako brushed irritably at the snow that blew into her eyes in the silence that followed. Ochiba broke it first. "None of it matters, does it?"

"It doesn't," Barako said softly. Her duty was unchanged. She would follow it to the end. "I needed to talk about it," she went on.

"So did I," said Ochiba.

In spite of her concern, Barako's blood warmed with joy. Ochiba was the only one to whom she could have said these things. But she also needed to say them to Ochiba. That Ochiba felt the same freedom, and the same need, was wonderful. "Maybe I can stop thinking about the succession now," she said.

"And resenting the fact that many lives will have to be risked to save a fool?"

"That too." *One life in particular.* She frowned, looking out into the falling snow. "Is it growing lighter?" she asked.

"I think it is. The wind doesn't seem as strong, too."

"You're right. Maybe the storm is finally ending."

"And those lives will be put at risk very soon," Ochiba said, her tone dry.

Together, they watched the fury dissipate. The wind dropped quickly. Soon it was not much more than a frigid breeze. The snow kept coming down. It let up much more gradually. Even so, it was ending. Gradually, the day became real. The mountains came into being once more. First the ground below the guard towers became visible, and then the path leading down the castle's mount, and finally even the roads Striking Dawn watched over.

"We must make ready," said Ochiba. "We will leave very shortly."

"It would be too much to ask of Haru that he comes back on his own," Barako muttered. Then she stepped forward with a jerk, startled. "Who…" she began.

She was interrupted by the guards in the west tower. They began striking the tower bell, raising the alarm.

Someone was approaching from the north. A single figure had appeared at the top of the rise into the pass, and was walking with halting, erratic steps.

Barako flew down the tower stairs, Ochiba a moment behind her. She ordered the guards to open the gates for her, and started down the path, cursing the deep snow that held her back. She heard Ochiba call for a squad to accompany them.

One person. One. A bad sign. They will need care. Or they will need destroying.

The figure fell several times, and rose again with obvious difficulty. By the time Barako had finally reached the bottom of the mount, the figure had barely covered a third of the same distance. She started north, uphill. She tried to walk on the top of the snow, but never managed a step or two before it gave way beneath her and she was up to her thighs and struggling to move forward. Behind her, Ochiba and the squad were not doing any better.

Ahead, the figure collapsed again, and did not rise.

Barako swore under her breath and kept moving, using all of her strength to advance with what felt like the pace of a glacier. It seemed it would take her days to reach the spot where the figure had fallen. *And how long will it take us to reach you, Haru, assuming it is not you who has just arrived, having abandoned your troops to freeze to death?*

At last, she reached the depression in the snow where the figure had dropped. It was a samurai, a man, his armor shattered, hanging in shards from tattered leather strips. He had fallen face-first. Barako rolled him over. It was Hachi.

His eyes had rolled up, revealing only their whites. He had lost his gauntlets, and his fingers were curled into tight balls, never to be broken, their skin unnaturally pale except where they were turning black. "Hachi," Barako said, softly, and then again, louder, "*Hachi!*" The samurai did not respond. Barako leaned over him and place her ear near his mouth. He was not breathing.

He had been wounded in the face and chest. There were deep gashes. From blades, Barako thought. She wasn't sure. Hachi's armor was stained black with his blood.

Barako leaned back. She would wait for the squad to carry him back. There was nothing more to be done here. *But there is much more we will soon have to do. Oh, Haru, you fool, what have you done?*

Ochiba caught up and crouched beside her. "Hachi," she breathed. "The state of him. And his armor. How did he make it back?"

"He didn't," said Barako. "He's dead."

"Even this far, then," said Ochiba, not offended. "In the storm. In the cold."

"Desperation," Barako said, not liking where the speculation was taking them. "He must have been fleeing something far worse than the storm."

The four guards who had come with Ochiba picked up Hachi. Their faces were masks of barely restrained horror, they started the slow process of carrying him back to the castle. Barako and Ochiba walked behind them.

"Only one," said Barako.

"That does not tell us the fate of the others," Ochiba said.

"It points in that direction. It tells us nothing good."

"It does tell us that we must hurry."

"It does," Barako conceded. Even if there were no survivors to be found, the danger that the City of Night's Hunger presented was real. It could not be ignored. It had to be dealt with, and soon.

"We must be clear," said Doreni, his voice echoing in the main hall. "The expedition certainly must deal with the danger presented by the City of Night's Hunger. But when it comes to Kakeguchi Haru, this is not a mission of rescue. It is a bringing to judgment."

"You speak for the daimyō?" Barako snapped. She could not abide the triumph in his tone, and the opportunism it revealed.

"Of course not. I make no such claim," Doreni said quickly, as if he realized he had overplayed his hand.

"Don't you?" said Akemi, her false mildness withering. "I had the impression you were making an edict."

Doreni flushed. He mastered himself before speaking again. "If I presumed too much, Lady Akemi, I apologize." He made a stiff, short bow. "My only wish was to establish clarity. I believe that is important. We are in crisis. No one in this room will deny that, I think."

"No, they would not," said Akemi.

"It gives me no pleasure to say what I must say," Doreni went on.

Liar, Barako thought.

"As I am not a Kakeguchi, it falls to me to point out the unpleasant truths that we must deal with. Your son disobeyed you. He has, it seems likely, caused the death of a third of a company of samurai, in addition to the cost of the caravan. That is not a loss the castle can easily afford. He has put Striking Dawn and the region it protects in danger. He has failed you, my daimyō. He has irrevocably stained the reputation of this family and this castle. He must answer for his crimes, if only to put an end to the dishonor he has caused and to prevent its spread."

Oh well done. That was very well done. Barako had to give Doreni credit for that speech. As self-serving as it was, it was also true.

"The judgment of Kakeguchi Haru has yet to be passed," Akemi said, formality masking her despair. "If he is alive, his trial shall not occur in his absence. He will be made to face his accusers when he has been brought back here."

Doreni nodded. "You are correct, Lady Akemi," he said. "I believe we all understand what must be done in this regard. I am satisfied."

You would be, Barako thought. *You can afford to be magnanimous in your victory. Akemi's heir is either dead or unworthy of Striking Dawn. Your accession is all but certain.*

She looked at Akemi, hoping the pity she felt was not visible in her face, and dreading the rule of Doreni. She prayed the ancestors granted Akemi a long life.

"We are discussing the aftermath of our mission," said Ochiba. "All of this must await our return. What matters now is the immediate action."

"Which has been made more difficult," Doreni pointed out. "You will now be venturing into the City of Night's Hunger with only two thirds the warriors you should have had."

"I thank the lieutenant for his skill in numbers," Ochiba said drily.

"It is true," said Akemi. "You will have to make do with that force," she added to Ochiba. "We do not dare deplete the castle's defenses any more than that."

"Nor would I ask you to," said Ochiba. "That strength will be enough. You have my word."

"The storm is done?" Akemi asked.

"It seems to be," said Barako. "The sky is clear to the north. We can ask for no better time than this to march."

Akemi looked thoughtful. "Junji," she said. "The lull in the storm and now its end. What do you make of them? Is this chance or design that we have seen?"

"I have been searching for an answer to that same question, my daimyō," said Junji. "I have not found it."

"If this was by design," said Doreni, "then Haru may have unleashed something on his first visit, and its power is great indeed."

"Whether that is true or not," said Barako, "our options are the same."

"We shall be wary and prepare for the worst," said Ochiba. "As we always do."

"As all of us *should*," Akemi said bitterly. "But not all of us remember that."

The rest of the council was silent. Even Doreni respected her pain. Or, Barako thought, he knew better than to plunge the knife deeper at this moment.

"There is another problem," said Ochiba. "Everyone who knows where to find the entrance to the cave left with Haru."

"We can help with that, don't you think?" Barako said to Junji.

"Yes," said the monk. "I still have found very little about the city, but thanks to the descriptions given to us by Haru and by samurai Ishiko, I think we can make a map."

"Do so," said Akemi. She turned to Ochiba. "When you have the map, go. Remove the shadow of that city from Striking Dawn. And bring him back, please. Bring my son back."

Chance or design. The question of the weather haunted Barako as she and Ochiba led their warriors north. The sky was a cloudless, brittle blue. The snow was blinding. The air was so cold, it was ready to crack. But though the progress was slow through drifts high and deep, it was not dangerous. On the high ridges, Barako could see the great vistas of the mountain peaks, their lines as sharply defined as if they had been cut out with a razor.

When the samurai found shelter under an overhang for the night, the stars and moon were so bright, there was barely any need for a fire except for warmth.

"What do you think?" Ochiba asked as they crouched

together before the flames.

"About what?" Barako asked.

"The ease of our journey."

So Ochiba was being troubled by the same thoughts.

"Are we being lured by the city?" the captain went on. "Or blessed by the ancestors?"

"Have you been reading my mind?"

"Or you mine, maybe."

Barako chuckled. "If we find our way to the City of Night's Hunger without incident, I will be braced for the worst."

"As will I."

There was a glint of eagerness in Ochiba's eyes when she spoke. Barako knew it well. That shine arrived with the approach of combat. It was there on the battlefield too. It was part of her lightning. Ochiba thrived in war. She was not foolish like Haru. She did not rush in without knowing what she was doing. Barako trusted her to be cautious in the City of Night's Hunger. Barako trusted her because she knew Ochiba would listen to her own caution, and temper her lightning, just as she would stir Barako's fire to a conflagration that would consume the enemy.

But we have to be careful. We have always faced traps. This one, though… This one feels terrible.

Ochiba said she would be braced for the worst. Barako was satisfied. They would be each other's bulwarks and blades.

They headed off before dawn. Even with the company huddled together for warmth, it was too cold to remain still any longer. They move on, through the end of a night glittering with reflected moonlight, marching north into a day that, when it came, was as searingly bright as the one before. Summer did not have this intensity of light. No land without a deep blanket of snow could reflect sunlight with such merciless clarity. The day jabbed at Barako's forehead. In the storm, she had stared and stared and seen nothing. Now she squinted, and shielded her eyes with her hand, and she still saw so much it hurt.

In the end, they barely needed the map. Barako consulted it frequently, and she had just said, "We should be near," when Ochiba said, "There it is." The mouth of the cave was a startling blot of darkness in the glaring white of the snow. It was hole punched into the day. It made the brilliance of the sun seem thin, as easy to snap as the first birthing of ice.

The company turned and fought through the drifts toward the cave.

"This was easy, wasn't it?" said Ochiba.

"As I feared."

"You think we have been lured."

"I don't know." She didn't want to think that. The implications of the enemy's power were too disturbing. "I am going to assume we have been."

"You were always the wise one."

"You don't think we have been lured?" Barako asked, surprised.

Ochiba gave her a gentle smile. "I'm acting on the same assumption you are. I just meant what I said. You are the wise one. And that makes me fortunate. That is all."

Barako smiled back, her cheeks hot even in the frost-biting cold.

"No signs that Haru came this way," she said as they drew near the mouth of the cave.

"We haven't seen any signs at all. Not surprising. The storm was a fierce one. He made it here. We know that."

Barako nodded. She thought of Hachi's wounds. It was not the cold that had sliced open his face and chest. And it was not clean blades that had carved such ragged tears.

They entered the cave, and then the passage. Barako felt the breath Haru had told them about. Ishiko had spoken uncertainly about whispers too. Barako did not hear those, but the breeze immediately had her on edge.

"The breath from the tunnels is wrong," she said.

Ochiba grunted. "Feels different from outside, doesn't it?"

"Malign," said Barako. And worse than that. Rotten. Knowing. The air that passed through the City of Night's Hunger was transformed.

"The Shadowlands taint of the city travels this far," said Ochiba.

"How much further, I wonder."

"To Striking Dawn?"

"I don't know. I hope not."

Their sense of the breeze's malevolence grew stronger the further they went. Barako tightened her grip on her hammer. There was nothing to hit. But the solidity of the weapon kept her grounded. Her pace was steady, a determined approach toward an enemy. She had fought in the Shadowlands. She had seen horrors, and she had bested them. She did not have the arrogance to believe she always would. She did have the resolution to face them without flinching.

Even so, she caught her breath when they emerged from the tunnel and saw the city. Ochiba gasped, and there were murmurs of alarm throughout the company. There was no shame in the startled displays of emotion. The samurai would not have been human if there had been no ripples in their calm.

It was night. Lord Moon shone over the tower and its domain. The stars were hidden by the turbulent darkness of the clouds.

"This isn't right," Ochiba murmured.

It had been late morning when the company had reached the cave. It was only early afternoon now. But it was night. Deep night. Night with no promise of dawn.

"Even Lord Moon is wrong," said Barako. The night before, he had been a waning gibbous. Now he was full, and baleful as a naked skull. "It is night here. Always night. Always the same night." She looked at the city, thinking about what Haru and Ishiko had described. She frowned at the emerald glare in the peak of the tower. "That light…" she said.

"Haru did not mention it," Ochiba confirmed.

"Nor did Ishiko. It was not there before."

"So *something* has changed."

"Since Haru came back?"

"Or because he came back." Ochiba nodded grimly, taking the measure of her opponent. "Very well," she said. "Very well. Very well. The City of Night's Hunger declares itself. We know each other, then." She spoke to the company. "The stain of the Shadowlands is on this land. Let us complete our preparations. Though we carry weapons and jade, let us truly arm ourselves as we must for what awaits us."

She kneeled with Barako beside her. The entire company kneeled. Ochiba prayed to the spirits of the Kakeguchi ancestors. Barako listened to the words, and through them found her core. All her actions, her very existence, would now be dedicated to the single goal of rescuing Haru. She prayed for the blessing of Lord Hida. With every step into the darkness before them, she would not walk alone. She would seek to be one with the perfection of action, and the purity of purpose.

"Are we ready?" Ochiba asked. In answer, her samurai rose and drew their weapons. "We are ready," she said.

They began the crossing of the ridge of claws.

The snow fell steadily, and had been forever, Barako suspected; endless flakes in the endless night. Yet it was not deep underfoot. There was not much more than a dusting over the rocky terrain of the ridge. "There are no footprints," she said. There was no sign Haru and his troops had come this way. She looked back. She left tracks in the snow. The company was tramping it down to the stone.

"He must have come this way," said Ochiba.

"Not enough snowfall to cover his traces, but there are no traces. He has been erased."

"You are gloomy, old friend."

"I wish I was not." The light in the tower bothered her more and more. She wondered just how badly Haru had failed. She wondered if there was any hope of undoing what he had wrought.

"With every sign, the scale of our task becomes clearer,"

Ochiba said. "I am glad of that. I would not want an inflated sense of our chances."

Barako smiled. "You have cast an aspersion."

"I do believe I have."

The banter was good. It was a relief to have the emotional space to be irritated with Haru. "He complicates our lives even when he is absent," she said.

"A good thing we're used to it then."

They were silent as they reached the gates, which stood slightly ajar. The city waited for them in silence. Its stillness was a lie Barako refused to believe, and it was belied by the squirming architecture. Ishiko had warned her about how hard it was to look at Night's Hunger. Barako had tried to picture what Ishiko had witnessed, had tried to prepare herself for what she would encounter herself. She realized now how badly she had failed.

Ochiba stopped inside the narrow space between the two gates, on the threshold of Night's Hunger. Barako stood at her side. They gazed at the narrow road, twisting away between the leaning shells of the ruins.

"Only a fool would march into so obvious a trap," said Barako.

"A fool and the greater fools sent after him."

Barako sighed. "He just walked right in, didn't he?"

Ochiba nodded. "Haru the intrepid, the fearless, laying claim to new territory for the Kakeguchis."

Perhaps they were being unfair. But the only sounds in the city were the keen of the wind and the tinkling of the glass snowflakes. If Haru's contingent was in combat, or marching, or doing anything at all, Barako should have been able to hear them. The silence was witness to disaster.

"Now he forces us to do the same thing," Ochiba muttered. Her anticipation of war was in her stance and in her voice, but caution was there too. She shook her head.

"No," said Barako. "I will not fight on the city's terms."

"We will not," Ochiba said, defiance and anger growing. "Night's Hunger does not command us." She looked up at the gate, exchanged a look with Barako, and nodded. "Our terms, then."

Barako took a vial from her pouch. Ochiba did the same. Junji had prepared it for her while she had been adding some finishing touches to the map. Behind them, the sixty samurai of their company lined up just outside the gate. In their training, they had not yet developed the wisdom and the skills needed for the ritual the two officers were about to perform. They recognized what was about to happen, though. They also recognized the need for it. Junji had performed the cleansing rite at the gates of Striking Dawn Castle, calling upon the blessing of the ancestors on the company. Ochiba and Barako, and their warriors, had marched as Haru had not, under the commands of their daimyō.

Barako walked along the line of her thirty troops, while Ochiba did the same with hers. The samurai removed their helms. From the vial, she took the sacred jade-infused oil and anointed their foreheads. "I call upon you, Lord Hida," she said. "Founder and defender of the Crab Clan. Bear witness to us, your children, in our struggle in your name against the machinations of Fu Leng, your great enemy." She paused, and then intoned, "The strength of Lord Hida" as she touched the head of each warrior.

When she and Ochiba had passed before all their samurai, they blessed each other, and then they turned to face the city. They extended the cleansing rite from the individual to the area, calling on the spirits to sanctify the land on which they stood.

"Spirits of earth and wood, of stone and jade, we beseech you. Bless us! Purify this place where we will take our stand, and drive out the evil spirits!" They dripped oil on snow and stone.

The City of Night's Hunger responded to their declaration of war. The tower blasted a terrible horn. Barako grimaced in anger and spiritual pain at the sound. The ground cracked where the oil had touched it. And the blood-red light in the tower shone brighter, hard with rage.

"Purify this place where we will take our stand," Barako repeated with Ochiba. "And drive out the evil spirits."

They dripped the sanctifying oil. The horn of the tower blared again. The earth shook.

Barako knew they could not remove the taint of the Shadowlands. Not so simply. The City of Night's Hunger was too deeply corrupt. They were only two mortals. But they inflicted a wound. And the city stirred itself, outraged.

They shook off their silence. They echoed with the tramp of feet, the jingle of armor, and the rattle of bone. There were voices suddenly, harsh, scraping voices that sprang from throats choking with the ruin of their own flesh.

"To the gates," Ochiba commanded. "But we do not go through. We hold them. Let the foe come to us, and be destroyed." Even wide open, the space between the gates was only about fifteen feet. The entrance to the city was an excellent choke point. It would keep enemies in as easily as it would keep them out.

The company formed an arc in front of the gate, blades and hammers at the ready. Barako and Ochiba took up positions closest to the entrance, on either side. Barako had the left. At a nod from Ochiba on the right, she took up the vial of sacred oil one more time. "Drive out the evil spirits! Begone, demons!" they chanted, and they anointed the open gates.

The horn sounded yet again. It seemed even louder, longer, and more doom-laden than before. From the approaching foe came shrieks of fury. The booted feet ran.

Barako hoisted her hammer. *Now we will see.*

The enemy arrived.

She saw.

She wished she hadn't.

CHAPTER 11

Barako knew the enemy that came for them. Days ago, these creatures had been her friends. Days ago, she had been preparing to march with them to the City of Night's Hunger. She had been expecting to fight side by side with them. Now the samurai who had left with Haru came charging to destroy her.

The samurai, or what was left of them.

Their armor was broken, hewn apart by the blows that had killed them. None of them had died easily. They must have fought hard. There was no comfort for Barako in that thought in this moment, because the hard deaths had created more hungry ghosts. The samurai were zombies, their skin pale and gray with death, their wounds hanging open, folds of flesh rippling as they ran. There was no blood left in their bodies. Their faces had withered, wrinkling as if aged decades beyond the years allotted to mortals. They were crumbling with decay. If time was meaningless in the City of Night's Hunger, ruin was not. The warriors who had been dead for a few days at most looked as if they had been in the grip of the city for an eternity.

The worst thing was that Barako could recognize them. She knew every shriveled, rotting face. She knew the names of every monster that rushed the gate, knew the qualities of the men and women they had been, knew the sound of their laughter, knew their skill in war, knew their dedication and their integrity.

All that she knew was gone. All that remained was the mockery of what these mortals had been.

She wished that was all that was left. She wanted to hope their spirits had found a way to pass on to the next life instead of being damned to this place for eternity.

Her hopes were irrelevant, though. What mattered now was her hammer.

The weapon was an old one. It had been passed down to her by her mother, from her grandmother, and from generations before them. It had been sanctified in the solemn rites that marked its passage from mother to daughter. It had kept Barako alive in the Shadowlands. It was the bane of tainted things.

There were fewer than thirty of the zombie samurai who came rushing out of the shadows to charge the gate, less than half the strength of the company that awaited them. The zombies did not come alone, though. Behind them came a horde of skeletons, the monsters who had killed them and turned them into creatures of the Shadowlands. They were what Haru's troops would eventually become. Almost all their flesh was gone. Leathery strips of skin and strings of muscle hung from bone. Fragments of armor clung to the bodies. Some of the skeletons wore helms.

Others had plates hanging from a single strap, swinging wildly as they ran. Others had a single boot, and still others had two. All of them had just enough fragments of armor to signal what they once had been. They were bone, but they had been samurai, and they hated those who still were.

The zombies rushed to the gate. Barako stepped into the gap with a huge swing of her hammer. The zombie in the lead was Hino, a fine warrior, one Barako liked and trusted, whom she had trained, and whom Ochiba had assigned to Haru, so he would have the best and wisest samurai under his command, a bushi who would temper his folly and buttress his strengths. In an eye-blink, Barako saw her friend's distorted face, and she knew it was no accident that had placed Hino at the front of the charge of the dead. What reigned in the City of Night's Hunger had made this choice, knowing the effect it would have.

Who the zombie was changed nothing. Barako knew all these monsters. If she could not give them peace, at least she would give them destruction.

She stepped, she swung, and she smashed the hammer into Hino's skull. The head blew apart in a shower of bone fragments and desiccated brain. Barako used the momentum of the swing to take half a step back, and then go forward again, swinging the hammer the other way. She crushed the flank of another zombie. The force of her blow hurled it into the creature beside it, knocking them into a tangle of bony limbs.

Ochiba had launched herself into the fray at the same moment as Barako. She wove between the zombies, slashing with her katana. Her attack had no pauses. It was a continuous movement, a whirling spiral that cut into the zombies and back out, in and out, always hitting them on their unprotected flanks, her blade slicing through necks, decapitating, and cutting chests in half. Her blade was as precious and holy as Barako's hammer. Tainted flesh burned at the touch of its sanctified steel. She fought with the same grim purpose as Barako. She too cut down what had been her friends.

Barako was the thunder. Ochiba was the lightning. Together they were the storm. Their assault was as precise as it was brutal. It blunted the rush of the horrors.

But the gate was wide. Other zombies pushed past them, and met the wall of samurai. The sixty fell on the enemy with calm fury. They avenged their comrades by destroying their bodies. Many of them did not have weapons that had become holy legacies, but every blade and hammer had been blessed by Junji, and every warrior called upon their honored ancestors for protection as they threw themselves at the zombies.

The tower sounded its horn, shaking souls and earth.

"Do you hear its anger?" Ochiba shouted. "Do you hear its frustration?"

"The enemy is in our trap!" Barako called to her troops. "Press them and do not let them pass! We have the advantage!" She blocked a sword blow with an upward swing, smashing the zombie's katana from its hands, and then brought the hammer down over her head, driving the monster's skull down between its shoulder blades and crumpling its spine. The zombie fell, quivering its last in the snow.

They were holding the dead things at the gate. Night's Hunger had tried to lure them in, but they had called it out instead. They had the enemy in a position where superior numbers did not matter. They could hold the gate almost indefinitely.

That was not enough.

"Do you see him?" Ochiba called to Barako. She ducked under a zombie's swing. The dead were clumsy. There was little of the skill that had been theirs in life, and Ochiba would have been too fast for them then. She came up under the zombie's reach, and with an upward stroke, split it in two.

"He isn't here," Barako said. Already they had destroyed most of Haru's contingent. There was no sign of him. It was the tide of skeletons reaching the gate that would challenge them now. "I haven't seen Ishiko either."

Two skeleton samurai rushed her from both sides, jaws hanging open, airless screams ringing in her ears. She grunted in disgust. With two strikes, she smashed the ribcage of one to splinters and pulverized the skull of the second.

"We have to search, then," said Ochiba, whirling and slashing. She was a lethal blur. Horrors collapsed in pieces in her wake.

"To the tower?" Barako asked.

"To the tower, with speed. Daizu, Goemon, Nahomi!" she called. "Join me and Barako. The rest of you hold the gate."

The three samurai she had named lunged forward. They were fast. They were from Ochiba's contingent, warriors in her mold.

"Now!" Ochiba ordered.

Barako barreled forward, shouldering skeletons aside, ramming with her armor and smashing the hammer down. She punched a hole into the horde. Ochiba and the three samurai rushed ahead of her and cut their way forward, slicing through dozens of skeletons. Barako followed, anchoring the rear.

At the same time, the rest of the company charged the gate, as if all would now invade the city. The monsters reacted to the threat and pushed back, concentrating on the greater numbers of their foe. Their error gave the squad the chance to break through and run deeper into the streets. In moments, a wail went up, the dead crying after escaped prey. But they had already lost the race.

The five samurai plunged into the dark. Ochiba ran at a full sprint, and the others matched her. She kept the great tower always in view, the death-green eye of its light staring down at them with baleful anger. Ochiba chose her paths at every intersection without hesitation. Barako trusted her instincts. They did not know the path forwards, but they had to keep moving. If they were fast enough, the forces in the city might not be able to prepare an ambush in time.

They used the secondary towers as landmarks, guideposts on the way to the center of the dark ruin. The winged eruptions of rock that surrounded them leaned over the street. The shadows beneath them were deep as oceans. The rattle of bones came from within, and the accusing wail of the dead, before the skeletons rushed out of the darkness and into the corpse-light of Lord Moon.

Ochiba's gamble paid off. The dead samurai were few in

number, and the squad tore through them without slowing down. Ochiba stayed in the light as much as she could. It was not, Barako thought, the light of comfort or of safety. It was the light of endings and despair. It also leveled the battlefield. There the warriors of Striking Dawn could see what was trying to kill them.

They drew closer to the tower. Its terrible horn thundered again. It was a summons to horror. It was also, Barako decided, a bellow of rage. Each blast shook her to her core, but she kept going. *Your roars are a sign of your impotence. You cannot stop us.*

The streets wound. They twisted. They writhed. They tangled up, and they looped back on themselves into intersections of illogic. Again and again, the samurai found themselves suddenly going away from their target. But Ochiba never hesitated. They ran, and they ran, and even with the setbacks they drew closer while the tower raged at them.

At last, with the horn sounding one more time, they arrived before it.

The tower gave birth to the snowdrifts of the city. Lord Moon shone on the vast structure. The green light blazed from its peak. The light of dead white and the light of dead green created the shapes of snow, and the drifts hung from the gables like long, ragged curtains, flowing down the height of the tower to spread across the city. From here, the unnatural snow reached every corner of Night's Hunger.

The tower was as massive as it was tall. Its gables were clawed, grotesque, reptilian. They were almost wide enough to be wings, as if the tower might yet rise up and cast its shadow over new lands. It looked as if, instead of being constructed, it had thrust up from beneath the ground, hurling the crust back like flaps of skin. From a distance, it had appeared dark, but up close it had the pallor of a thing dead but malign, and Barako saw that its substance was the same as the talisman's. She shuddered to think they had once mistaken it for white jade.

The tower's entrance had no door, and was wide open. It was edged with spikes, and looked like a lamprey's maw. Inside, profound shadow wrestled with jagged slashes of diseased emerald light. The interior pulsed like a living thing, a heart that hated and hungered.

A slope of shattered rock led to the entrance. On it, blocking the way, was a large group of skeleton warriors. Unlike those who had rushed the city gates, their armor was largely intact. They were also larger. As the squad closed with them, Barako saw why. They were made from more than one body. They had three arms or four. Some had two heads. Multiple femurs and ribcages had been fused together, creating hulking giants. Each hand clasped a pitted, rusty sword, the kind that had torn Hachi's flesh so hideously.

Dedication to purpose turned Barako's horror to anger. I am your bane, monsters.

Ishiko was at the head of the fiends. She was a zombie, and though she had not been turned into a giant, she was different from Haru's other fallen comrades. The venomous light coiled around her. Her shriveled, mottled features were pulled back in a rictus of anger. She quivered with the rage of betrayal. She had been destroyed on a fool's errand, and now she meant to bring all others down into her abyss.

Her face struck Barako in the heart even more than the blasting of the horn. In that anger, in that pain, there was still a trace of what the samurai had once been. This horror was more than just a body that was forbidden to rest. It was a ruin of Ishiko. She had been one of the most respectable warriors Barako had ever known. It chilled her to see a blasted reflection of that now. This creature's hatred was pure. She sought destruction with the same absolute commitment with which she had once followed her duty. This was her new duty. Her jaw dropped open and she wailed, the sound an awful, cracked echo of the beloved comrade's voice. Everything Ishiko had believed in had been taken from her. Now her anger was not directed at the thing that had robbed her. Instead, as if the evil had shown her the truth of the world, she sought to tear the same beliefs from all before her.

After the last sounding of the horn, a scream came from inside the tower. It was so weak a sound by comparison. It was pitiable. It had no power. Even another hundred yards away, it would be inaudible, its horror and fear and pain lost, swallowed by the city's hunger. It was small and human. It was mortal.

It was Haru.

The skeletons howled with Ishiko and they charged. They formed a wall between the samurai and the tower. Squad and monsters clashed. There would be no rushing past this foe.

Ishiko ran first at Ochiba. At the last moment, the zombie feinted to the left, the speed and agility too horribly like those of the living warrior. She skittered around the squad and came at Barako's flank.

One of the giant skeletons reared in front of Ochiba at the moment she had been prepared to fight Ishiko. Four arms and four blades slashed at the captain from both sides.

Barako turned on her heel. She blocked Ishiko's strike with the shaft of her hammer. The blow was powerful. Green light flared. The zombie burned with the power that infested the corpse. Her eyes blazed with the flame of their terrible truth. She howled again, jumping back out of the way of Barako's swing, then darting in again with her katana. Barako turned and caught the hit with her shoulder plate and swung again. Ishiko lunged away, but received a glancing blow on the shoulder, hard enough to spin her around.

Ochiba leapt to one side, dropping low, out of the way of the blades. The skeleton used the four blades to stop her counterstrike. The monster was not as fast as Ochiba, but fast enough, and it used its bulk to absorb her blows. It was determined not to let her pass.

Haru screamed.

The other skeletons fought with Daizu, Goemon, and Nahomi. When the monsters screamed, Barako thought she heard a trace of a mimicry of the tower's horn. They were its guardians. They would defend it as she would Striking Dawn.

Nahomi lured a two-headed monster forward. It stumbled into an awkward lunge, and she smashed her hammer against its elbow, shattering the arm. Goemon took advantage of the moment. He had just forced back one of the other giants, and he made a vicious turn to plunge his katana at the staggering monster's neck. The creature jerked at the same instant, spoiling his aim. The blade went between the heads. One of the skulls whipped around and snapped its jaws closed on his blade. He jerked it free, but the extra second it took him to do so was enough for the opponent he had forced into retreat to storm back. Its three arms wielded a massive, two-handed zanbatō sword. It slashed the enormous, curving blade into Goemon's back, severing his spine. Nahomi hurled herself at the twin-headed creature, and with a shout of vengeance, shattered both of its necks with two swift, punishing blows of her hammer.

Ishiko hissed. The zombie sprinted around Barako and made a swift run at Nahomi. Barako leapt after it. She was slower, in her armor, than Ochiba. But she had speed of her own when she called upon it. Her hammer strike was awkward as she ran, but hit the zombie in the shins. Ishiko rolled, screaming a rage that was worse than the death cry of an animal, and came back at Barako while Nahomi jumped from the fallen giant and clashed weapons with another.

Barako blocked Ishiko's flurry of strikes. She retreated, buying time, looking for an opening. As she did, she glanced toward Ochiba.

The captain feinted, sidestepped as the monster skeleton tried to counter, and thrust her katana through a seam in the monster's armor, into the joint of its knee. She twisted the katana, pulled it out in a slashing move, and cut the leg out from under the monster. It fell at her, screaming. She avoided it easily.

She was on the uphill side of the enemy. There was nothing blocking her access to the tower.

Haru screamed again.

Ochiba's eyes met Barako's.

The moment was the briefest. It was sliced so finely from the measure of time that it had no dimensions at all. Next to it, a single heartbeat was the passing of an age. Barako looked across the battle into Ochiba's eyes without distraction, without a twitch in the smooth movement of her defense against Ishiko. The tiniest fragment of time. Not even a spark against the dark of night.

Yet it had the weight of a glacier. It pressed down on Barako. It was so massive, it wore down mountains, so how could she shoulder it? Its weight came from absences, of words, of gestures, of confessions, of touch. Of hopes, and of laughter and of the dreams of what might be. All that had been left undone was gathered together, and the other side of the moment was too late to think of them.

The look and its weight were beyond bearing. Barako should have gasped. She should have shouted. But the instant was too short. There was no time for anything that was not happening already.

No time for anything except a decision.

Ochiba was going into the tower alone.

No, Barako would have shouted, had the moment been long enough. *You must not. Do not divide the forces. Do not go in alone. Please. Please. Do not go in alone.*

Except in truth, she would not have shouted. So many times, in so many battles, Ochiba's battle joy had balanced with Barako's caution. This time, though, there was no balance to seek.

Time in the moment to make a decision? No, that was not so. Because there was no decision to make. Fate had decreed what must be done. Haru was in the tower. Ochiba was the only one with the opportunity. It was nothing like recklessness that commanded her to turn from Barako and run for the entrance. It was only duty that called. It was honor that commanded.

And in that fragment of time, before Ochiba turned, while Barako still looked across in horror to see her eyes and know what was about to happen, Barako cursed the tyranny of her duty.

In time yet to come, in the uneasy dark of sleeplessness, Barako would think about that curse, and realize that she understood the rage that burned in the thing that had been, and in a terrible way still was, Ishiko.

The hobbled skeleton tried to drag itself after Ochiba. There was a new pain in its scream without breath, as if in its failure it too knew the meaning of duty and felt its loss. Ochiba sprinted up the slope and vanished into the green and black storm beyond the threshold. The doorway quivered, its spiked circumference twitching inward briefly, then stilling. It did not close.

Barako snarled. She turned her wrath on Ishiko. Barako was here when she should be at Ochiba's side. She could not know what was happening in the tower. The fear that she had seen Ochiba for the last time fueled her speed and the power of her blows. Now the zombie was on the defensive. Barako struck and struck and struck with the hammer. The horror and grief that came with seeing what

Ishiko had become were forgotten. Ochiba's absence was the worst of all absences, the reason why everything else became an absence. Barako had no other will now than to smash these creatures of the Shadowlands to dust, and to fulfill a duty, *her* duty, the one whose precise shape was hers and hers alone, and that was to be at Ochiba's side.

The Ishiko horror was in the way, and so it must be destroyed.

Haru screamed.

And Ochiba yelled.

CHAPTER 12

Barako had never heard her roar like that. In battle, Ochiba was as silent as her katana. She shouted orders, but in her duels with the foe, her concentration was absolute. There was no room for the excess of an exclamation.

To hear her yell… To hear that shout of anguish and defiance…

And the expression of the zombie changed. The Ishiko-thing pulled her lips back. The snarl turned into the corpse of a smile.

Barako roared in her turn. She saw red. The City of Night's Hunger vanished from her view. Her vision came down to nothing but the immediate instants of struggle. The only thing that mattered was taking apart the enemy that prevented her from aiding Ochiba. When she came at the zombie this time, the zombie that had dared to mock her and Ochiba's pain, there was no stopping her. Could a creature that was dead know uncertainty? Could it know fear? Barako made certain this one did. She towered over Ishiko, her armored shape a dark, brutal instrument of war. She brought the hammer down with the force of her desperate fury. Her blow would have shattered mountains. It did shatter Ishiko's blade. And it smashed the zombie's face, obliterating hate and mockery, caving in the front of the skull.

With the zombie fallen, Barako disappeared into the frenzy of battle. She kept her focus. She was not reckless. She had never been reckless. What she lost was all sense of self that extended beyond the necessity to destroy what she fought. She barely sensed the presence of the other samurai. They were violent, flickering shadows at the edges of her perception, projections by lanterns upon a paper screen. They were not her concern, except when their fights brought them to an intersection with hers, and they became part of her arsenal, a factor in the moment of the fight that she could use against the foe.

Even the nature of the enemy became vague. The giant skeletons lost their substance. They were abstractions, forces she contended with, conditions that strove against her waging of destruction.

Forces that could not stand before her.

She became her hammer. She was a weapon, and nothing else. The weapon was speed married to violence. She struck and she struck and she struck. Somewhere in the distance, unholy creatures were screaming at her. Somewhere even farther away, broken monsters were falling, bones clattering against rock, in a distant place where night was eternal and snowflakes broke like glass. Barako did not care about that place. She did not care about victory. She did not care about glory. She only cared about one thing. And the only action left to her was violence.

Barako came back to herself with a jolt when she swung the hammer and it swished through air. There was nothing for it to hit. She blinked. She was surrounded by shattered bones. She was breathing heavily. Her right flank ached, and there was warmth trickling down her waist.

She looked around, her movements quick and jerky as she struggled to adjust to the absence of combat. Nahomi and Daizu were still alive. They were wounded. Daizu had lost his helm and the right side of his head was badly gashed. Part of his ear dangled. Nahomi was stooped, looking as if standing was difficult, and that walking would be worse.

Barako turned to the tower. Haru's screams had stopped. There had been no other sound from Ochiba. The blackness and the foul, blinding emerald still pulsed and flashed. The chaotic beat and war of light and shadow had grown more intense, Barako thought.

She began to run towards the tower. She could not suppress the terror that she was already far, far too late.

The horn sounded. The blast was colossal, so much louder than any that had come before. The jagged rock formations that surrounded the tower cracked and fell away, huge white slabs of stone falling like shards of shattered bone. Their fragments exploded across the square, stinging shrapnel. The noise of the horn struck Barako a physical blow. It was like running into a wall. She staggered and dropped to her knees, the breath knocked from her. She gasped for air, her lungs grinding. Blood poured from her nose and ears.

The horn went on and on, drowning out the thunder of the collapsing rock. The earth vibrated like a drum.

Fissures opened in the slope. Barako used her hammer like a cane and struggled to her feet. She managed to take a step forward, pressing into sound that slammed across the City of Night's Hunger like a god's fist. She could hear nothing else. It was easy to believe that she would never hear anything else again.

Then the horn stopped. The tremors ended. Barako's ears popped.

Ochiba emerged from the tower. Haru was with her. She had his arm draped around her shoulder. She was supporting him, but only barely. He moved like a drunken man. He did not seem to know how to use his legs. They were rubbery, his steps splayed and uncertain. His head hung forward, wobbling violently from side to side.

Barako could run again. She did, her eyes on Ochiba. As she drew closer, her sudden, ecstatic flare of joy turned to concern, and then to alarm. Ochiba's face was covered in blood. She wore lacquered armor rather than the plate that Barako favored. Its leather foundation gave her better mobility. Much of it, and the Kaiu-forged steel plates riveted to it, had been torn away. Her arms were bare to the cold. Her flesh was blackened with burns. There was so much blood, and the blood was so dark, Barako could not see where she was injured. She had the heart-wrenching impression that the wounds were everywhere.

Barako reached Ochiba and opened her arms to help. The captain opened her mouth. She tried to speak. She could not. Her breath rattled, and a string of blood dripped from her lower lip.

"You did it," Barako whispered.

Ochiba rolled her eyes at Haru. Barako looked at him. He had been screaming. She did not know what terrible things had been done to him. But she could see no injury. The only blood on him was Ochiba's. At that moment, Barako hated him with a viciousness she had not known she possessed.

You bastard. You should be supporting her.

Ochiba fell. Barako caught her. Haru, left without support, wavered but remained standing. He raised his head, and looked around, his face stunned and stupid.

"Captain," Barako whispered. It was not the word she wanted to use. It was the one she could use here, in the midst of war, with warriors under her command, and a fool to haul back to his mother. So she used that word, and she invested it with what she felt. She held back the storm surge of her grief and anger. She focused on what was necessary. She tried to see what Ochiba needed. The blood was everywhere, and kept flowing. There were too many wounds to staunch.

Ochiba grasped her forearm. The grip was horribly weak. She shook her head. "Out," she managed to croak. "Get us out."

Still cradling Ochiba, Barako turned to the stunned Haru. "Can you walk?" she said.

He blinked at her stupidly.

"*Can. You. Walk?*" she snarled.

He backed up a step before her anger.

"You can walk," she said. Ochiba could not. She had used the last of her strength in whatever she had fought to pull Haru out of the tower.

Daizu and Nahomi were with them now. Nahomi would not be able to help. She could barely keep herself upright. Barako nodded to Daizu. They lifted Ochiba up, each putting one of her arms over their shoulders.

"This is not going to be quick," Barako said.

Daizu nodded, uncomplaining. "If you need to fight, I can hold her."

Ochiba said nothing. Her eyes were closed.

"Walk ahead of us," Barako told Haru. When he didn't react, she shoved him with the butt of her hammer. "Now. *Go!*"

He moved forward at a stumble. He didn't have the coordination to run. Barako did not mind, as long as he moved. With Nahomi and Ochiba's injuries, none of the squad was going any faster.

They began the long walk back.

"Do you remember the way?" Nahomi asked.

"I do," said Barako. It had been Ochiba's duty to find the way forward, Barako's to know how to return. She had kept track of every intersection Ochiba had taken. She could see the secondary towers, too, landmarks of the route back to the gate.

Speed had been their weapon before. They had lost it now.

"If they rush us in great numbers," Daizu muttered.

"Then we will fight them in those numbers," said Barako, though she shared his dread. If anything like the tower guards came for them, there would be nothing to be done except try to die with courage.

They headed back through the streets, in falling, stinging

snow. Barako followed Ochiba's example and kept them in the center of the roads, in the moonlight, away from the drifts, as much as she could. Nahomi struggled along beside Haru. Even racked with pain, she was able to keep him from wandering off the right path. He shuffled along like a puppet, as if he were still learning how to use his legs. Ochiba tried to walk, but she was barely conscious.

They passed the signs of their first passage. The pieces of broken skeletons littered the road as if left to mark the route out of the City of Night's Hunger. Sometimes, in the depths of the shadows, Barako heard the bone-rattle again. She clutched her hammer, ready. No skeletons emerged.

At the rear, the tower sounded its great horn. More structures crumbled near the path, narrowly missing the samurai. If the horn was a summons, this time nothing answered. Barako dared to allow herself a small fraction of hope, a sliver of relief. Then, on an especially narrow street, where the line of moonlight was barely six feet wide, she saw that she was wrong. Something had answered the call.

The snowdrifts answered. Barako had been suspicious of them during the run to the tower. They were more than places of concealment for the city's dead warriors. Until now, they had kept secret how close their connection was to the sinuous, squirming engravings on the city's architecture. Now they were no longer hiding what they were. Through them, the city hungered. Through them, the city fed. They were part of the fabric of the night. They were its white veil, and its appetite.

The snowdrifts moved. They had their own being. Their

edges rippled and coiled. They slithered along, and Barako saw a texture to them that snow should not have. They were cold and white, yet they seemed reluctant to let light fall on them. Struggling down the thin path of moonlight, almost at the edge of the cold illumination, she felt like she was moving along the shore of a pale, venomous sea. Its ripples were tentative. The tide was out. But it would soon come in, and it would come in on the fury of a tempest, and release the ghosts it concealed.

"Stay in the light," Barako warned the others. "Do not touch the drifts."

Haru jerked at her words. He was beginning to respond more, and show understanding of what he was told. He stared down at the shadows for a moment, then shuffled closer to the center of the road.

Ochiba muttered wetly. Barako could not understand her. "I'll get us there," she promised her captain. "I promise I'll get us there." *I will not let you die for the sake of a fool.*

They reached another intersection. Then another. Then another. The path turned and twisted as it had before. Barako was certain she was taking the right branches. She was less certain the streets had not changed. The way her squad had to work its way back toward the tower, or follow curves that tightened into spirals that led nowhere, seemed different, a variation on a theme instead of the unchanged route she had run down less than an hour before. Time had no meaning here. Perhaps space did not, either.

Yet they were getting closer. They had already passed one of the other main towers. There was one more to leave behind before reaching the gate.

Up ahead, Nahomi paused. "Are you sure we came this way?" she asked.

"I am."

"This feels different."

"It might be."

"Then..."

"It doesn't matter. Changed or not, the roads are not stopping us. We are getting closer to the gate. That is what is important. Everything else is this cursed place is lies."

Nahomi nodded. She started forward again, almost doubled over. Bones chattered in shadows to either side. Rusted metal scraped against stone. The enemy stayed in the dark, and the darkness quivered in anticipation.

The snow fell and fell and fell, softly, gently, caressing and grazing. Where it touched Ochiba's exposed flesh, it cut tiny lines, and called up new beads of blood.

The squad reached the other secondary tower without an attack. The shadows grew deeper all the time, and gathered more and more substance.

"I think we're getting close," Daizu said.

"We aren't far," Barako told him, cautious. The gate's towers were visible now over the tops of the distorted shrines. Now that the goal was almost within reach, she was even more wary. She recognized hope for the enemy it was. The city wanted them to think they could escape. Their agony would be all the more succulent.

The next crossroads revealed the trap. Here, the walls of the ruins rose too high and too close on all sides. The moonlight could not reach the intersection. It lingered in slivers at the edges, and it grew stronger again after a few dozen yards down the road Barako knew they had to take. "Wait," she said.

The samurai stopped in the light, a few paces from where it fell away into the waiting shadows. They caught their breath. Haru was looking more alert now. He kept glancing back at the green gaze of the central tower, his face twitching in apprehension. "There are ghosts in the snow," he said. It was the first time he had spoken since the tower. Barako suspected it was shame more than anything else that had kept him silent until now.

"I know," Barako said.

"How do we fight them?" Nahomi asked.

"We don't. Not now. Our only victory is in retreat."

"We can't run, either," said Daizu.

"We have to."

"How…" Daizu began.

"If we can't run, we still move as fast as we can. And if we can't walk, we crawl. We keep moving, whatever happens. There is nothing else to do, except stand here and wait. I am not stopping. I am taking Captain Ochiba to Striking Dawn Castle." *And its heir. Though I would hurl him from the mountains if the choice were mine.*

Nahomi grinned through her pain. "Run, walk, crawl. Understood. Simple enough, lieutenant, even for me."

"Ready?" Barako asked Daizu.

He nodded.

"Ready, captain?" she asked Ochiba.

There was no answer. But Ochiba's hand twitched in Barako's.

"Go," Barako whispered.

They plunged into the drifts. Barako felt their texture immediately. Instead of snow, it was like splashing through a puddle of water that was turning into tar.

White tar that stirred, currents turning into spirals.

Spirals that turned into clutching hands.

The ghosts grabbed at Barako's boots. They clung to her steps, slowing her down. Ochiba's feet dragged in the snow, and the spectral hands grabbed at her boots, at her ankles, and reached higher for her legs. Daizu hissed. His gait became jerky as he tried to pull himself free.

Barako felt a drift coil around her shin like a rope. The rope grew teeth. The ghost bit into her leg.

Ochiba moaned but did not wake. Something tried to pull her down, to yank her from Daizu and Barako's grasp. Barako tightened her grip on Ochiba's left arm. She swung her hammer down with a sharp jerk. Its head smashed through a substance that felt like taut flesh and rang against stone. The ghost released her leg. She moved more freely, and so did Daizu.

They had only covered a few yards. They were halfway to the light.

Ahead, Nahomi cried out and fell to her knees. Ghostly limbs swarmed over her. In moments, Barako could only see her because of her struggles. Haru was a few paces further on, within reach of the dubious safety of the moonlight. He looked back when Nahomi shouted.

He hesitated.

Barako's hatred of him turned incandescent. She should have been blazing with her own source of light.

Haru turned back. He rushed to Nahomi. When he

hesitated again, Barako remembered the darkness inside the tower. Haru might know more about what the ghosts could do than anyone.

Even so. He hesitated.

Haru reached into the snowdrift. He reared back, and pulled Nahomi up, holding her under her arms. He pulled harder, staggering back. The ghosts did not want to let her go. They covered her lower half in whiteness.

Nahomi gasped in sudden, shocked pain. The horrors in the drift yanked, hauling Haru forward a step. Things crunched, and tore, and cracked. Nahomi spasmed violently, as if caught in a seizure. Then blood burst from her mouth and she went limp. Haru stumbled back, almost losing his balance as the drift suddenly dropped down again.

The ghosts pulled Nahomi's lower half down into their snow. They began to feed.

Haru shuddered. He dropped the half-corpse he held and rushed for the gate. As he turned, Barako saw his face contorted by horror and shame.

I do not care that you tried. I do not care what you suffered. I only care that you hesitated.

She slammed the hammer down again, and leaned forward. Daizu pulled with her, and they dragged Ochiba faster. They angled around the spot where Nahomi had fallen. The ghosts there boiled, frenzied with the joy of flesh. Phantom currents in the snow lashed out at the samurai, snapping at their heels. Teeth scraped at the plates on Barako's boots. She struck again with the blessed hammer, and the ghosts pulled back, satisfied with their prey.

Then they were in the moonlight, and the way was clear.

Haru was staring at the ground. He refused to meet Barako's gaze. "I tried," he murmured.

"You failed," she said.

"I..."

"Go. Walk. Every samurai who dies in this city increases your debt of blood. I have no interest in sparing you anything, but for the sake of the noble bushi who have risked their lives and souls for you, I do not wish to see that debt grow any larger. Now *go*."

Haru obeyed.

They moved on, struggling much too slowly back along the route they had raced through before.

"I can hear them," Daizu gasped, out of breath and hopeful, truly hopeful now.

"So can I," said Barako. The sounds of the battle at the gate were audible. She heard the clash of arms, the shouts of samurai, the wails of skeletons.

They came around another bend, and at last the gate was in sight. The company had held the position, and the numbers of the dead had greatly diminished.

Perhaps there were limits to the city's army, Barako thought. Perhaps it had been too well hidden, and too few had discovered it to their cost. Perhaps there was yet a way of destroying its threat.

That struggle was not for this day. She would have to return to Striking Dawn with only a partial victory. Ochiba could not correct her caution now. Barako would save the company she still had. She would save Akemi's worthless son.

She would save Ochiba.

And she would not fall into a trap of unearned confidence. The skeleton samurai might be limited in number. The shadows were not.

The horn blasted over the city again, at the same time that Barako raised her hammer high, hoping someone in the company would see her before the skeleton samurai did. If the force in the tower thought to urge its forces to greater effort, to destroy the Kakeguchi once and for all, its efforts backfired. The blast forced the mortals to face the tower, and some of them saw Barako.

The company had followed her orders, standing firm against the attacks of the dead, holding the gates, and not venturing into the city. At the sight of the returning squad, the samurai hurled themselves at the monsters. The forces were much closer to even, and the sudden charge knocked the skeletons back.

"Go," said Barako. She and Daizu pulled Ochiba faster, the captain's feet dragging. Ochiba was completely unconscious, her body dead weight, her breathing gurgling and ragged. "Go," Barako said again. "Go." She was speaking to herself, repeating the word under her breath, urging herself to go a little faster, a little further, for a little bit longer.

End this. Pass the gate and end this.

Haru had lost his weapons. As they ran down the last stretch toward the gate, he grabbed a blade lying beside a fallen zombie.

The samurai of Striking Dawn broke through the barrier of the skeletons. They charged across the distance that separated them from the squad. The dead howled, and sought to cut into the line of warriors. But more of the company came through the gate, protecting the flanks, holding off the skeletons.

"Go. Go. Go," Barako whispered. And in a few more steps, she was surrounded by her troops. A moment later, Ochiba's weight was lifted from her. She almost resisted, afraid that if she let go, she would never see Ochiba again, that by holding her, Barako was preventing her from slipping away. Then she let go. She let others carry the burden. It hurt to be apart from her, but now she was free to fight again, free to smash more of the enemy, more of the tainted filth that emanated from the city, the city that had laid Ochiba low.

She held back from any battle frenzy. She fought for one purpose, and that was to get her company back through the gate.

And she did.

She led the way through, and then stayed at the rear, crushing skulls and limbs until the gates were closed.

"Will that stop them?" Daizu asked.

"We can only try," she said. There was no way to block them from this side. There was no reason why the dead could not pull them back open. Yet the horrors ran up to the threshold of the city and stopped. They wailed at the samurai of Striking Dawn. They reached out with grasping hands, though even their fingers did not pass through the gates. They shrieked. They raged.

They did not pursue.

"The race is done," Barako called to the company. "Do

not dare, any of you, fall now." The warriors listened to her caution, and they crossed the ridge again carefully, resisting the urge to flee.

"We have struck a hard blow," Barako called. "We have our victory."

She did not really believe what she said. Not until she heard the City of Night's Hunger sound the horn one more time. And though the sound was terrible, though the mountains trembled in their fear of it, though it battered her soul again, as it had every time, she heard something new. She heard what she had prayed to hear.

She heard the notes of anger, of frustration.

Of defeat.

CHAPTER 13

The screen slid back, and Akemi entered Ochiba's room. Like Barako, she often stayed in the barracks, but had a chamber in the main part of the castle too. Here there would be quiet. Here she might heal. Barako was sitting beside Ochiba's mat, where she had been since they had arrived at dawn, keeping watch over the unconscious, heavily bandaged captain. She looked up, ready to expel the intruder. When she saw the daimyō, she rose, bowed, and sat down again by Ochiba's head.

Akemi kneeled at the foot of the mat, lowering herself slowly with the help of her cane. The single lantern in the room cast a quiet, amber light over the spare surroundings. It invited whispers, and Akemi spoke quietly.

"How is she?"

"As you see her." Barako's fingers hovered near Ochiba's shoulder. She did not touch.

"Will she live?"

"She might." She was verging on insulting, but she was exhausted, and some of her hatred for Haru was spilling over into testiness with the daimyō. Barako recalled herself to duty and spoke more gently. "The wounds are many. It is hard to say how deep they go. We shall see."

"Are they more than physical?"

"Junji has examined her. He is not sure. We will have to wait for the physical injuries to heal before we know if there are others." The rest of the survivors had completed the rites of purification and submitted themselves to a full examination. They had been judged untainted. Even Haru. Barako was almost as surprised as she was relieved about that.

Akemi said. "You were reciting a poem to her just now. I interrupted you. It sounded familiar."

"'The Courtier's Lament.'" It was a beautiful verse, and mournful. It was a song of love made impossible by family and by the strictures of the imperial court.

"Ah yes. I should have recognized it."

"It is her favorite. She has known it all by heart for many years. She has recited it enough that I know it now too."

Akemi smiled. "That does not surprise me."

Barako's cheeks burned.

"I am sorry for what Ochiba has suffered," Akemi said solemnly. "Sorry for what has happened. There will be an accounting."

Barako said nothing.

Akemi looked at her steadily when she spoke again. "Thank you for saving my son."

"It was Ochiba who rescued him."

"Thank you for returning him to me, then. For bringing him safely out of the City of Night's Hunger."

"That was my duty," Barako said. Then, out of a sense of

another duty, she asked, "How is Haru?"

"He has barely spoken since you returned," said Akemi. "Or emerged from his quarters." She grimaced. "I have no illusions about my son, Lieutenant Barako. I know you do not, either. I do hope, though, that you know that he feels the weight and obligations of his duty as acutely as you and Ochiba. It is shame that binds his tongue. Of this I have no doubt."

"I understand, Lady Akemi." *I understand, but I do not forgive. I don't need to be told that he is deeply conscious of his reputation. Ochiba is lying here because of his concern for his reputation.* "Has Haru said what happened to him in the tower?" Barako had not exchanged more than a dozen words with Haru on the long march back to Striking Dawn. Ochiba had not woken since the retreat from the gates of the city. Barako needed to know what was inside the tower. For many reasons.

"He doesn't remember," said Akemi.

Barako frowned. "That is troubling."

"You may think that is convenient for him," Akemi said. "In your place, I would. But though we know his shortcomings on the battlefield, have you ever known him to lie?"

"I have not," Barako admitted. "Not to me. But I was not among the samurai who obeyed him when he told them to leave with him for the City of Night's Hunger. I did not hear what he said to Ishiko." *She was the most honest of us all. That is not even a tribute. It is a simple truth.* "No one who marched with him is still alive. There are no witnesses to what he said." The words felt cruel, yet necessary.

"I know," said Akemi. She sighed. "I know. Even so I believe him. His sense of pride has led him astray, but I believe that loss means that he is truthful now. And he will be judged, lieutenant. He will be judged."

The last of the resentment Barako had felt toward Akemi melted away. A new wave of sorrow rushed into its place, and with it came all the anxieties for the future. What hope could Akemi have now that Striking Dawn would remain in Kakeguchi hands? Barako could imagine no plausible way that Haru could retain any form of claim on the castle; even if his punishment for his disobedience and the disaster he caused was no more than a censure, he no longer had any moral authority. If he were made daimyō, every samurai in Striking Dawn would be forever on edge, waiting for their leader to doom them all. No, he would never be daimyō now. The castle would pass to Doreni. Akemi would resist that outcome. She might adopt another heir, but Doreni's claim would be strong all the same. Akemi would do what she could to keep the castle in the hands of the Kakeguchis. Barako would aid her in every way she could. Yet the end of the struggle was already clear.

"If Haru cannot remember what happened to him," said Akemi, "we will have to wait for Ochiba to wake to tell us."

"If she wakes."

"Yes. If she wakes."

"If she does not, what then?" The prospect was so awful, Barako retreated into anger to shield herself from the thought of Ochiba's death.

"We will deal with that situation only if it arises."

"This is about more than evidence for or against Haru."

"Of course it is." Akemi was not offended by Barako's directness. Her voice never rose above its soft, calm tone. She would not be the one to disturb Ochiba's rest. "We must know what we are fighting. For that we must know what is inside the tower."

"I will return there," said Barako. "I will return and end its threat."

"You almost sound like my son."

"I will not return the way he did."

"No," said Akemi with a sad smile. "That is certain. But no one is returning yet. For the time being, then the defense of Striking Dawn Castle is in your hands."

Barako thought about this. She had been so focused on Ochiba's state, she had not considered its immediate consequences for herself and for the castle. She felt like she was sinking in a mire of fatigue and dread. "I am not a captain," she said. "And I will not be captain while she lives."

"Of course," Akemi said.

"Will Doreni accept this?"

"He will have to." Akemi stood up to go. "This is still a Kakeguchi castle."

The mood in the main hall was too solemn for a victory feast. Yet the success of the mission had to be marked. Though winter had come, and the stores were not as full as had been hoped, the troops in the barracks had an extra ration of rice and fish. In the hall, the rice was also plentiful, and there were plates of roast pheasant brought out on trays to be served to the samurai on low, individual tables.

Akemi sat near one end of the central floor, her table in front of her, Haru to her right, Barako opposite him at the daimyō's left. Junji was at the other end, so wrapped up in his thoughts, he was barely present. Doreni sat beside Barako, and next to him was his wife, Rekai. Facing them, sitting next to Haru, were his two children. They were younger than Haru, only recently come to adulthood. The eldest, Chuai, was a bushi, his initial warrior training barely finished. He seemed promising, from what Barako had seen, though he had yet to be truly tested. His sister, Mioko, was a courtier. Two years younger, she already had the polished grace of a veteran. They both had their father's sharp features, tempered by their mother's wiry delicacy.

Barako looked at the two Hiruma, and at the sullen, silent Kakeguchi next to them. *Doreni will be better served by his offspring than Akemi.* She could already see the power configuration to come. Chuai would inherit Striking Dawn. Mioko would ensure that he kept it. Doreni and Rekai had groomed them well. Akemi's failure had not been for lack of trying. The grooming had simply not taken. Haru lacked talent. These two did not.

"Has there been any improvement in Captain Ochiba's condition?" Doreni asked Barako.

"There have been no changes."

"I am sorry to hear it. I hope to see her amongst us again very soon." He sounded sincere. He was being unusually conciliatory. Perhaps he was speaking with the generosity of a victor.

"We are all praying to the ancestors for her recovery," said Rekai, just as sincere.

Barako caught the careful glance she gave her husband, and wondered how much instruction Doreni had been given about how to behave.

Doreni poured himself some more sake. "Lady Akemi has informed me that you will command in Ochiba's place."

"That is correct." Barako kept her voice neutral.

"I am glad," said Doreni. "That is as it should be." He faced her, and his stern face was calm and open. She saw no hint of resentment.

"I am glad, too," said Barako, "that this will not be a source of friction between us."

"It will not be," Doreni said firmly. "The disagreements I have had with our daimyō are no secret. I will never conceal what I feel to be right." He turned to Akemi. "But I hope I have never been disrespectful."

"You have not," said Akemi.

"Good." To Barako he said, "The situation that faces us is a dangerous one."

Which situation? The City of Night's Hunger or the political circumstances in Striking Dawn? "I agree with you," she said, still neutral.

"We must work together. To do otherwise would be foolish, and irresponsible."

Impressively, his eyes did not so much as flicker Haru's way.

You still aren't saying what situation you mean. Then Barako realized his vagueness was deliberate. He meant both. He had every intention of meeting the threat of the Night's Hunger with all due seriousness. He was telling her that he would not use the danger for his political ends.

And yet he was, because he was also referring to Striking Dawn's future. He was telling her that he would work with her now, and that he hoped she would work with him then. He wanted unity, especially unity on his terms. He wanted her on-side.

"We must all be one as we work to preserve the present and future of this castle," said Chuai.

Mioko put a hand on his arm. "Lieutenant Barako does not need that pointed out to her," she said, silencing him before he said any more. Unlike what Haru would have done, the young man nodded apologetically at Barako and went back to his meal.

"All of us are aware of the need for unity," Akemi said coldly. "Now and in the future. There will be no future if there is no present."

"Your words are a wise reminder," said Rekai. "Where you lead, Lady Akemi, we will follow."

Doreni was still looking at Barako. "Let us discuss what we must do, then," she said. She would keep the conversation focused on Night's Hunger. If Doreni thought she would agree to a future alliance with him, here and now, and so insult her daimyō, he was even more arrogant than she had thought.

Maybe, though, that is not what he's doing. Maybe he wants me to think about what is inevitably to come, and show me that I will have a place at Striking Dawn.

As long as I know my place, that is.

It doesn't matter. None of this matters if Striking Dawn does not survive.

"The tower is the key," Barako said. "It was from there

that the shadows spread over the city. Its horn seemed to issue commands. It is the heart of the city. I don't know if taking it will lead to victory, but I am certain that victory is impossible if we do not defeat what is inside."

"Agreed," said Doreni. "So we need to know what is inside."

Haru stirred to life. He looked up as if he had only just discovered where he was. He glared at Barako and Doreni. "I would tell you what is in the tower if I could," he said. "I will not say it again."

"I will not ask you to," Doreni said mildly. "No one disputes your truth. Your honesty is not in question." He did not add for now. He did not need to.

Haru's expression darkened even further. He looked, Barako thought, like a man torn between twin storms of anger and guilt. If there had been any way of construing Doreni's words as an insult, he would have erupted. But he was a samurai who had lost his blade, a shame that diminished him in the eyes of all in and of itself, but also was symbolic of the scale of his failures. There was no moral high ground for him.

The silence in the hall trapped Haru. He could not accuse Doreni of lying without accusing everyone else of collusion. Instead, Doreni's reassurance turned his fury back in on himself. His face reddened with embarrassment. He had made himself look ridiculous, and he knew it.

Barako watched Haru's warring emotions with little interest and no sympathy. He hunched his shoulders, lowered his head and started eating again, concentrating on his rice with an intensity meant to block out his awareness of his company.

"We may not be able to find out what is in the tower until we enter it," Barako said to Doreni. "Ochiba may not remember either." She refused to say, *she might not wake.* "We can reach the tower, though. We did it once. We can do it again."

"What do you recommend?"

"We will need at least as many samurai as we were originally meant to take. A full company."

Haru stabbed at his bowl with his chopsticks.

"That will mean pulling more from the castle's defenses than any of us would like," said Doreni.

"It would," said Barako. She looked at Akemi.

"That is a risk we may need to take," the daimyō said after a moment. "Go on."

"At least half the company holds the gate," Barako continued. "Depending upon the initial resistance we encounter. I am hopeful that we have already greatly reduced the enemy's numbers. We divide the rest of the company into squads. They break through and make for the tower. Speed is vital. If we move fast enough, and stick to the moonlit paths, we should be able to reach our target."

Junji spoke for the first time since the meal had begun. "You have made many assumptions, Lieutenant Barako. Has the enemy's strength truly been depleted? What if your victory on this occasion was but a ruse? Perhaps the City of Night's Hunger wants you to return with still more troops, so that it may destroy them with the forces it has hidden from you, and then find Striking Dawn vulnerable to them."

"If the skeleton samurai would not cross the gate," Doreni said, "could it be that nothing of Night's Hunger can leave its boundaries?"

"Perhaps," said Junji. "And perhaps something wishes us to believe in such a comforting weakness."

"That could be," Barako said. "It could also be that the city will rise up and walk against us when we attack. Should we stay here, then, and hope for the best?"

"That is not the way of the Crab Clan," said Akemi.

"No, it is not," Junji agreed. "I do not suggest ignoring the danger of Night's Hunger. I mean, instead, to emphasize it. Nothing about that city can be trusted. What has been seen there may be nothing but deception piled upon deception."

"What do you recommend, then?" Barako asked him.

"I can recommend nothing except caution. I do not have the knowledge to say more than that."

Barako clenched her jaw in frustration. Doreni's eyes narrowed. For once, she shared his feelings completely. Junji's refuge of neutrality was turning into a fortress. He would not even speculate now, if that meant people would take action based on what he had said. *He's growing worse. Is it Night's Hunger that has done this to him? Does he dread the city that much? He wasn't even there. Doesn't he realize he's making things even more unstable?* She couldn't believe Junji was acting out of cowardice. She had seen what he could do, when necessity took him to the battlefield.

She'd had enough of his evasiveness. She tried to pin him down. "Junji," she said, "will you tell us what is troubling you? Is it something that we do not already know?"

He was silent for so long that Barako thought he wasn't

going to answer at all. He stared down at the table. He seemed to be gazing through the floor, and down through the earth to the roots of the mountains. Finally, he looked up. "I am troubled, yes," he said. "I have not said so because I have not been sure of the nature of my trouble." He took a deep breath. "Perhaps it is necessary that I set aside the caution to avoid speaking when I know nothing. Well then. Well then. I am worried because the ground shifts beneath my feet. It melts into air. The more I seek to learn about the city, the less I know. What you have seen and fought, Lieutenant Barako, may be the truth of the city. Yet since your return, I have been plagued with a sense of premonition that is as vague as it is insistent. Something is wrong, yet I know not what."

"I can tell you what is wrong," said Chuai. "We have lost thirty bushi and possibly our captain."

"Be still," Doreni snapped. "My apologies," he said to Junji. "My son remains a student when it comes to wisdom."

"So do I," said Junji. "So do we all. And he is correct. Our losses disturb me. But something else does too. I do not know what it is. And so it disturbs me even more."

He's afraid, Barako thought. Then we should all be. What is coming? She turned back to Akemi. "The decision is yours, daimyō. I respect Junji's concerns. I do not see how to act on them. I believe our best recourse is to act on the basis of what we have seen."

"I concur," said Doreni.

"So do I," said Akemi. "We have opportunity right now to make our attack. The skies are clear. We cannot waste that chance. Lieutenant Barako, you have barely returned. Even so, I will ask you now to lead the march at dawn tomorrow."

Haru looked up. His eyes were wide with pain. He seemed on the verge of begging to be allowed to be part of the mission, to have this chance at redemption. He said nothing. He must know, Barako thought, how utterly beyond the pale his request would be. Or maybe he was just afraid. Maybe the thing that he could not remember was too monstrous even for his injured pride.

Haru shrunk back in on himself, and hunched over his table once more.

"I will take us back to the City of Night's Hunger," Barako said. "I will do so gladly."

"I wonder–" Doreni began.

The blast of a terrible horn cut him off.

Haru gasped. Barako's fist closed convulsively around her chopsticks and snapped them in half. Junji leapt to his feet. His face had turned to chalk. His lips were pulled back in agony. He was a man whose soul had been dealt a crushing blow.

Plates and bowls rattled against the tables. The floor and walls vibrated.

"Is that…" Akemi croaked. She could not finish, and Barako could barely hear her.

The sound of the horn went on and on, as if now that it was heard over Striking Dawn Castle, it would never fall silent again.

"Yes," Barako said. "Yes." She lurched to her feet and ran from the hall, Doreni and Chuai a few steps behind her. She flew out the castle doors. She wore kosode robes over her hakama skirt, no defense against the cold, but she did not feel the bite of winter. She was already cold, frozen to the core by the voice of Night's Hunger.

She ran to the outer wall and pounded up the stairs of the guard tower. All she could think of was what she had said to Junji. *The city will rise up and walk against us.* It could not be. Surely it could not be. Surely she would not look out from the ramparts and see the City of Night's Hunger bearing down on Striking Dawn.

But as she had neared the gates, the guards were shouting, and they were ringing the bells in the tower, sounding the alarm. The shouts went on while she climbed the stairs. And what was that she heard in the voices? Was that wonder? Was that awed, fearful wonder?

It was.

That was an awful thing to hear.

She burst into the top of the tower and looked north. Twilight was falling, and the torches burned along the walls in the dimming light.

There was no walking city coming through the pass.

Doreni and Chuai joined her, and the younger man gasped, because what they did see was bad enough.

The horn sounded again, and a storm surged down the north slope. It had swallowed the sky and the mountains. It barreled towards Striking Dawn, pushing winds ahead of it, winds that rose from chill breeze to a screaming gale in seconds, and then grew stronger yet. They slammed into Barako, throwing her and the guards back from the parapet. She hit the wall behind her with a grunt.

The horn's blast ended. In its place, the wind's howl was

the frenzy of the damned, as if it blew directly from Jigoku itself.

Then the clouds arrived. Low, thick, hateful, they rolled over the land, boiling with rage and snow. They smashed into Striking Dawn, and they brought night with them, night slashed with ice, night without stars, without hope, without mercy.

The siege had begun.

CHAPTER 14

During the hour of the rooster, there was only the storm. For Barako and everyone around her, it seemed as if there might never be anything again *except* the storm. It had consumed the world with finality.

Barako and Doreni made their way back to the guard tower's staircase and descended, beginning their long walk back to their quarters to arm themselves. Even inside the tower, the wind found ways to get at them. It was so powerful, it found every chink in the walls of the tower. It keened mournfully down the stairs, caressing Barako, and rubbing freezing fangs against the back of her neck.

"I did not wake when Haru left for the city during the night," said Doreni. "When the storm came then…"

"It did not hit like this," Barako answered the suspended question. "It came quickly. Not unnaturally, though."

"Or at least not visibly so."

"Yes."

And that storm had nothing of this one's intensity. The first screaming blast of wind had blown out all the torches on the north wall. It caught the lantern hanging in the east tower and hurled it away into the night. The guards were still struggling to get and keep torches lit.

Barako and Doreni reached the bottom of the stairs. They opened the door and stared into a black limbo streaked with fine lines of silver.

"The storm then was never this dark," said Doreni.

"All that tempest had to do was keep us behind the walls long enough for Haru to reach Night's Hunger."

"You think the earlier storm was unnatural too?"

"I didn't then. Now I fear it might have been. And this one wants to knock the walls down. It wants to destroy us."

"It may yet succeed," said Doreni. "We could lose our way in that blackness and freeze to death long before we reached the castle."

"We have no choice," Barako told him.

"No, we don't. Ancestors, watch over us and guide our way," Doreni prayed.

They ran from the tower. Barako put her trust in her sense of direction. She knew where the castle was in relation to the gates. All she had to do was run in a straight line.

So thought every victim of a blizzard ever.

She had grabbed a lantern from the guard post. She lifted it before her and moved out of the tower. The lantern illuminated no more than a couple of feet in front of her. She would have to hope that would be enough to help her walk that straight line.

The wind tore through the courtyard with such force, it was as if the walls were already down. Barako leaned into the wind. The pain of cold dug into her cheeks and forehead. Her ears burned with the freezing bit. Ice formed on her lashes. When she breathed, the cold reached into her lungs and stole the warmth from her core.

She and Doreni staggered forward. She kept looking back before she took another step, trying to make sure she held the line. But she could never see more than a single footstep behind her, and the vague shape of Doreni. He was no more than a struggling shadow, though he was barely a yard away.

The darkness surrounded her. It howled at her. It buffeted her from side to side. It wanted her lost and frozen and dead. It swallowed the world, and it swallowed time. She might walk through nothing forever. The snow blew into her face like a hail of needles. It kept forcing her eyes shut. She had to stop and pry her lids open with her fingers.

She was numb everywhere, her hands stiff and clumsy, when, to her shock and relief, they reached a building wall. They could see so little of it, they could not tell where they were.

"Is this the castle?" Doreni asked.

"I don't know."

They worked their way along the wall, and when they reached a door, Barako realized how far wrong they'd come, despite her efforts.

"These are the merchant quarters," she said, and banged the door open.

They rushed inside, pursued by the wind, and closed the door. The lanterns blazed, casting their light over the gathered crowd. The merchants had divided into two large clusters, one gathered in fearful fascination at the windows, the others huddled together in the middle of the hall. Barako stepped into a din of gabbled prayers and sobs. Chen detached himself from the center group and rushed over to the two bushi.

"Save us, masters!" he pleaded.

Doreni pushed him back. "What are you mewling about? The castle has not fallen. Do you see any invaders?"

"But the storm…" Chen began.

Barako beat caked snow from her robes and rubbed circulation back into her hands. She felt more sympathy than Doreni for the merchants, but there was no time to indulge them and their terrors. "The castle is well defended. It is provisioned. If you do not think we can survive a storm, then you insult us."

Chen backed away, head lowered in shame. "Please, please forgive me. I did not mean–"

Doreni cut him off. "I'm sure you didn't," he snapped. Then he and Barako left the merchants to their weeping and their fears.

The two lieutenants hurried down the corridor that ran the length of the merchant quarters. At the far end was a storehouse, and from its exterior door was a short distance to one of the servants' entrances to the castle. Even that door, so close, was invisible in the storm, but Barako could just make out the castle's bulk. There was no chance of getting lost this time.

She and Doreni rushed in the shrieking cold again, across the space and to the castle. They found the servants' entrance easily enough, and hurried on to their quarters on the second floor.

"How long has this taken us?" Doreni asked.

Barako shook her head. She didn't know. "Too long," she said. That was her only certainty. "We'll hit the barracks first. All bushi, without exception, must be on the wall. You will command the defense of the south."

"You think the storm is just the start of the attack."

"Yes. What better cover for an assault could there be?"

"Agreed. And the flanks?" Normally there would be an officer on each side of the castle during a siege. But Ochiba was unconscious. "Do we trust Haru? Is he in any state to fight?"

Barako thought for a moment. In this darkness, deeper than any night, communication along the walls was going to be difficult. The wind was so loud, it would whip shouted commands away into the whirl of the snow. Lantern signals would be invisible more than a dozen yards apart, at best. The defense of the walls, even those with an officer in command, would come down to the actions of the individual samurai, responding to conditions in the immediate vicinity. They would have to trust the training and skill of their warriors. She did. They were all samurai of the Crab Clan. Their lives, from birth, had been governed by the single, overriding purpose of defending Rokugan from the Shadowlands.

"We'll have to use runners to relay messages," she said.

"I suppose," Doreni said. "The truth is that we'll be isolated from each other."

"Yes, we will be."

"And Haru?"

"He is physically weak. He won't be of any use on the

ramparts. Let him find his use inside the castle." *If he has any use.*

"So he can defend the daimyō, or she him."

Barako shrugged. She thought Doreni was right, but Haru was still, for the moment, heir to Striking Dawn. She would not disparage him before the Hiruma. Not before his trial.

She left Doreni, donned armor and weapons. She made her way to the barracks to give her orders, and then headed back to the north wall, this time with a full company. The warriors carried enough lanterns to make it possible to find the gate in the storm, and she climbed the stairs of the east tower until she reached the doorway to the wall. She led the company onto the ramparts. She commanded that siege defenses be readied, and ordered the squads to spread out as far as possible without losing contact with each other.

"Beware the dark," she said. "It will seek to conceal the enemy's approach."

Daizu was at her side. The blood-stained wrappings around his wounded ear poked out from his helmet. He shielded his eyes with his arm. The snow pattered against his gauntlet. "I fear we will see nothing until it is upon us," he said.

"Likely so. But even if the foe is invisible to us, we are facing it. We will not be surprised."

"Could this storm be the attack? It would be bad enough, if it does not end. What if time has stopped like in Night's Hunger?"

Then we are doomed. The same awful possibility had occurred to her. If that was what was happening, there could be no hope. The people of Striking Dawn would starve. Night's Hunger would not have to do anything other than bury them in cold and snow and darkness. "I do not think that is what we face," she said. She had to believe that she was right, or embrace despair. "Striking Dawn has already weathered two storms. Both ended."

"Were they both sent by Night's Hunger?"

"The effect of their timing, especially of the second one, is too much to be a coincidence. And now this one. Perhaps the influence of the city outside its borders grows stronger. Perhaps we have made it stronger. But if the power ranged against us were infinite, we would already be dead. We would not have survived to escape the city. Night's Hunger has limits. This storm will end. What we must dread is the opportunity that it provides the foe. The attack will come, Daizu. It will come, and soon."

The watch was long. It was painful. Barako *did* feel as if the timeless space of the City of Night's Hunger had engulfed Striking Dawn. She had to issue more orders, to be sent slowly along the ramparts, that the troops rotate in and out of shelter. She would not have her samurai freeze to death while they waited for the enemy to declare itself. She forced herself to go inside the tower periodically, to warm up by the fire in the guardhouse. Staring into the furious, white-streaked darkness was as hypnotic as it was numbing. She could imagine anything in the frenzied patterns of the snow. In the misery of the cold, it was hard to stay alert. Duty kept her going. Duty to the daimyō, and to the castle.

And to Ochiba. Barako would keep her safe.

She lost track of time. Night had fallen, she knew that.

She did not know what hour it was. She did not think it was dawn yet. For as long as the storm lasted, day and night would have no meaning. All would be darkness.

A short while after the second time she had sought warmth, she heard something. It was hard to make out, or even to be sure she was not imagining things. The howl of the wind rose and fell but never ceased. It held all other sounds captive. Now, though, she thought she heard something from the north, blown towards her by the storm.

Barako grabbed a lantern and held it up, waving it back and forth to warn those who could see it that all was not well. She looked out beyond the ramparts, desperately trying to pierce the black shroud of the storm.

The noise continued. She had not imagined it. It sounded like the cracking of ice. In its rhythms, it reminded her of the rattling of bones in Night's Hunger.

She leaned over the parapet. She could not see the ground.

"Get me a torch," she called.

A guard lit one from the pile they kept in the shelter of the rampart walls. They had not managed to keep any lit more than a few minutes in the storm, and were keeping them back in reserve. Daizu took the torch and brought it to Barako.

"Throw it down there," she said, pointing at the ground.

Daizu tossed the torch over the parapet. It turned end over end, and landed in the snow. The flames flickered madly, ready to go out. They lived long enough to show Barako the origin of the noise.

There was movement at the base of the wall, where the

drifts were more than five feet high. The snow writhed and cracked. Powder burst into the air. Skeletal hands thrust up from the surface. They scrabbled at the snow, struggled, then heaved the full body into view.

As if the ground below were a white graveyard cursed to release what should be held, it was giving birth to skeletons of snow.

Barako ordered more torches thrown down as the first began to gutter.

The skeletons crawled over each other, fighting to be first on their feet and first to the wall. They wailed as had the ones in the City of Night's Hunger. There was a difference in their cries. There was even less of a trace of human pain. In its place was the voice of the wind. If the spirits of the damned inhabited these forms, the bodies were made of snow and shaped by storm.

"Lord Hida protect us," Daizu hissed.

"He is our strength," said Barako, hate and determination leaving no room for fear. "We are the protection." She raised her voice. "The enemy is here!" she called. "Send word! Send word!"

Wielding blades of ice, the skeletons advanced on the wall. They grasped its face. They stuck to it. The began to climb, ice forming around their hands and feet, holding them to the wall, then shattering when they moved the next arm or leg. There were so many of them rising in the night. That was why Barako could hear their movements. An army was coming into being.

Barako picture the endless expanse of snow beyond the wall. This army could be infinite.

Then fight it forever, if you have to.

Her shout was taken up to the left and right. The warning was passed from samurai to samurai, and the bushi at each end of her company's position ran to the other walls and spread the alarm.

Barako raised her hammer, waiting for the first of the snow skeletons. She wondered if the assault had already begun on the other walls. This foe could form on all sides of the castle, and attack everywhere at once.

Everywhere…?

Torches and lanterns were being lit all along the wall, illuminating the ascent of the skeletons. The monsters were relentless, but they were slow, like a creeping vine. She had a few moments yet.

Barako rushed to the other side of the wall and had more torches thrown into the courtyard. The ground below was undisturbed, a featureless field of gray in the flickering light. Nothing cracked. Nothing shifted. Nothing rose to slaughter the inhabitants of the castle.

Daizu had come to look with her. The relief on his face mirrored her own, even with an army of unnatural horrors scaling the wall. "Then there are limits," he said.

"What knows limits, knows defeat," Barako said.

"But why does the wall act as a barrier? Why aren't we invaded inside as well as out?"

"The castle has been blessed by generations. The ground is sanctified by our shrine." Barako turned back to face the attack. "Or maybe there are other reasons. What matters is that the taint has not yet spread into Striking Dawn."

The first of the skeletons had reached the top of the

parapet. Barako swung her hammer, striking the nearest climber in the head as it clambered over the battlements. The blow pulverized the monster. It disintegrated, powdered snow swirling away into the dark.

"They are weak!" Barako shouted. "They are fragile! Strike them and they vanish!"

She could barely see ten feet in either direction, but she heard shouts from further away, and the clash of weapons. Skeletons howled, and they vanished by the score. Barako moved back and forth, smashing every creature that closed with the parapet. With every hit, a skeleton vanished, some bursting apart so close to their goal that Barako ran through sudden clouds of snow. For several minutes, she began to hope that they could keep the enemy breaching the defenses at all. But the cracking below went on. The army of the dead kept forming. The creatures stalked toward the wall and began to climb. There were too many, and there were not enough samurai to plug every gap on the ramparts.

The skeletons began to reach the top.

The first one was destroyed as soon as it arrived. Then more came, the pressure from below relentless as a rising tide. And though they were fragile, they were dangerous. To Barako's right, Tanako slashed her katana through a skeleton as it scrambled over the parapet. The burst of snow blinded her for a moment, and she was slow to turn as another monster came over behind her. Its ice cleaver slammed into the back of her neck and she fell, half-decapitated, blood pumping from the wound, a dark fountain turning almost immediately to ice.

Barako destroyed the second skeleton a moment later. She swung her weapon in a wide arc, turning herself around to explode the chest of yet another monster that was trying to catch her by surprise. She took out two more still climbing, then moved to cover Daizu's flank as he protected another few feet of wall. The scope of her thoughts narrowed to the violent needs of the next heartbeat of time.

The siege reached a stalemate. The samurai held the skeletons back. The skeletons kept coming. Their wails sounded like taunts. Their numbers could not be counted. They would never tire. The defenders would. And every fallen samurai thinned the defenses, making the struggle more desperate.

Then runners from the other walls arrived. The skeletons were attacking all four sides of Striking Dawn.

"At least our defenses are holding," Daizu said. He shattered another skull and jerked back to avoid the stinging blast of snow.

"Holding is not enough," said Barako. She moved rapidly to and fro, smashing her hammer down with an unwavering rhythm. They had to do more than break the monsters apart as they drew near. They had to stop them earlier. They had to stop them from forming at all, if such a thing were possible.

She felt as if her hate for the skeletons should have been enough to melt them from a distance, so powerfully did it heat her blood.

But if they could hold back the skeletons a bit longer, until her counterattack could be launched...

"Cauldrons ready, lieutenant!" Umsau shouted.

It had taken longer than she would have liked to heat the cauldrons. It had been hard to light the fires under them, and hard to keep them lit. It had taken long, too long, to bring the water to the boil. But they were ready now.

CHAPTER 15

"Cauldrons, go!" Barako shouted. Once more, the order was echoed and re-echoed along the wall.

The siege teams pulled down on heavy levers, and the cauldrons, supported by iron frameworks, tilted on their axes. Cascades of boiling water poured down the walls. The skeletons caught by the flow vanished, exploding into sludge and steam. The scalding waterfall struck the snow drifts, melting them down. A thick, cloying fog rose up the wall.

"Fill them up again!" Barako ordered. "More water, and move the cauldrons down." Not for the first time, she wished for the presence of shugenja in Striking Dawn.

The respite the cauldrons provided was a small one. The skeletons continued to climb everywhere. But where the water had fallen, nothing new emerged to scale the wall, at least for the moment.

Limits, Barako thought. It all came down to limits. If the power that was attacking them truly could summon skeletons for as long as there was snow, then Striking Dawn was doomed. She had to believe there were limits.

She redoubled her efforts. She moved with the cauldrons, concentrating her attacks on the skeletons climbing to their positions, endlessly smashing the snow creatures until the water was boiling again. It took less long this time for the cauldrons to be ready. The firepits built into the frame were glowing fiercely, the blazes steady, and the metal already so hot that the snow shoveled in melted instantly. Wherever a cauldron stood, steam enveloped the ramparts.

More skeletons reached the top before the water was ready. Another few defenders died. The company's line stretched and thinned. Barako's arms burned from the effort of incessant strikes. Her helmet gave her some protection from the cold, but her nose and cheeks throbbed with a numbing pain. Her skin was freezing. Her limbs, though, were warm.

War kept her warm.

The water boiled, and the water fell, an anointment of oblivion descending on the skeletons.

And the pattern continued. Barako fought with a mechanical precision as cold as the storm. She moved from skeleton to skeleton, always rushing to the nearest immediate threat. She hardly had to give any orders now. Every samurai with her knew what was asked of them. The conduct of the war was clear. Hold the line, and protect the cauldrons until they could pour again. And then repeat, and repeat, and repeat.

Barako found it harder to think about anything past the next second, and the destruction of the next enemy. Part of her mind detached itself from her body and the struggle to stay alive. It floated above the walls, wondering at the cycle of repetition, and wondered if it could ever end. It wondered if Daizu had been right. It wondered if the first victim of the storm had been time, and if Striking Dawn was caught in an infinite struggle. As the snow fell forever on the City of Night's Hunger, and the drifts never rose, and the sky never cleared, so perhaps was Striking Dawn doomed to an eternity of siege, never to fall, and never to triumph.

No. Do not believe that. Believe we can win. Know we can win.

The cauldrons poured scalding destruction yet again. Barako stayed by a cleared strip of the wall long enough to throw another torch to the ground below. She waited for the worst of the steam to clear. *Lord Hida, grant that our strength is enough. Look kindly upon our struggle in your name.*

The wind blew away the steam, and before the torch went out, she saw what she had prayed for. A portion of the snow against the wall of the castle was gone, leaving bare rock. No skeletons came forward to climb here. And in the snow beyond, no more of the dead things arose. Wherever the drifts lay against the wall, the skeletons spawned. But not here, not below her.

Limits. You have limits!

She did not understand what configurations of forces created this chance for victory. She could not guess why the snow had to touch the castle wall for the skeletons to rise and attack. Was there something in that connection that somehow both summoned the enemy and led it to its prey? That was for Junji to discover, if Striking Dawn survived this siege of darkness. Barako did not need a reason. She needed only a path to victory.

"Melt the snow at the base of the wall," she ordered. "Give us a border of bare rock around the entire castle. Send a runner to Doreni and let him know. Melt the snow, and we break the siege."

She turned to her left, rushing to block another skeleton surge. Her energy was renewed. An end to the struggle was possible. They could win.

The struggle was long. The strips of rock each cauldron could expose at one time was only a few feet wide. But each incremental step narrowed the regions the skeletons could climb. Barako coordinated the movements of the siege cauldrons to make the most progress. She had each pair start twenty feet apart, and then move together, driving the skeletons in that section into a more restricted space of wall, making it easier for fewer defenders to hold them off. The progress seemed so gradual at first, it would have been easy for it to seem pointless.

The Crab Clan, though, was familiar with the grinding interminability of struggle. Life was struggle. Existence was defined by the eternal siege of the Shadowlands. The promise of victory was enough. How far away it might be was irrelevant.

Step by step, victory came nearer. Barako and her samurai fought beyond exhaustion, entering a state of near trance. They fought until they surely could not fight any longer, and then they kept fighting, because that was their duty and the alternative was destruction. The skeletons wailed, and now Barako laughed at them.

"Listen to them," she said to Daizu, who had been fighting close behind her all along the wall. "They scream because they know they have lost. We can push them back until there are no more of them to come. Even the wind knows it has lost."

The keening of the storm was filled with frustration. The Kakeguchis had outfought it.

Daizu grinned. He weaved briefly with fatigue, then lunged past Barako, sword piercing the neck of a skeleton that had just leapt onto the top of the ramparts and was raising its ice cleaver to attack the team of a nearby siege cauldron. In the eruption of snow, Daizu struck again, destroying another monster as it came up behind its comrade. With the second snowburst, Daizu disappeared for a moment from Barako's gaze. She smashed a creature below her position and moved forward to find Daizu.

He emerged from the cloud of snow with a slow, unsteady gait. His arms hung limp. The point of an ice blade stuck out from his chest. He had been stabbed from behind. He dropped his katana. He frowned, puzzled by pain and the refusal of his body to obey him. He looked down. Blood poured from his mouth. Then he toppled sideways, over the rampart and down the wall. The wind dropped for a moment, as if in mockery, and allowed Barako to hear the crunch of his body when it hit the ground.

The snow skeleton that had killed Daizu bent down and picked up his blade. It held the blade before its empty eye sockets, contemplating its prize. It turned on Barako, its wail stuttering as if turning into laughter. Barako charged at it. Her blow smashed the arm that held Daizu's sword. The laughter stopped, and she was covered by another layer of snow.

She paused. For the first time since the siege had begun, there was nothing within immediate reach for her to attack. She blinked, confused that she had nothing to kill. The siege cauldrons poured the boiling water down again, and they sealed this section of the wall. Here, at least, there was only the blizzard now. The wind shrieked, and the snow hurled itself in anger at the wall and at Barako. Their fury was impotent. There were no monsters of snow to answer it. Not here.

A few hours later, there were none anywhere.

CHAPTER 16

The storm raged on, and it was impossible to keep the strip of stone clear everywhere. The snow blew in to cover it again. But the skeletons did not return, at least for now. Barako left instructions for the cauldrons to be kept full, the water boiling and ready for another attack.

"I am sorry your watch is not over yet," she told the guards she assigned to the first shift after the battle. "You will be relieved before long. There will be little rest for all of us while this storm lasts."

"This is the first watch after victory," one of the samurai, Sakimi, told her. "That will make our burden a light one."

Barako placed a gauntlet on the bushi's shoulder. "You fill me with pride, sister. Well said."

She led the rest of the company back to the castle. The storm was as strong as ever and as dark, but a line of lanterns had been set out between the gate and the castle doors, lighting the way. While her troops headed off to the barracks and the promise of sleep, however briefly, Barako trudged to the main hall. She arrived there a few steps

ahead of Doreni. He carried his helm under his arm, and
his gait was slow. His face was gray with fatigue. He smiled,
though, when he saw Barako.

"A good battle," he said.

"I don't know if I would call it that." She was glad to see
him. The feeling was a novelty. She suspected it would not
last.

"Any battle that ends in victory is a good one."

She thought of Daizu and the other samurai she had seen
die. "I would like to think that."

"It is the way I know to ward off despair."

She nodded and opened the door to the main hall.
Akemi was alone.

"If you are not on the wall, you bring good news, I hope,"
said the daimyō.

"Striking Dawn is safe, for the moment," said Barako.

"Though this unnatural storm continues."

"It does."

"With no end in sight," Doreni added.

"Then the siege has not ended," said Akemi. "We have a
reprieve, at best."

"So it would appear," Barako said. "I fear it will not end
until the power that reigns in the City of Night's Hunger is
defeated."

"Do you propose marching there in this?"

"No. That would be impossible. Earlier, Lieutenant
Doreni and I got lost going from the gate to the castle door.
While this darkness persists, we must remain here." *Did you
hope I would say we should go, and so mimic your son's folly?
You know me better than that.* The daimyō must feel her grip

on Striking Dawn growing very slippery if the thought that Barako would be that reckless had crossed her mind, even if only for a moment.

"We do nothing, then?" Akemi asked.

"Doing nothing is painful for me as well," Doreni said. "Lieutenant Barako is correct, though. We have no choice but to keep to the shelter of Striking Dawn."

"Until it falls?"

"There is some hope it will not come to that," Barako said.

"I would welcome such hope."

"The evil that besieges us is very powerful. It is, however, not all-powerful. Its skeleton warriors did not appear, at first, to be limited in number. They were, though. So I do not think this storm can last forever. The being that caused it will have to rest. Even in Night's Hunger, there were limits to what it could do. If we wait, and we defend the walls, the enemy will have to retreat eventually. The storm will end, and then it will be our turn to lay siege."

"It is clear we do not have any choice but to do as you say," Akemi said. "Much as I wish it were otherwise."

"This not a time for recklessness," said Barako.

"I don't think it ever is," Akemi answered, her voice sad.

"Where is Haru?" Doreni asked.

"Resting. He was too weak to wait out the entire siege with me."

"And Chuai? I gave him instructions not to leave you alone."

A guard for the guard, Barako thought. Chuai had no doubt been told to keep an eye on Haru too.

"I sent him away," said Akemi. "I wanted to be alone."

"With respect," Barako said, "was that wise?"

"If I was attacked, then the situation would have been far more dire than what could be dealt with by one or two bodyguards."

The scream cut through the main hall as if in mocking answer to Akemi. It was a long cry, ringing in the halls of the castle with an immensity of pain and terror. The voice was so distorted by agony that Barako could not recognize it. The scream went on and on, the extremity greater than the victim's need to draw breath. It ended in a gurgling moan. There was an awful, wet quality to the final moments.

"Strength of Lord Hida," Akemi gasped. "What was that?"

"I think it came from upstairs," said Barako. That was not Ochiba's voice. Ancestors grant that it was not Ochiba's voice.

The three left the hall. Akemi, her cane tapping sharply on the floor, hurried after Barako. Doreni brought up the rear. They took the stairs behind the main hall. The corridors were crowded with terrified servants, and Barako ordered them back to their stations.

On the second floor, she headed first for Ochiba's chamber, closest to the stairs. The captain was unharmed, and still unconscious. Thank you, Lord Hida. From there, the next doorway was the library. She entered, and found Junji standing near the entrance. He had the look of a man who had feared the worst, and knew it had come.

"Do you know whose cry that was?" she asked.

He shook his head.

"Was it from nearby?" Doreni asked.

"From above."

"Are you sure?"

"No," said Junji. "It seemed to be everywhere. But I don't think the victim was close by."

"So loud," Akemi murmured in horror. "To be in such pain…"

Junji went with them as they headed down to the next sliding doors. Doreni had been silent, but Barako sensed his rising tension. The quarters he and his family occupied were next down the hall.

Barako let him take the lead. He tapped first on the entrance to his chamber and called gently to his wife. After a moment, Rekai pulled the panel aside. She was pale, her eyes wide. "Who was that?" she pleaded.

"We don't know," Doreni told her. "Stay here. I'll be back soon."

The next room was Mioko's, and she was safe too. And then it was Chuai's.

There was no answer to Doreni's knock. He gave Barako a look glittering with anxiety, and slid the door open. The chamber was empty.

"He may be at the wall," Barako said. *Only he isn't. You know he isn't. Because that would be too much good fortune.*

"His duty was with the daimyō," said Doreni. "He would have waited here for new orders when she dismissed him."

Barako was about to suggest that Chuai had been detained on his way here. She stopped herself. Such reassurances were hollow. They helped nothing.

They headed up to the next floor.

"There is no reason for him to be up here," said Doreni.

"Then perhaps he isn't," Barako said, then cursed herself. *That means nothing. If that scream was Chuai, the fact that he should not be on this floor is meaningless.*

The halls were darker here. Most of the lanterns were out. Somewhere, a window was open. The wind had found its way into the castle here. It shrilled to itself, banged shutters, and blew snow along the floor. The door to Akemi's quarters was open, the chamber within black and cold. Junji lit one of the lanterns and stepped inside. Frost silvered the furnishings. There was no one here.

The wind keened and caressed. It leeched away at the last of Barako's warmth. Premonitions gathering, she followed the corridors that led past the daimyō's quarters toward the shrine in the south-east corner of the third floor. She held her hammer tightly, all the while certain, with rising dread, that she would not be using her weapon. There would be nothing to fight. Where she was going, all had already been accomplished.

She smelled the blood before she saw it.

Chuai's body leaned against the wall next to the entrance to the shrine. Beside him was a statue of Lord Hida.

Chuai's face hung like a torn glove over the head of the Kami.

CHAPTER 17

An entire company, divided into squads, searched every room and corridor in Striking Dawn Castle. Barako oversaw the hunt, and she had Doreni involved as much as he wished to be. She needed him to see that every corner was scoured, that she was taking the murder of Chuai as seriously as if the victim had been Haru or Akemi. She foresaw the splintering of the unity that had been forged during the battle on the walls. She feared the consequences.

The search began on the top floor of the castle and moved down. The entire population of the castle was moved to the ground floor for the duration of the hunt. After each floor was cleared, guards were posted at every stairwell, preventing any movement to or from the regions that had been searched. Then the company moved through the ground floor, the barracks and the merchant quarters. The squads searched the storehouses and the stables. They swept through the guardhouses and over the wall. They formed a line, with every warrior holding a lantern, and moved across the courtyard.

Do this properly, Barako told herself. Hold Striking Dawn together.

They forgot nothing. They ignored nothing.

They found nothing.

It disturbed Barako that she was not surprised. She had to guard against fatalism.

She watched Doreni closely. His grief and rage were dangerous. His family was stunned by shock, and unable even to begin mourning. The body had not yet been taken away from its position outside the shrine. It would have to stay until Junji had finished his examination, and performed initial cleansing rites.

When the search ended, Doreni went to his wife and daughter. He would be demanding his son's body soon enough. Barako hurried to the third floor to speak to Junji before that happened.

The monk knelt before the door to the shrine, a small finger of jade in his hands. He stood when Barako approached.

"Is it done?" she asked.

"As much as can be here. The family can prepare for cremation now."

"Good." That was the smallest of mercies, but at least she would not have to ask Doreni to delay. "And what have you found?"

"Nothing that would surprise you, I fear."

"Then the murderer is not mortal."

"No." He gestured quickly at the limp, hanging face. "Never mind that no blade did that." He turned to the corpse, still upright, as if the pain of its death was so great, it could not rest. The chest plate of Chuai's armor had been cut down the middle. "Look at this." Junji moved one half of the tunic aside, revealing the wound to the chest. It looked as if a single blow had torn through armor, skin, muscle and bone.

Barako's jaw clenched. So much power. The killer must be huge. How can it be hiding?

There was an answer to that. She wanted Junji to tell her she was wrong.

"There was snow on the floor," said Barako. No longer. The window was closed now, and some heat had returned to this part of the castle. "But this does not look like the handiwork of the snow skeletons we fought. Their blades were ice. Lethal, but fragile."

"I don't think this was done by any blade. Look how thick the wound is. This was done by a claw. A big one."

Barako looked at the flayed skull, and then at the face again. "Yet that mutilation was skillfully done." She did not say *elegantly*, yet the word rose in her mind, hissing.

"Quite." The sickened look on Junji's face suggested he was trying to avoid the same word.

"This is the work of an oni, then," said Barako.

"It is."

An oni. A demon from the hell of Jigoku. The answer she had guessed, and prayed to be mistaken. She had fought an oni before. One had led the assault on the Wall during which Haru's father had given his life. The battle against the monster had been terrible, and that had been on the great rampart built expressly to hold back such evil.

An oni on this side of the Wall. Inside the castle… The

implications of this kind of attack were dark. To think too deeply about them would be paralyzing. "How can such a thing be here? How did it escape from Jigoku? The Festering Pit is far from here. The Wall still stands."

"The City of Night's Hunger must have given it a way in."

"I realize that."

"I know you do," said Junji. "You do not want to say Haru's name, do you?"

What do you mean? That he led the oni here? By accident? By design? That he is the oni?

"No, I do not want to speak his name," Barako said. "But I must." If she did not, Doreni would. If she had suspected the killing to be the work of an oni, he would too.

"His behavior has changed since he emerged from the tower at Night's Hunger."

"The change is not abnormal. He behaves as one might after what he experienced." She did not enjoy defending Haru. She was as angry with him as she had been from the moment Ochiba staggered out of the tower. The person she was truly defending was Akemi, and through her, the Kakeguchi family.

"What *has* he experienced?" Junji asked. "We do not know. It is possible he opened the way for the oni, even without knowing he had done so."

Barako remembered Haru's awkward movements when he was first out of the tower. The clumsy walk. The uncertain limbs. That might not mean anything. It might mean everything. "He might have," she conceded. She decided to put the worst surmise into words. "You believe it is possible he summoned the oni, unintentionally or not, and with the storm it has come to Striking Dawn."

"That is my fear. It bothers me that we do not know what happened in the tower. If only Ochiba were awake."

"I pray for her awakening with every hour that passes."

Junji smiled gently. "I'm sure you do."

"An oni," Barako said, hating the sound of the word. "One we cannot find."

"It will not have left," said Junji. "There are many ways one can hide. Its work has only just begun."

"So I fear. And if this storm is its doing…"

"Yes. It must have great powers." Junji looked down at the body again. "Powers to deceive, and powers of attack. We must let the daimyō know. She awaits word in the main hall."

"Yes." Barako thought for a moment. "Will you come with me? If Doreni is in his quarters, I want to speak with him first."

"It is his right to know," said Junji carefully. "It was his son. The family must know they can take the body away. Why do you wish to speak with him before the daimyō, though?"

"We will pass his chamber on the way to the main hall."

"You have not answered my question."

"I want to tell him as a mark of respect."

"That is still not an answer."

"I believe the more respected he feels in this terrible moment, the better things will be for all of Striking Dawn. Is that enough of an answer?" *If I am forced to play at being a politician, it is partly because of your damnable neutrality.*

Junji lowered his head. "I understand now. Thank you."

They descended from the third floor. They found Doreni in his chambers. He filled the doorway when they knocked. Rekai and Mioko were hunched, grieving figures at the far end of the room.

"My work is finished," Junji said. "You may begin the funeral rights for Chuai."

With a short bark of command, Doreni sent four of his servants to begin the work. When they had gone, Doreni stepped out of the room and slid the door shut. "What do you have to say to me?" he said.

"There are matters all of us must talk about with Lady Akemi," said Barako. "And that you should know first."

Doreni nodded curtly. They walked toward the stairs together. Barako could tell how well this conversation was going to go. In spite of Doreni's political maneuvering, there had been the beginnings of a genuine bond between them as a result of the battle on the ramparts. That was gone now, as if it had never been.

"Hiruma Chuai was killed by an oni," Junji said softly.

Doreni grunted. He did not seem surprised. "And where has it gone?"

"It is hiding," said Barako. "We have looked. You have looked with us. We cannot find it."

"That is unfortunate." His tone made an insult of the words.

"The oni is still here. We must assume that. We must be on our guard. The attack by the snow skeletons was a diversion. The real assault on Striking Dawn Castle is happening now." She descended the staircase slowly, praying without hope that she could make Doreni an ally in what lay ahead. "Do you see, lieutenant? We must be united."

Doreni snorted. "I see very well. I see you acting in the interests of your family."

"I think you misunderstand me."

"I think you are the one without understanding. You ask this of me? And what you are asking is for me to follow along without objection to whatever you and Akemi decide. You do not understand anything. You have not lost your son."

"I have suffered losses too, in this struggle." She had no wish to deny Doreni's pain. She did need to keep him from disappearing into the selfishness of grief. He was still a lieutenant in the guard of Striking Dawn.

Doreni gave her a look of enormous contempt. "I will not dishonor my son's memory by doing nothing."

"That is not what I am asking. I am asking you to think about the goals of the evil that is at work here. The oni will seek to sow confusion and distrust. Can you think of a better way to achieve that end than what it has already done?"

Barako knew immediately that she had said the wrong thing.

"You speak as if the murder of my son were the placement of a piece in a game of go."

"I expressed myself badly. I apologize. I intended no insult. My only concern is the safety of Striking Dawn and all within it. I believe you are an honorable samurai, and I–"

Doreni interrupted. "Do not play with my emotions. Do not seek advantage that way. Do not dare."

I am not. It is you who are refusing to listen. It is you who will not understand. She bit back all of her replies. At this point, it was better to say nothing at all. Doreni would take anything she said in bad faith. She would try again in council, though she did not hold out much hope. She had lost this battle. She worried that perhaps Doreni thought he had won it. He had not. The victory had gone to the oni.

She looked to Junji for support. He was caught up in his own thoughts again. Either he had not listened to any of the conversation, or had chosen to give that appearance.

In the main hall, Akemi received the news solemnly. "The search was a thorough one," she said after Junji had finished speaking. "Where can it be hiding?"

"I cannot guess, Lady Akemi," said Junji. "Oni are clever. We looked everywhere, but there are places even human killers could conceal themselves. The oni could be in the walls or the roof. It could be somewhere we cannot imagine. We do not even know its shape."

Doreni started. He looked at Junji sharply.

"It will be moving around," Junji continued. "We may be seeking it, but we must remember that we are not the hunters. We are the prey."

Barako watched Doreni, braced for what he would say next. She knew what he was thinking. The same idea was torturing her. It was one she did not want to countenance, for the sake of the daimyō, though she knew she had to.

"We do not know the oni's shape," he repeated. "Are we sure, then, that everyone in the castle is who they appear to be?"

There. The words were spoken. Soon other words would

be too, forcing the idea into the open. Barako had hoped to temper Doreni's anger before this moment. She had failed. If his ambition was married to his rage, then everything would become far worse than it already was.

Doreni continued, "The silence of this council speaks volumes."

"We three were together when Chuai was killed," said Barako.

"And everyone else?"

"I was alone," said Junji.

"So were many people in the castle," said Akemi. "Those who were not fighting in the siege took refuge in their quarters."

"Some would be together," said Barako. "Like the merchants. And many of the samurai returning to the barracks. And those who were still upon the walls."

Akemi closed her eyes for a moment. She had aged years in the last few days. Barako felt her own fatigue grow heavier to see Akemi's weariness. The daimyō had not been in combat, but every repercussion that had come from the discovery of Night's Hunger had struck her like a blow.

The daimyō opened her eyes and straightened on her chair. "And so the threads are tangled," she said. "It will take a great effort to learn who was seen by whom, and who can be trusted. The oni might have the face of almost any of us."

"Is that so?" Doreni asked Junji.

"Some oni are known to be mimics," the monk said carefully. "They are cunning. But they are not mortal. Their mimicry is not perfect. They will make errors."

Barako's mouth dried. *The way Haru walked at first. It can be explained by the agonies he suffered. But what if that awkward gait should not be explained away? What if it were the walk of something unused to the human form?*

"Then there might be a faster way of finding our foe," said Doreni. "Is there anyone amongst us who has not been behaving normally?"

The question was a leading one. Doreni already knew his answer, Barako thought.

So do I.

She kept silent. She would do nothing to put Striking Dawn at risk, but she would not be the one to wound Akemi either. And she was not sure. She was a long way from being sure.

"None of you will answer?" Doreni said. "Will you put family pride before the protection of the castle and the duty of the clan?"

Akemi glared at him. "Speak plainly," she said, carving her syllables from ice, "since that is what you wish to do."

"Clearly I must. There is one in the castle who *must* be considered. Haru has come into contact with the forces of the Shadowlands. No one knows to what extent. No one knows the *nature* of that contact."

One of us does, Barako thought. *But she cannot tell us.*

"You have made your point, lieutenant," said Akemi.

Doreni continued as if she had not spoken. "He has also not been the same since he returned to us. Has he?" He waited. No one spoke. Those who most wished to contradict Doreni could not. Tension built in the silence. "Haru has changed," Doreni resumed, merciless. "He has said very little to anyone. All the better to avoid making a mistake that would give him away?"

"You are wrong," Akemi said.

"I am sorry, daimyō. If you have lost your son in Night's Hunger, then we are comrades in grief."

"We are not, because you are wrong," she insisted. "I mourn for you, Hiruma Doreni. I will not rest until you are avenged. Wherever the oni hides, it will be found. Whoever it hides as, it will be discovered. But I tell you this. As certainly as I draw breath, my son is my son." She turned to Junji. "You say the oni mimicry is imperfect." She was almost pleading.

"It is."

"There. There is your proof," Akemi said to Doreni. "Don't you think I know my own son? Don't you think I would see at once if an imposter had returned?" She looked at Barako and Junji, seeking their support.

Barako said nothing. She could not. There were doubts she could not shake. She kept seeing that uncertain figure in Night's Hunger, staring around blankly, moving like a puppet. She did not know. She wanted to be convinced by Akemi. But she did not know.

"You see your son because the agony of not seeing him would be too much to bear," Doreni said, his voice hoarse with pain.

Akemi shook her head.

"The oni know us," said Junji. "They know our weaknesses. They will show us what we wish to see."

"He is Haru," said Akemi. "I know he is. I will not permit it to be said otherwise."

"You have suspicions," Barako said to Doreni. *So do I. And wouldn't that just be like Haru, to be the cause of an even greater catastrophe than we thought?* "You do not have proof."

"I will get it."

"You forget yourself, lieutenant," Akemi snapped. "You are not daimyō of Striking Dawn Castle. I am. You will be respected because of who you are. You are due respect for your actions for your family. Your words will be excused because of your grief. But I will be obeyed."

He glared at her. She met his gaze. Neither flinched. The tension in the hall tightened. It became a thrumming wire. In a few moments of silence, the political currents of Striking Dawn grew turbulent, grew dangerous.

Doreni ended the confrontation with a perfunctory, rigidly shallow bow. He said nothing. He conceded nothing, except in the most minimal display of respect.

"No one will act against anyone without proof," said Barako. "If we did, we would be handing the oni its victory."

To her surprise, for once, Junji supported a position. "That is true," he said.

"What are we to do?" said Akemi. "Even if none of what has been said in this room is repeated, there will be rumors. If the enemy is not found right away, suspicion will spread. What we seek to avoid will happen anyway."

"Then we will have to manage the inevitable," said Barako. "We will continue with the search. We will have patrols, frequent ones, on all the floors day and night."

"Day," Akemi said bitterly. "What is day? Does it still exist? Does anyone here know what hour this is?"

"It is the hour of the serpent, Lady Akemi," said Junji. "It is day."

Barako was almost as surprised to learn it was day as she was that Junji was managing to keep track. "Along with the patrols," she said, "we must take a special precaution. Other than we four, no one in the castle must be alone. Ever."

Barako nodded a greeting to Sakimi. The samurai who had taken the first watch on the walls after the battle was now guarding the door to Ochiba's chamber.

"Have you not had any rest?" Barako asked.

"I have, lieutenant, thank you. I had a few hours' sleep after the search."

Barako fought off a wave of dizziness. She had lost track of time again. More hours had passed since the council than she had thought. The eternal darkness was confusing her, and she could not remember when she had last slept herself. She would have to sleep, and soon. It was just that there was always something else she had to do. There was an enemy loose in the castle, and she could not bear to surrender her watch to anyone else. Someone had to keep track of what Doreni was doing. Someone had to help Akemi.

She had to accept that, at least for a short time, that person could not be her. Otherwise soon she would not be able to help anyone.

Sakimi slid the door open, then closed it softly behind Barako, who sat down in her place at the head of Ochiba's sleeping mat.

"Can you hear me?" Barako asked.

Ochiba did not stir. Was her breathing easier than it had been? Barako hoped so. It was still labored, still slow. The

Legend of the Five Rings

pauses between exhalation and inhalation were so long, they made Barako hold her breath, fearing the silence would not end.

"I hope you can hear me," Barako whispered. "I want you to know what is happening. Then, when you wake up, you can take up command again. Striking Dawn needs you."

She lowered her head. She stared at her hands. "I need you," she said, so quietly that she barely heard herself. "I do not ask you to break your oath. I would never ask such a thing. But I need you. I need to be at your side. I'm so tired. This burden is so heavy. I don't know if any of my decisions are right. I think I may have made Doreni into more of a threat to Akemi when I was trying to do the reverse. I've had enough, Ochiba. I need to follow you again."

She sighed. She leaned her back against the wall. Her body ached with all the combat pains she did not have the time to indulge. Her limbs were bruised and heavy with exhaustion. "All right. I have my moaning out of the way. I don't think I have the energy to recite 'The Courtier's Lament' this time. I'm going to tell you more about what is happening. Is that all right? I think you would want to know. So, I think it is night again, for all the difference that makes. The storm is as strong as ever. There was another attack by the skeletons of snow again. Two hours ago, I think that was. It was a minor assault. Easily dealt with. Not too many of the enemy. So that's a good sign, do you think? I hope it is."

She listened to Ochiba breathe for a bit. She got used to the pauses. The rhythm was regular. That was a good sign, too. She held it close. It was the promise that Ochiba would recover. "Come back," she murmured. "Come back soon." She matched the rhythm of her breathing to Ochiba's. She wanted to stay in this space of comfort forever.

"Ochiba, there's an oni loose in the castle," she said. "You won't be alone, though. There will be a guard." She would have preferred to have two guards posted at the door, but between the watch on the wall and the patrols in the halls, the defenders of Striking Dawn were stretched thin. Barako's instinct was to protect Ochiba as thoroughly as she could. She also knew what Ochiba would have said about wasting resources. So she assigned a roster of guards chosen from the samurai who had been with her on the wall, and had stayed there when she returned to the castle after the battle. She was as certain as she could reasonably hope to be that none of them was the oni.

"I've set up the patrols. Doreni has too. They're separated into Kakeguchi and Hiruma pairs. I don't think that's a good idea. It won't help the unity in the castle. He may not believe in unity right now, and I don't blame him, but we need it, more than ever." She drummed her fingers on the floor, thinking of the fault lines between the families in Striking Dawn.

"I'm having trouble with time. Every hour is the same now. It feels too much like the City of Night's Hunger. I worry we might lose time completely. What we have of it is broken into shifts instead of day and night, and that doesn't help much. Too many people on too many shifts. There is no cohesion, no unifying cycle. I don't know what will happen if the distinctions created by the shifts break down. At least we're doing something. It isn't enough, captain. It isn't enough, and I don't know how to do more. We're ready for an attack, but the attack is already happening."

Before she could go on, she heard raised voices in the hall outside the chamber. She heaved herself to her feet and pulled the door aside. Sakimi was confronting two Hiruma bushi, Nisobu and Tsuru.

"What is it?" Barako snapped.

"They insist on inspecting Captain Ochiba's chamber," said Sakimi. "I told them it already had been, and that I answered for it."

"You're not Hiruma," Tsuru said to Sakimi. "It wasn't the heir of your lieutenant that was killed."

"We answer to Hiruma Doreni," said Nisobu. "If he orders us to look in every room, we will look in every room."

"Of course, of course," Barako said, utterly tired of everything. Wearily, she stepped aside and waved at the room. "There. Go. See. Are you satisfied?"

Aware of her anger, and of how close they had come to shouting at the commanding officer of Striking Dawn, the two guards shuffled past her, glanced into the chamber, and withdrew. They turned to go.

"No," Barako said. "Stop. Wait one moment."

The Hiruma samurai looked at her, puzzled.

"Sakimi," she said. "Go with them."

All three bushi opened their mouths to object. The impropriety of doing so stopped them.

"You will complete your patrol together," Barako said. "This way, both families will be satisfied. Isn't that so?"

"Yes, Lieutenant Barako," said Nisobu. "But…"

"We are all here for the same purpose. We are all of the

Crab Clan. Are we not?"

"We are," Tsuru said reluctantly.

"Good. We fought side by side on the wall, and we fought well. Now it is even more crucial that we stand with each other." Doreni's suspicions were spreading like poison. She had to do what she could to counteract them. "Go," she said to Sakimi. "I will stay with Captain Ochiba."

She watched the three samurai head off down the hall. They obeyed reluctantly, but they obeyed. That was a victory for this moment, and one moment at a time was all she had energy for.

Barako shut the door again and slumped down beside Ochiba. "Can I tell you what I'm afraid of? I'm afraid that even if the oni has left Striking Dawn forever, it has already won." The words felt like a death knell. She could say them to no one else. She had to say them to Ochiba. Perhaps, if she gave voice to the worst, she would find the strength to fight it.

She stared at the wall opposite, eyes mechanically moving from one panel to another. It had been days since she had slept. Her body was a sack of lead she had to drag around.

She should sleep.

She didn't think she could.

They didn't speak to each other for the rest of the sweep of the second floor. Sakimi walked a step behind the Hiruma guards. She glared at their backs while they refused even to glance at her. All three of them put aside their animosity as they checked each room, though. Death crouched in dark potential behind every door.

The second floor was quiet. Two more floors, and the samurai could return to ground level, pass their duties on to the next shift, and relieve themselves of each other's presence.

They reached an intersection. To the left, the hall ran past the servants' quarters. To the right, it went along the wall of the audience chamber and ended at a staircase. The lanterns in both branches had gone out. The corridor was dark.

"There was light when we first came this way," said Tsuru.

They drew their blades.

Snow hurled itself, a swarm of clicks, against the shuttered windows in the wall opposite. The eyes of the castle were blank with night.

Sakimi strained to see to the ends of the corridor. The shadows were too thick. Light from the lanterns in the intersection only reached a few yards.

Down to the left, there was a smash of breaking shutters. The wind blew into the hall, sudden in its fury. It knocked the nearest lantern to the floor, and its light went out. The samurai stood in near total darkness.

There was movement to the left. There was a shift in the black, a glimpse of something pale crossing the corridor toward the invisible shattered window.

"It's there!" Tsuru shouted. "It's trying to escape!" He and Nisobu ran into the dark.

At the same moment, Haru called for help to the right.

"Wait!" Sakimi shouted to the other two.

They ignored her, or they didn't hear. The wind shrieked

at her, the gale in the hall almost as strong as it had been outside.

Haru called again. His voice was desperate and weak. It was a wonder she heard it at all.

Why is he here? Sakimi wondered. He had been keeping to his quarters since his return. She hesitated, then turned right. Haru was the heir to Striking Dawn. He needed her help *now*. The oni would be long gone before Nisobu and Tsuru reached it.

She rushed into the dark, slowing almost at once. She knew the hall well. She had run its length countless times as a child. But the shadows were dangerous, and Haru sounded as if he were under attack. There was a side entrance to the audience hall just before the stairs. Perhaps the lanterns in the hall were still on. If she could find the door, she might be able to see what was happening.

Haru cried out. This time there were no words, only pain. Sakimi advanced with her katana out in her left hand, her right brushing the wall, searching for the door.

Haru's cry became a moan.

"Lieutenant Haru," she called. "I am here!"

She found the door to the audience hall and threw it open, bracing for an attack. The great chamber was empty. The glow of its lanterns shone through the doorway and filled the end of the corridor. Sakimi could see to its end, and to the stairs.

There was no one there.

"Lieutenant Haru?" she called again.

Silence. There were no signs anyone had been here. There was no blood on the floor or the walls. She was alone in an empty corridor.

Sakimi turned around. She looked back down toward the other end of the hall. There was only darkness. The wind blew hard against her, its shriek as hollow as a tomb. "Tsuru!" she shouted. "Nisobu!"

No answer.

She thought she saw paleness again. Movement that was sinuous, and very tall. It was there for only a moment. She might have imagined it.

Sakimi rushed into the audience hall, grabbed a lantern, and started down toward the servants' quarters. The light that surrounded her felt like a shield. She was banishing darkness as she advanced, destroying the shadows where things could hide.

She called out to the Hiruma samurai again. Still there was no answer, but shortly before she reached the intersection of corridors again, she heard noises from the far end. There was a cluster of sharp cracks. A rapid drumming, like fingers of iron tapping against wood. The taut flapping of a flag in wind.

The cracks stopped. The rattling stopped. The flapping kept on.

She was walking slowly now. She did not see the pale movement again. After another few steps, she saw the flapping motion. She went forward a little more, and the light showed her everything.

Her eyes widened in horror.

The samurai had been skinned. Their flesh, unrolled into long banners, hung over the broken window, toys for the wind. The bones of their arms had been splintered into spikes and driven into the wall over the window frame, holding the strips of skin.

There were more bones in the center of the floor. They were arranged in a spiral that seemed to move. At its center were the skulls, wet with blood but so cleanly scraped of tissue that the bone gleamed in the light of Sakimi's lantern. Their jaws interlocked, as if they were devouring each other, the dead at war while the spiral turned and turned and turned, pulling them deeper into damnation.

CHAPTER 18

Barako's eyes snapped open. She leapt to her feet, hammer in her hands, ready to fight. The sounds that had woken her began to register properly. There was shouting nearby. Voices raised in anger and fear. But no clash of arms. No fighting. She took a moment to rub the last of sleep from her eyes. Her neck was stiff, her back aching from sleeping in her armor. Her rest had not been long. It would have to do, though. She was needed now. At least she felt some strength had come back to her.

She knelt beside Ochiba long enough to make sure her breathing was normal. Then she left the chamber.

She stepped out into frigid air. A breeze blew against her face, and it grew to a strong wind as she ran down the halls.

She found chaos outside the servants' quarters. The wind raged down the hall from the broken window. The servants were shrieking at the horrors in the corridor. There were at least a dozen samurai there too, Hiruma and Kakeguchi, some shouting at the servants to be silent, the rest shouting at each other. Doreni was there too, standing still in the middle of the riot, ignoring the violence of unleashed emotion around him. Barako shouldered her way through the bushi. Beside Doreni, she took in the butchery, feeling numb with despair. In the arrangement of the bones, she saw the same design that was everywhere in the City of Night's Hunger. Seeing it here felt like the spread of a disease.

She looked at Doreni. His face was thunderous. Though he was staring at the skulls, his eyes were unfocused. He was seeing something else, something that consumed him completely. Barako stepped away, leaving him to his dark meditations. If she could take the initiative and gain control of the madness, she might contain an eruption.

She spotted Sakimi leaning against the wall a short distance from the crowd. The samurai straightened when she saw Barako approaching.

"Did you see what happened?" Barako asked.

"No," said Sakimi. "I heard Lieutenant Haru calling for help." She pointed to the other end of the corridor. "He wasn't there. When I came back, Tsuru and Nisobu were dead." She was still looking toward the staircase. "There's another window broken down there," she said. "It wasn't when I was looking for Haru."

Barako ran down to the other window. There were splinters of wood on the floor. The shutters had been smashed in from the outside.

The oni breaks the shutters at the other end, she thought. *But not these ones until later.* "Are you sure Haru's voice was coming from inside the castle?" she asked Sakimi.

"No," Sakimi admitted. " But it came from this direction."

Barako tried to picture the movements. The creature visible near the servants' quarters, then jumping out the window, and scuttling down the roof to the other end of the hall to mimic Haru's voice and lure Sakimi away. It must have gone back again to kill Tsuru and Nisobu.

"Doreni!" Her shout cut through the din and snapped the Hiruma lieutenant out of his trance. He stormed down the hall toward her, fire in his eyes. She pointed at the window. "The roof! The oni was on the roof!" She had caught his interest now, diverting him, at least for the moment, from his path of anger. "Get us rope," she said to Sakimi. "Rope and hooks."

The samurai rushed off.

It could have come back for Sakimi, Barako thought. Why didn't it? Why did it let her live?

Because of the discord it would sow by only killing Hirumas.

Doreni toed the splinters of wood. "Then it is in the castle again," he said, fully in the present moment again.

"Unless it has left again from elsewhere. We looked everywhere for it. Everywhere *in* the castle." The roof was almost perfect concealment. It was impossible to see anything other than darkness and snow outside.

When Sakimi came back with the rope, Barako attached one end to a grappling hook. It took several throws before the hook latched onto the eaves of the roof, catching something more solid than snow. She tested her weight on the rope. It felt solid, and she went out first, dangling in the shrieking darkness. She climbed as quickly as she could, and heaved herself onto the steep slope of the second-floor roof. It ended at the wall of the third floor, which she could just make out thanks to the lantern light shining through its windows. Its roof was invisible to her. Barako was grateful for the snow. With her feet sunk into it, she was able to stand and not be thrown off the slope by the wind.

Doreni came next, and then two of his samurai, bringing lanterns with them.

"Look," said Barako.

In the light, they could see the tracks in the snow. They had cut a path from above the far window to this position. They kept going too, heading around the corner of the roof.

"You were right," Doreni said. "It ambushes us this way. How does this help? We can't post guards here."

"No, we can't." It was too cold, too exposed, and there were too many places the oni could hide. If she sent warriors out here, she would be sending them to their deaths. "We'll have to barricade the windows. We can try to limit its ways in and out. And seal off portions of the castle completely."

"That won't be enough."

"I know." She looked up into the darkness. "It could be perched on the castle peak." *Watching us. And we can't even see the top of our home.*

"Or it is inside now, mocking us," said Doreni. "Even if it is not, this is foolish ground on which to challenge it."

He was right. But they knew something more, now. And at least by bringing him out here, she had diffused the conflict in the corridor for the moment. And she was unsatisfied. The oni had been too obvious, almost as if it had hoped to lure them onto the roof.

Why leave the signs to lead us here? What does it what us to see?

Barako took one of the lanterns and turned around slowly. She spotted another track, leading away from the edge of the roof. She followed it up the slope toward the third-floor wall. When she drew near enough for the light to reach, she saw the design. It was another spiral, painted in blood. It was huge. It glistened, dark and wet, in the light. It should have been frozen. It was not. The blood flowed, coiling around in an eye-scraping spiral, pulling the Barako's vision around and around to the center, the center that seemed to be burrowing deeper and deeper, not into the wall, but into the fabric of being, plunging into a fathomless abyss. The sinuosity of the spiral extended off the wall and onto the snow below it. The blood ran here too, a current pulling the eye, and with it the soul, into the tainted spiral.

The darkness at the center sought to devour. This, Barako thought, was the hunger of the night. It was what everything in that cursed city had been created to do. The spiral drew all it caught into the maw of the night, and the hunger there would never be sated.

It wants us. It wants our souls. It wants everything.

Simply standing here, close to the spiral, felt dangerous.

Doreni caught up to her. He stared at the twisting, luring blood. "The same as the bones," he said.

"The mark of the City of Night's Hunger," Barako said. "The oni has staked its claim. This is what it has come to do. It has come to make Striking Dawn Castle part of Night's Hunger."

Doreni swore. He took a step toward the blood on the roof. He kicked snow over it, trying to bury that part of the sigil. The snow turned to steam as soon as it touched the blood. The sign refused to be hidden.

"The taint will only grow stronger until we are rid of the oni," Barako said.

Doreni turned away from the sign with a snarl. He shuffled down the roof to the rope. He moved quickly, with sharp purpose. Barako hurried after him, but he moved recklessly fast and reached the rope well ahead of her. By the time she was back inside, Doreni had already done what he intended. A squad of Hiruma guards had Sakimi surrounded, with Doreni at their head. Kakeguchi samurai crowded uneasily forward, outraged at the treatment of their sister, but held back by Doreni's authority.

Barako approached carefully. "What are you doing?" she asked.

"Bushi Sakimi is the only survivor of the latest attack. I am ensuring she is protected." Doreni's eyes were cold and full of challenge.

"That is a wise precaution," said Barako, trying to gauge her next move. *What game are we playing now?* "She will come with me. You do not need this responsibility at this time."

"I will keep her under my protection," Doreni declared.

Barako took a single step forward. She looked down on Doreni. She let the silence stretch out before she spoke again. She used her height, and the physical fact of her presence. She saw the other Hiruma become uncomfortable as she loomed over them. Doreni did not blink.

"It would be much better for all if she came with me," Barako said quietly.

Doreni said nothing. His right hand was at his belt, and he moved it very slightly. The gesture could have been casual, a simple shifting of stance. But his hand was now just that small bit closer to his katana. The warriors around him altered their stance. They did not touch their blades, but they were standing ready now.

The corridor was silent. Kakeguchi and Hiruma samurai eyed each other, animosity needing only a single word from either lieutenant to turn into violence. No threats were uttered. There was no need. They coursed like lightning through the silence.

Barako locked eyes with Doreni. They fought each other without words or motion. With every passing moment, the reality of open conflict drew closer. If the war was not decided in the clash of wills, it would be with steel and blood.

Don't force my hand, Doreni. This is what the oni wants.

And Barako wondered what she was doing. Was she not playing the oni's game too? Yet she could not abandon one of her samurai in this way.

She felt the struggle with Doreni go back and forth, each of them seeing the precipice they were on, how easy it would be to fall over, and thinking *why, why, why*, because it was so unnecessary. If only the other would see that, if only the other would understand what was at stake, and this was not the time, of all times, to let passion overrule reason.

Doreni spoke first. "Two of my samurai are dead," he said. "The Kakeguchi lives. All of the oni's victims have been Hiruma." Every syllable was dipped in a venom of suspicion and anger. He spoke quietly, his tone flat with false calm. Each declarative statement was the thinnest of veils cast over a threat.

Barako forced herself not to smile. Doreni had ceded ground to her without realizing it. He had given voice to his grievances. She saw the shape of the battlefield, and its disposition of forces, and how to counter him. For this round. He had given her the means to appear to give ground. This was not the battle she wanted to fight. The only one that mattered was the struggle against the oni. She loathed the fact that the political struggles in Striking Dawn were being tangled into that conflict, and there was very little she could do to keep them separate.

"I understand," she said. "And I think you are right. The oni is not attacking at random. Can you imagine a better way to pit us against each other than to begin by killing only the Hiruma?" She paused after the question only briefly, giving Doreni no time to answer, and continuing to speak as if he had agreed with her. "The protection you offer is accepted with gratitude. Now we must speak with her together. Somewhere quiet." *Away from a crowd that could be ignited.*

She held Doreni's gaze the whole time she spoke. His eyes narrowed slightly as her words backed him into a corner. She was the voice of reason now. He would do his cause no favors by appearing perverse. There were twice as many Kakeguchi as Hiruma in Striking Dawn. No matter his grief or anger, Doreni would be conscious of the numbers. He was too ambitious not to be.

"Yes," Doreni said, doing his best to sound authoritative, and imply that what Barako had said was what he had demanded in the first place. "Let us go and conduct this... conversation." His hesitation made the word *interrogation* hover in the air, a petty victory for him to claim, yet he took it all the same. "My guards will come with us."

Barako nodded to Sakimi. Remaining silent, she followed as Barako led the way, heading toward her chamber in the south-east corner of the floor. It was at the opposite end of the castle from the site of the killing.

They had only just begun to walk when Barako saw Junji standing quietly a short distance up a branching hall. He bowed to Doreni as they drew level with him.

"Lieutenant Doreni," he said. "I mean only the fullest respect to you, your family, and your samurai of the Hiruma. I know you understand the need for rites of purification to be performed. I hope you also understand that any insight, small though it might be, that could help us in the fight against the oni is essential, and that you will not object to me studying the remains of the honored fallen."

Doreni glared at him. Then he paused and shouted back to one of the Hiruma warriors at the intersection. "Let the monk do what he must."

"Thank you," Junji said. "I will see the bodies are taken away and prepared for cremation."

Doreni grunted.

Find something, Barako mentally urged Junji as she started walking again. *Find something. We are losing this war.*

CHAPTER 19

Barako took them into her room, inviting Sakimi to sit on the matted floor, while she kneeled behind her writing desk. It was her one possession of pride outside of her armor and weapons. It was dark, the lacquered surface scarred from heavy use.

Barako looked up at Doreni and invited him to sit too.

"Wait outside," he said to the guards. He slid the door shut behind them and kneeled too.

Good. We are as calm as the situation permits. What Sakimi had to say was not going to make things easier. At least Barako had ensured that Doreni would not be surrounded by his kin when he heard what had happened.

"Tell Lieutenant Doreni what you told me," Barako said. "Explain to him why you were not with the Hiruma bushi when they were attacked."

Sakimi looked at her uncertainly.

"Leave nothing out," Barako said. "That is most important." It was. Sooner or later, Doreni would hear what had lured Sakimi to the other end of the hall. Better he find out this way. Better he see that she wanted him to know it all, that she was concealing nothing.

"Haru," Doreni said, when Sakimi had finished her account. "You had us climbing around on the roof," he said to Barako, "to no purpose at all, when you had proof the oni was Haru?"

Barako delayed answering him directly. "Should we first agree that Bushi Sakimi is quite capable of protecting herself?"

After a moment, Doreni gave a curt nod.

"You have both our thanks for your help," Barako told Sakimi. "You may resume your other duties."

She waited until Sakimi had seen herself out, then asked, "What proof? Sakimi heard Haru's voice, and Haru was not there. Why would we think he was?"

"Someone was."

"Some*thing* was," she corrected. "Certainly. But why think it was Haru? Isn't this evidence of his innocence? If the oni has disguised itself as him, why make it obvious? Why expose the disguise? Isn't it far more useful to its ends to use Haru's voice to sow discord? Are we not falling into its trap?"

"And if it is Haru," Doreni countered, "it could count on precisely this defense, and so achieve the same ends."

She did not have an answer at the ready for that.

"Haru disappeared into the City of Night's Hunger," Doreni went on. "No one saw what happened. He was gone for days before you and Ochiba arrived at the tower. Why think that was him that came out?" Doreni was remorseless, using reason against Barako. He had not been as weakened by his anger and grief as she had thought. "You have very little reason to believe that Haru is what he claims to be."

"You have as little to show the contrary."

He shook his head. "You know better than that, Lieutenant Barako. I'm sure you do. But your loyalty to Daimyō Akemi prevents you from seeing clearly. Your loyalty does you credit. But it is leading you astray. You do not believe Haru is the oni because you do not want to believe it." He pressed the attack. "No, that's wrong. I think you do see more than you say. You *do* believe he is the oni, even though you do not wish to."

Barako stared at him, marveling at the scale of his ambition, how he followed its ends even now. His grief for his son's death was real. His anger over the death of his samurai was real. And yet, he had seen the opportunity the killings created for him, and he was seizing it. He was working to make her his ally, as he had at the feast before the coming of the storm.

Am I any better? Have I not been trying to make him my ally?

Only, she thought, because she was trying to head off this sort of power game.

Then she thought that rationalization sounded thin. She felt a wave of disgust, for herself, for Doreni, for all the machinations of mortals that played into the hands of the powers of the Shadowlands.

"You presume to know my mind," she said. *I don't even know it myself.* "You go too far."

"I am prepared to go further. Haru's trial has been delayed because Ochiba cannot speak for or against him.

There can be no more delay. I will see to that, and I do not care at what cost."

We are already here. At open defiance. Barako thanked the fates that this conversation was private. "You mean to have him answer for his foolishness now? Don't we have better uses for our time?"

"Not for his foolishness, no. That action, we know was committed by Haru. I charge this being with murder. With being an oni."

"Do you know what you are doing?"

"I do."

"Your intent is to engulf the castle in a political war?"

He looked uncomfortable for the first time. "No."

"Then will you listen to caution? You have sworn an oath of loyalty to the daimyō too. Remember that. Do not bring shame upon yourself and disorder upon Striking Dawn." She held up a hand before he could respond. "Your questions must be answered. They *must*, if we are to survive. But consider what will happen if you push us to the brink. What will happen if you are seen to attack Haru for political ends, and you are wrong? Let me speak to Akemi. We will go to her together, but *let me speak.*"

"We will go together." He would grant her nothing more.

She nodded.

They left her chamber and went up to the third floor. The daimyō's chambers took up most of it. Four Kakeguchi guards were posted outside the door.

"Is the daimyō awake?" Barako asked them. "Has she heard what has happened below?"

"She has received the news," one of them said. "She left

word that you should be admitted at once."

She drew Doreni aside. "You *will* speak to her," she said quietly. "You have my word. All I ask is that you let me speak with her first."

"You demand a great deal of trust when I have none to give."

"You have nothing to gain by storming in and making demands. What could I possibly say to her that would turn her *against* you, when you are here to charge her son and heir with being an oni?"

After a moment's thought, he gave her that quick, sour nod again, as if any concession, no matter how reasonable, was an intolerable wound to his pride, one that incurred a debt he intended to collect.

Barako went back to the guards. They opened the doors for her and she went in alone. The flickering of the lamps casting dark shadows across the ornately painted screens that partitioned the room. The daimyō was sitting on a low cushion, next to a small sunken hearth that had been covered with a wooden platform and a heavy quilt to keep her warm, she still looked cold, hunched and old. Without looking up she said, "I can guess that you bring me still more ill tidings."

"I do." Barako stood before her at the hearth. "Doreni waits outside. He insists that we interrogate Haru, and I'm afraid he is right." She spoke gently but firmly.

"No." Akemi shook her head with a violence that sent a tremor down her frame.

"Doing so may exculpate him."

"No. He is my son. He will be the daimyō of Striking

Dawn Castle. He is not an oni. He will not be subjected to a politically driven suspicion." There was little authority in Akemi's voice. She became weak, querulous.

"Doreni follows the path of his ambition," Barako told her. "But he has lost *his* son. Two more Hiruma are dead. He is within his rights to demand an accounting."

"Not from my son."

Remain patient, Barako told herself. You may be the only one who still can. "You know I am loyal to you, Lady Akemi. I will fight for you to the death. It is out of love for you, for our family, and for Striking Dawn that I speak now. If you refuse Doreni's request, the divisions in the castle will grow worse. We will come closer to being defeated by the oni."

"Haru is Haru," Akemi said. "He did not kill those Hiruma. He was with me all the time."

Barako looked around. "Where is he?"

"Asleep." She gestured toward a closed panel door. "He is still very weak."

"Where have you been?" She hated herself for questioning her daimyō.

"Here." Akemi seemed too worn to object.

"Did you sleep at all?"

Akemi did not answer.

Barako sighed. "Then you don't know if he has been here all along."

Akemi stirred in the chair. "He *has*," she cried.

"We have to be sure."

"How? How will you be sure? Will Doreni stab him, and if he dies, we will know he was innocent?"

Barako said nothing.

"I am not shielding him. He *will* answer for the disaster at Night's Hunger. Didn't I say he would be judged?"

"And now he must be," Barako said softly.

Akemi slumped lower. "He *is* my son." She was barely audible.

Barako knelt beside her. She took Akemi's hands in hers. The daimyō's hands were cold, and fragile as parchment. They trembled. "What if he isn't?"

Akemi aged another ten years before Barako's eyes. With a struggle, she got to her feet. "I'll wake him," she said. "Fetch Doreni. Let him do his worst."

The interrogation took place in Akemi's chamber. Akemi had removed herself to a low chair. Her gaze did not waver from her son once. Haru remained standing. He was pale, his skin sheened with sweat. He faced Doreni with brittle defiance.

"Go on, then," Haru said. "Ask me what you will."

"No," said Doreni after a long moment, his face hard. "If your guise has been this convincing, your answers will be too."

"Then what is the point of this?" Akemi asked wearily.

"He must be placed under guard," Doreni told her, as implacable and cold as if the castle were already his.

"You would imprison my son?"

"Yes."

"I will not permit it." An ember of Akemi's internal fire flared up.

"Doing so would decide things one way or another," Barako said, hating herself. *This is the only path forward.*

This is what has to be done to save Striking Dawn. "If the oni strikes again while Haru is…" She forced herself to say it, "… is imprisoned, then his innocence is proven."

Haru looked at her, his eyes wide. "You don't suspect me, do you?" he asked.

"We have to be sure," she said. *And I am not. The neediness in his voice certainly sounded like Haru. But that was not enough.*

"Do *you* think I am the oni?" he demanded.

"I know only that your mother, Lieutenant Doreni and I are not." *I don't know what I think. The more you seem like Haru, the more I fear the oni's skill at mimicry.*

Haru's face crumpled in pain. His shoulders sagged. "Lock me up," he said. "If that is what it takes, let it be done."

"*No!*" Akemi cried. "I forbid it."

"It will be done because it must be," said Doreni.

"I have forbidden it. That is an end to the matter."

"You will force me to break my oath of loyalty for the good of the castle."

"Are you threatening me?" Akemi rose from her chair.

The ember had ignited a blaze. Akemi was seeing the consequences of what Doreni was demanding, Barako thought. She was looking to the longer-term effects, becoming a political animal again, as any daimyō had to be. Haru's position was precarious enough. Outright imprisonment would give substance to the worst suspicions about him. His claim to Striking Dawn would all but evaporate.

She was right, Barako thought sadly. But it didn't matter.

The oni had destroyed Haru's future. Nothing could change that.

Except Akemi refused to accept this.

"If you have so far forgotten yourself," the daimyō said to Doreni, "do not forget that you Hiruma are a minority in this castle."

"We are now," Doreni said, calm in the certainty of victory. "If you refuse, everyone will know that you protected what may be the oni. If you refuse, and it kills again, what do you think will happen to your authority?"

Akemi wilted. She sat back down, her head in her hands.

"Perhaps," Barako said, before something was said that could not be withdrawn, "there is room for compromise?" Look at me, Ochiba. Look at me trying to sail the political waters. Are you laughing yet?

"Compromise how?" Doreni asked, skeptical.

"It is not necessary to bring Haru out of these quarters in chains."

"I had not suggested we do that."

"Having him visibly under guard would amount to the same. Can there be some flexibility about *where* Lieutenant Haru will be guarded?"

Akemi raised her head at the sound of even the smallest hope. Haru did not react at all. He was staring at the floor, sunk in apathy.

"What do you have in mind?" Doreni asked.

"I was thinking about him staying in these quarters?"

"With its windows?"

Barako shook her head. "I was thinking of the shrine. It has no windows, and only one door. A strong one. Well-guarded, it is as secure a prison as any chamber in the castle." She used the word *prison* for Doreni's benefit, to get him to agree.

He looked thoughtful. "The shrine…" he repeated.

"If he is the oni," said Barako, "that will not be a place of comfort." She gave up trying to convince herself that her argument was solely to convince Doreni. To her dismay, she realized that she fully believed in what she was saying. They *had* to know about Haru, one way or another, and shutting him in the shrine would, she thought, be a blow to the oni if that was what he was.

Still Haru said nothing. He did not move. He appeared utterly disinterested in his fate.

The weight of the hammer strapped to Barako's back was suddenly reassuring. She was glad she had it at hand. The more disconnected Haru seemed, the easier it was for her to imagine having to swing her weapon with intent to kill. Until the killings had begun, she had only thought about Haru with anger for what he had done, and the harm his foolishness had caused. Now, she was not sure if she thought of him as Haru at all.

"Very well," Akemi said, grateful in defeat that she and her son would be spared the worst humiliations. "Let it be the shrine."

Doreni took a step toward Haru. That jerked him back to life. He snatched his arm away from Doreni's grasp. "I know the way," he muttered. He straightened, seemed to gather his dignity for a defiant walk to the shrine. Then he deflated. He shrank in on himself. It was not the heir to Striking Dawn who left the hall, just ahead of Doreni. It was a prisoner.

When Haru was sealed in the shrine to Lord Hida, with three Hiruma and three Kakeguchi samurai assigned to guard the barricaded door, Barako and Doreni left Akemi's chambers. Barako felt the daimyō's eyes burning into the back of her neck. It did not matter that she had done the right thing, and that she had saved Haru from worse ignominy. Akemi saw Barako's role in the imprisonment of Haru as a betrayal. Barako wondered if Akemi would ever trust her again.

Outside the daimyō's quarters, Barako began, "If Haru is not the oni…"

"Yes," said Doreni. "We must take other precautions." His political victory achieved, the exhaustion of grief was catching up with him. He suddenly looked worn, a statue eroded by wind and rain.

"Every window is a chink in our defenses," Barako said. "We cannot stop it from coming in where and when it wishes. So we must be strong. Full squads, then. No patrols with fewer than five bushi."

"Do we have the numbers for that?"

"We will have to see that we do. If the shifts need to be twice as long, then so be it." Even as she spoke, she knew such an effort could not be sustained indefinitely.

"There will be little sleep in Striking Dawn."

I know. Oh, how I know. "Let us pray to the kami that sleep will return."

CHAPTER 20

But she had to sleep. Regardless of the demands Barako placed on her troops, she needed rest. The few minutes she had stolen in Ochiba's chamber were not enough. With no sun, the day was marked by the watch shifts, and a full cycle passed without violence. That was a victory. The cremation ceremonies for the dead took place in the ground floor shrine to all the kami, and they were not disrupted. That was a victory too. Doreni seemed to be satisfied with what he had accomplished and allowed himself to grieve formally for his son.

That he was not, briefly, doing more to undermine Akemi was, as far as Barako was concerned, still another victory.

She took them in whatever minor form they appeared, and she was grateful for them.

And though it was just as hard as it had been before for her to relinquish the responsibilities of command, even for a few hours, she was grateful too, that she had carved out some time to sleep. She could not go on. With Haru under guard, Doreni was satisfied for the moment. He'd had some rest earlier, and she could trust the defense of the castle to him. The raids by the snow skeletons continued, but they remained sporadic, and easily repulsed. The patrols were organized.

She had felt all this before. When she had gone to sit with Ochiba, she had felt the defenses were in place, as best they could be, and for a short time there would be nothing more for her to do. She had been wrong.

Was it different now? Did she feel something almost like security with Haru locked away? Was she that convinced he was the oni?

No. I'm not. I don't think he is. I just am not sure that he isn't.

Then why did she think she could sleep? If Haru was not the oni, the monster was loose, prowling the outside of the castle, unreachable, invisible until it was too late. The patrols could not be everywhere. A full squad might very well not be strong enough to fight the horror. So why should she sleep?

Because I have to. I have nothing left.

In her chamber, Barako lay down on her sleeping mat. She was asleep in seconds.

When she woke, it was not to the sounds of a crisis. She woke of her own accord. She knew it was hours later, because she felt genuinely rested. The weariness would not leave her until this war was over, but she was ready to do battle again.

As she rose, she began to grow anxious. She donned her armor and took up her hammer. She listened intently to the sounds of the castle while she hurried to be ready. She was convinced she would have to charge into a fight. But the halls seemed quiet. Not too far away, she heard the tramp of feet of a patrol that had passed her door not long before. She heard the murmurings and shifting of the castle's life. It was the pulse of blood running through the body of the building, the sign of health. The shriek of the wind continued outside the walls. When she stepped out of her quarters, no breeze greeted her. On this floor, at least, the windows were unbroken.

Her anxiety deepened. It grew without reason, without evidence.

She carried her hammer. She walked quietly, beginning her own patrol. It was the hour of the monkey, late in the afternoon, a meaningless division of time in a world of eternal night. Yet people still behaved as if day mattered, as if there were a safety during its hours that vanished during those of the night.

She did not feel that safety now. The security that had let her sleep was gone. An event was closing in. Its anticipation gathered in air, tightening around Barako's skull. Her pulse began to pound.

Then the pounding was outside her head. It was outside the castle, the boom and crunch of massive blows pulverizing wood and plaster. The impact shook through the walls and floor. It was hard to tell where it was coming from. Barako ran down the hall, trying to locate the source. It seemed to be level with this floor, but it resonated so far and wide, and was caught up in the howls of the storm. There were two more booms, more splintering of wood. Barako thought she heard a scream, but it was so brief, it could have been the voice of the wind. Then the pounding stopped.

She stopped too, listening. The patrol she had heard earlier came around the corner. The samurai's alarmed looks mirrored her own. They were by the entrance to the library, and Junji emerged, his face confused with broken sleep. Barako had barely seen him since the murder of the two Hirumas. He had been immersed in the scrolls, searching for a way to fight back against the oni. She had told him about Haru's imprisonment, and his only response had been a brief nod before returning to the scrolls. He must have passed out from exhaustion, but he was awake now.

"What was that?" Junji asked.

Barako shook her head. She was still listening, waiting for the booming to start again. And it did. It was further away now. Another part of the castle under attack.

"I think that's higher up," one of the guards said.

The third floor. Where the daimyō's quarters were. Where Haru was.

Barako sprinted for the stairs, adrenaline giving her speed despite her heavy armor. The squad and Junji followed close behind. She tore up the stairs to the third floor. The sounds of the blows and the smashing of wood grew louder.

The sliding doors to the daimyō's quarters were wide open. Shouting came from inside. Barako charged in, already raising the hammer to strike. The guards who had been posted outside, and those who had been guarding Haru, were struggling to break down the door to the shrine. Something had jammed the heavy sliding door. Akemi was on her knees, shouting at them to hurry, her voice ragged with fear. The pounding and the splintering came from inside the shrine, and so did Haru's shouts for help.

Barako barreled into the door, ramming it with her shoulder. The wood cracked, and the door budged a fraction of an inch. The guards stepped back to give her room. She was the only one armed with a hammer. She swung it again and again, shattering the lacquered wood. After a few hits, the upper portion of the door seemed to be breaking more easily, as if something very heavy had fallen across the lower part.

The cracking sound on the other side stopped. The storm was screaming inside the shrine. Then Haru was screaming too, the desperate courage in his shouts gone in an instant. Then they stopped, and the only sound from the other side of the door was the keening of the storm.

Barako smashed the door until the wood gave way. Once it started to go, it went quickly, and she punched through a hole big enough to climb through. She replaced the hammer on her back, grabbed the lower edge of the hole and heaved herself up and through.

The shrine was a square chamber, about thirty feet to a side. Haru was curled in the far corner. The destruction of the shrine was total. The altar and the idols were in fragments, smashed by timber. There was a breach in the castle wall, almost ten feet wide and stretching the full height of the room. A chunk of broken plaster and timber had fallen against the lower part of the shrine door, jamming it into the frame and holding it closed. All sanctity in the shrine was gone. It was a space of rubble now.

Haru, his face a gray mask of horror, was staring at the

hole, at what turned in the wind.

The body of Hiruma Mioko dangled there, one hand impaled by large splinters of wood wedged into the top of the gap. Barako had trouble recognizing Doreni's daughter. Her flesh was rumpled. Her body hung so slackly, it looked as if it were melting. For long, awful seconds, Barako stared without understanding. Her vision felt blurred, as if she were back in the City of Night's Hunger, facing the architecture that defied the direct gaze.

And then she understood. She saw what the oni had done to Mioko. It had flayed her, as it had done to her brother's head, and to the two guards, but with a difference. It had pulled her skin off, and then it had pulled it back on.

Backwards.

The hair on the back of Mioko's head pushed out of the empty eye sockets of her face.

Lord Hida, watch over us. Lord Hida, grant me strength. Lord Hida, do not abandon us!

Barako's flesh crawled. A cave of ice opened up in her chest, as if the sight had blasted all emotions from her.

She looked at Haru, keeping her distance for the moment. He was covered in splinters and dust, and shivering in the blast of the storm. He appeared to be unharmed. He felt her gaze, and tore his eyes from the corpse. He turned to her, his face pleading for help, for comfort, for absolution. Pleading for anything at all.

She had nothing to give him. Not yet. Perhaps not ever. She did not know if she believed the agony she saw.

Barako took her hammer from her back. On her guard, ready to smash his skull to pulp, she turned away from

Haru and approached the gap in the wall. She looked at the splintered edges. She saw where the wood and plaster had been punched in by powerful blows.

And she saw where the wall had been punched *out*.

CHAPTER 21

"Give him to me! He dies now! He dies at my hands!" Doreni's roars filled the daimyō's chambers. *"Where is she? Where is my daughter? Does he have her? Let me pass!"*

There was a scuffle. Some guards were trying to hold Doreni back. They had looked through the hole in the door. They had seen. They knew what would happen when Doreni saw.

Barako lunged for the remnants of the door. *Keep him out.* She was too late. Doreni had shoved the guards aside, and they would not dare do more to stop him. He was at the breach. He looked past Barako at the corpse swaying in the wind.

He froze. A low, animal moan rose from his chest.

Barako stepped out of the way. She backed up until she was halfway across the shrine, between the door and the curled Haru.

Doreni struggled through the hole in the door. His movements were uncoordinated. A man numbed by too much horror, he staggered forward and fell to his knees at the edge of the gap in the wall. His mouth opened wide. His cry was silent. It was too great to escape from his chest. It had claimed him. He would belong to it forever. It had banished peace. It had devoured joy.

Pain held Doreni. Barako could almost see the sinews of its grip beneath his skin. Pain this great was a fist. It constricted the lungs and heart. And then the pain opened its claws. It pushed out the ribcage until the bones shattered. It turned breath into a stone that could not be expelled. Pain rippled, reveling in the fury it gave birth to.

Barako adjusted her stance, readying herself. Pain this great was death too. Death for its victim and those who came near.

Doreni reached out a hand. His fingers brushed Mioko's foot. The wind pulled her body away from Doreni, then pushed it back at him. Her foot bumped into his fingers, and her loose, flapping skin bunched up. Doreni yanked his hand back as if stung.

He struggled to his feet. His mouth was closed now. His lips pulled back over clenched teeth. His breath emerged as a long, harsh whine.

The storm sent eddies of snow around him, the flakes dancing in vicious mockery.

"Rekai," Barako said, trying to break through the dangerous vortex of pain that was swallowing Doreni. He was turning into a creature of instincts. She had to summon the thinking man again. "Where is Rekai?"

Doreni grunted. He drew a breath. It rattled like stone.

"Is Rekai safe?"

Another grunt. Doreni straightened. When he spoke,

it was to his daughter's body. "I came to our quarters. I looked for you. There was a hole in the wall, just like this one. You were gone. Your mother was there. She was in our quarters."

"You should be with her," Barako said. "You need each other."

Doreni turned around slowly. "She was in every part of our quarters," he said in a terrible monotone.

Barako felt the blood drain from her face.

Doreni clutched the hilt of his blade with both hands. "Stand up," he said to Haru.

Haru neither moved nor spoke.

"Put down your blade, Lieutenant Doreni," Barako ordered.

Doreni ignored her. "Stand up," he repeated. "Shed your disguise. Face me as you are, or I will destroy you in that sad guise."

Haru shivered. "I didn't…" he muttered. That was all.

Doreni moved away from the rubble-strewn end of the shrine. He closed in on Haru. Barako stood before him.

"Let me pass."

The guards on the other side of the door made a move to enter the shrine, but at a look from Doreni, they stopped.

"Leave this place," Barako said to him. "Go. Let us do what must be done. We will return your daughter to you for cremation."

"What must be done," Doreni spat. "If you had done what must be done, I would still have a family."

"For the last time–"

Doreni did not let Barako finish. He lunged forward,

sweeping his blade at her neck.

It was a warning feint, and she dodged it easily. He had not tried to kill her with his first attack. There was still some part of him that was using reason. But when she dodged his next strike too, his restraint fell away. He pressed her hard, his slashes as furious as they were fast. He was a ferocious fighter, and he was not holding back. She was. She did not want to kill him. She fought defensively, dodging every strike and using her greater size and strength and heavy armor to her advantage. She made herself into a wall between Doreni and Haru. Maddened by grief and anger, Doreni's attacks were wild. They lacked discipline and precision. The few strikes that Barako did not dodge bounced off her armor.

As she struggled to save Haru's life, Barako felt his presence at her back like an active threat she could not confront. She fought in the expectation of betrayal. She was braced for the brutal discovery that she had given her life to protect an oni.

Except she did not know. So she had to stop Doreni.

Doreni shouted, incoherent in frustration, broken in grief. His blade flashed. It collided with her hammer. The weapons clashed again and again. Barako moved forward slowly, gradually maneuvering Doreni toward the other corner of the shrine. She met his frenzy with patience and an implacable refusal to take a single step back. Soon she had forced him onto the uncertain footing of the rubble near the door. Then she kept him in a stalemate. He was expending more energy than she was. He would tire first.

He did. His slashes became expressions of frustration

more than real attacks. She barely had to move to dodge them now.

"Give him to me!" Doreni pleaded. He was almost sobbing. "Why are you protecting him? He is the oni!"

"I don't know that he is," Barako said calmly. "You don't either."

"Oh, you are a fool!"

"He was attacked too."

"Then why isn't he dead?"

She didn't know.

Doreni stopped fighting. He bent over, panting. He swung away from her, and his eyes fell on the broken plaster of the hole. He pointed. "Broken out!" he shouted. "These are broken out! What more proof do you need?"

"I have not yet spoken with him."

"Tell us!" Doreni shouted at Haru. "What is this? *Why is the wall broken out here?*"

Haru finally stirred. He stayed pressed into the corner, shivering in the cold, his arms clasped around his knees. "It smashed the wall," he said. "The oni smashed it, and came inside. And then it broke more of it, struck at the wall, sent the wood into the night. It… It did that." He pointed at Mioko without looking at her. "Then it left."

"You saw what it looked like?" Barako asked.

"The lanterns were all smashed…"

"What did you see?" she insisted.

Haru took a long, shaking breath. "Nothing," he said. "The lantern was smashed by the wall. There was no light. I sensed a huge shape in the breach. That's all."

"Why are you alive?" Doreni snarled. "*Why?*"

"I don't know."

"The oni smashes its way into your prison and makes you the gift of *my daughter's corpse*, and then leaves without touching you, and all you can say is that you don't know why?"

Haru shook his head. "I don't... I don't..."

Barako advanced on him, ready to block Doreni if he attacked again. "Tell me what happened in the tower in Night's Hunger," she said.

"I don't remember."

She crouched in front of him, blocking his view of the light from the hall, making of herself a looming, massive silhouette in steel. "*What happened?*" she growled.

"*I don't know!*"

This was futile. She straightened. Is this Haru or not? She still didn't know. But until she was sure he was not, it was her duty to protect him.

"I will have justice," Doreni said. "I will have his life."

"Wait," Barako said.

Doreni was not listening. He climbed back through the door. "His *life!*" he shouted and stormed out of the daimyō's quarters.

Barako lifted enough of the rubble away to make it possible to slide the door open. She let the guards in. "Put Lieutenant Haru in chains," she said. "Take him to the prison." There were cells in the basement of the castle. There, the walls that encased Haru would be the castle's foundations. If the oni wanted Haru, or if he were the oni, it would have to break through iron bars and stone walls. Yet it was not protection from the oni that Haru needed, or that Barako could provide. Imprisoning him was the only way she might be able to save his life from his fellow mortals, if there was a life here worth saving.

She left the shrine. When Haru was led out, Junji slipped inside to examine the body. Akemi stepped in front of the guards. They stopped, uncertain, and looked to Barako for guidance.

"No," the daimyō said. "No. Not this."

"We have no choice, Lady Akemi," Barako said. "Not anymore."

"If we put him in another room here…" Akemi was grasping at delusions.

"The oni has made that impossible." *Whether or not he is the oni.* "He has to be seen to be imprisoned. I doubt that will be enough for Doreni now, but I have to make the attempt." To the guards, she said, "Take him."

They obeyed, walking around Akemi. She stood still, alone and helpless.

Hating herself, Barako left the daimyō there and went to Junji, who was just stepping away from the corpse. "Anything?" she asked. "Here or in the library. One way or another, you've had plenty of time to look. Is there *anything* that can help us?"

"Not yet," Junji said.

He had hesitated for the blink of an eye before answering. *He knows something.* Barako pushed him harder. "Are you sure? The slightest chance is better than none at all."

"Not yet. Not yet."

"Very well. As long as you understand that *not yet* is soon going to be *never*."

Akemi had withdrawn to the heavy blanket beside the sunken hearth when Barako left the shrine again. It would have been easy to leave her there. It would have been merciful.

We do not have the luxury of mercy any longer.

Barako made herself walk over to Akemi. She made herself do what she had no desire to do. She was going to have to push the daimyō down a painful road. "Lady Akemi, you must address the people of Striking Dawn."

"What?"

Barako had not realized a word could be haggard.

"You must speak to as many of the samurai as we can assemble in the audience hall. You must tell them what you are doing."

"What am I doing?"

"You are imprisoning Haru. You will do all that is necessary to determine whether or not he is the oni. You are putting Striking Dawn before family, which is your duty as daimyō."

"Are you telling me my duty?"

"No. I am telling you what you need to do if you want to save the castle, and if you want even a hope of saving Haru's life." She was this close to giving orders to the daimyō. Everything about this situation was wrong.

Akemi shook her head. "Why should I listen to you?"

"I understand why you do not wish to. I wish there were other choices open to you. There are not."

"Yes, there are. I refuse. You have imprisoned my son, not I."

"It must be seen to be you."

Akemi shook her head again. She hunched over. She would not look at Barako. The attack on the shrine had broken her. The attack, and perhaps the doubts that even she had now about Haru, but could not face.

There would be no convincing her. Not like this.

The longer Barako stayed here, the longer Doreni had a free hand elsewhere in the castle.

What is he doing?

He said Haru would be his.

What does he have to do to make that happen?

What the oni has been pushing him closer and closer to doing.

Barako abandoned Akemi to her withdrawal into hopelessness. She ran down the stairs to the ground floor. The uproar of voices from the main hall made her heart sink. She knew what she would see before she crossed its threshold.

CHAPTER 22

The hall was full. There were so many Hiruma and Kakeguchi samurai present that Barako wondered for a moment if there were any still on the wall. But no, on that count, at least, she had no doubt about the courage of the bushi and their commitment to protecting the castle from the one enemy they had so far managed to keep out.

Doreni stalked the center of the hall, turning as he shouted, exhorting every samurai in the hall. He had gathered his troops around him, but it was the Kakeguchi he was specifically addressing.

This is the moment, then. He has moved to open rebellion. He cannot see what the oni has done to him. It has destroyed his caution. All he had to do was wait. Haru had sabotaged himself completely. The castle was Doreni's. He is destroying himself. He is shredding his reputation.

She wondered what the oni was doing to her. She wondered what she was becoming.

"Hear me, samurai of the Kakeguchi family," Doreni said. "I tell you that you are freed of your oaths of loyalty. By her actions, the daimyō has shown herself unworthy of them. She protects the oni. She refuses to destroy it. She cannot see that this thing is not her son. Kakeguchi Haru died in the City of Night's Hunger. The thing that came back is not him. It has killed only Hiruma until now. But when we are gone, then what? Do you think you will not be next? The oni plays on your integrity. It believes you will stand by Lady Akemi and what you believe to be Lieutenant Haru because that is what duty demands. It is using that against you. It will use it against you until you are all dead."

Barako raised her voice, her thunder cutting across Doreni's bluster. "And what, Hiruma Doreni, would you have these respectable bushi do?"

He whirled, startled out of his rant. He had not seen her come in.

A day ago, I would not have surprised him. He is not seeing any further than his immediate need.

"They must do what is truly right," Doreni said.

"Which is follow you? Should they rebel against their daimyō because the oni's victim, confused with grief, tells them so?"

"No. No. No." Doreni laughed bitterly and pointed at her. "You are the one abandoning the path of righteousness. Hiruma and Kakeguchi, we are Crab Clan, and we do not always have the luxury of following Bushidō. We are the ones who are called to stand against the Shadowlands. We must do whatever is necessary to hold the Wall."

"That's right," said Barako. She spoke more quietly now. *Let Doreni appear the wild one. Be the voice of calm and reason.* "And we must guard against those who would dress their own ambitions in the robes of false necessity."

Doreni's eyes widened. Fury choked him and he struggled for words. "You would accuse me…" he croaked. "My family…"

Barako cut him off and addressed the room. "Lady Akemi, daimyō of Striking Dawn Castle, *your* daimyō, will speak to you, to all of you, in the audience hall. She awaits you in five minutes."

She was rolling dice.

She was rolling against a certainty. If she failed to convince Akemi to enter the audience hall, the daimyō's situation would be no worse than it already was. All she had done was grab some leverage to use on Akemi. If she could, Barako would save the daimyō despite Akemi's plunge into surrender.

She ran back upstairs. In the time it took her to reach the third floor, she thought about how the oni could attack again, now while so many of the inhabitants of Striking Dawn were consumed with their political struggle. The oni could strike, and render all of this pointless.

That would not suit it, though. It is attacking us just enough to make us turn on each other. The battle on the wall gave us a unity just so the oni could show us how brittle it was.

Akemi had not moved since Barako had left her. Barako moved to stand directly in front of her, close enough to fill her vision.

"Doreni is moving against you," Barako said. "He has called for your overthrow."

"He wouldn't dare."

"There is nothing he would not dare now. He has lost

everything except his ambition. He has vengeance to goad him onward now, too. He is in the main hall right now, denouncing you."

"What is this to you?"

"You are my daimyō."

"Yet you take my son from me. You destroy my chance of a legacy."

"Your son may have died in Night's Hunger. I am trying to prevent your legacy from being the fall of Striking Dawn."

Akemi turned her head. Barako moved to stay before Akemi. *Do not look away from me.*

"In a few moments," Barako said, "the bushi of the Kakeguchi and Hiruma families will climb the stairs to the audience hall. I have told them that you await them."

"They will be disappointed."

"This is your surrender, then?" Seeing her daimyō so broken stabbed at Barako's heart.

Akemi said nothing.

"My entire life as a warrior has been dedicated to you. I have fought for you, and have been willing to die for you. I refuse to accept that was for nothing. I refuse to accept the daimyō I believe in was a lie. Doreni has forgotten himself in his grief. Will you as well? Are you that weak?"

"Go away."

"If I leave, I leave with your last chance to remain in command. If I enter the audience hall alone, then Doreni will become daimyō of Striking Dawn. There will be nothing I can do to prevent it. There will be nothing I *should* do. He will deserve it. You will have proven yourself unworthy of their respect."

Her words sank in at last. Akemi focused on her. "You have never spoken like this to me before."

"I never had reason to. I do what I do now to save you and our family. This is your struggle. Take the battlefield and defend the castle from its besieger. Fight or capitulate. And if Haru is your son, he will surely die."

Akemi was coming back to herself. It was as if she had surrounded herself with a thick fog, and Barako had finally burned it away. Withered, injured in her soul and her heart, Akemi still looked more like the daimyō as she pushed herself out of the chair. "Fight how?"

"The wars of politics are the ones you know. They are not my domain."

"I need your counsel, Barako."

"Do not defend Haru. No one can trust him. Show that you understand. Because I think you do, and that is what has caused you so much pain."

Akemi gave her a look that mixed determination, agony, and hatred. Then she walked away, stiffly at first, then with growing strength, her cane changing from a support to a staff of office as she went out of the hall, heading for the stairs to the second floor.

Barako watched her go. *You will never forgive me, will you?*

Sorrow was a luxury she could no longer afford either. She pushed away the worry of what Akemi thought of her and followed the daimyō out.

The audience hall was smaller than the main hall, and even more crowded. Akemi and Barako entered from the rear door. Barako took up a position next to the door while Akemi kneeled on the raised platform that took up the eastern end of the hall. The samurai who had come to hear her were kneeling too, in descending rank away from the platform. Doreni was at the front.

The painted wall panels created a mural of the mountains in spring. Pink blossoms floated on gentle breezes. The hall was a place of serenity and decorum. Already, the ceremony of the audience hall had one effect Barako had counted on. Doreni was kept still. There would be no pacing here. Alone in the center of the platform, Akemi's authority was given a spatial and physical manifestation. Talk of her overthrow would be more difficult to her face, in her elevated position, and with her most powerful guard in full plate armor in the background.

"I have heard the accusations leveled against my son," Akemi said without preamble. "I do not believe the evidence against him is compelling. I do not believe he is the oni. But my first duty is to Striking Dawn Castle. Before my flesh and blood, I must first do everything in my power against the foulness of the Shadowlands." As she spoke, her voice grew stronger. "So I have given orders. Kakeguchi Haru is to be imprisoned until it is confirmed that he *is* Kakeguchi Haru. If he is not, then that thing will be destroyed."

Barako contained a sigh of relief. That was the Akemi she knew. That was the Akemi who could make the hard decisions, and stare them in the face as she did so.

Doreni scowled. "That is not enough," he said.

"What more do you demand, *Lieutenant* Doreni?" Akemi asked, making a show of the courtesy he had denied her.

"This imprisonment is a sham. It is an attempt to save

face when it is far too late. This is how he should have been held yesterday."

"You agreed to what we did do yesterday."

"It was not what I wanted. I was wrong to compromise. There can be no compromise with this kind of enemy. We have been making the tragic mistake of letting our personal needs interfere with the needs of this struggle."

"Have we?" said Akemi.

"*You* have," Doreni said, voice booming. He pointed at the daimyō accusingly. "You were more concerned with defending your claim to Striking Dawn than with defending the castle itself."

Do not rise to his bait, Barako pleaded with Akemi.

"I have not used the death of my family as an opportunity to further my ambitions," Akemi said.

Barako winced.

"You will throw their deaths in my face?" Doreni exploded. He leaned forward, barely restraining himself from leaping to his feet. He was flanked by his samurai, and those closest to him moved their hands closer to their swords. "My daughter still hangs outside the ruined shrine of *your* chambers. I will take no lessons of duty from you."

As the Hiruma stirred with their kinsman's anger, the Kakeguchi samurai shifted too. The air in the audience hall hummed like a strummed biwa string. The calm beauty of the murals turned into expressions of bitter irony.

"I have had enough of your self-serving, hypocritical displays of righteousness," Akemi said.

No, no, no, no, Barako thought.

Unlike Doreni, Akemi did not move at all. She seemed

to become more and more utterly still, more statue than flesh, her kimono draped about a stone idol embodying pure authority. Behind her frozen calm, Barako perceived the same anger and desperation that had reduced her to a shell a few minutes earlier. Akemi was here because Barako had told her this was the only way she could save Haru. But in lashing out, she was dooming what she sought to preserve.

"I have done what is needed," Akemi said. "I have done more than that. I will remind Hiruma Doreni of his oaths. I remind all of the Hiruma of the same."

Mutters of anger greeted her demand. It did not matter that Doreni had openly called for the end of her rule a short time ago. Akemi had insulted them. She had directly questioned their integrity.

"She who has broken her oath has no authority over others," Doreni snarled.

"You will withdraw that accusation," said Akemi.

"I will not withdraw the truth. You protect the oni. You are unfit for rule. Prove me wrong. Turn over the killer of my family to me. See that the monster is put to death."

"Never."

"We will sit by and wait for the oni to kill us all."

The audience hall was one wrong word from erupting into violence. It would be a slaughter, and Barako was not sure all of the Kakeguchi would fight for Akemi. More than a few were looking convinced by Doreni's arguments. They were ready to believe their daimyō had turned away from her duties, whether her reasons were good or not, to protect the enemy in the castle.

Barako saw how events were about to unfold. She saw the blood on the walls of the audience hall, and then the blood in the cell where Haru was held. She saw chaos engulf Striking Dawn. The oni's sigil on the roof would prove a true mark of ownership. The castle would fall. It would become an outpost of the City of Night's Hunger.

The Shadowlands would gain a foothold on this side of the Wall, one that was not contained by a hidden bowl in the mountains, but one that controlled the route to Hida Castle.

She saw the future dropping into darkness. She thought she heard inhuman laughter at the back of her mind.

Perhaps the tragedy taking shape in front of her eyes was the work of that spiral of blood tainting the castle and all within it. Or perhaps what was coming was the fault of simple human folly, that unerring instinct to face disaster and make it infinitely worse.

The cause didn't matter. Only the result did. She was the only one to see what was coming, and she did not know how to stop it.

Then she spotted Junji. He was a few rows back from the front, kneeling next to the wall. A flight of painted blossoms arced over him, as if he had sought refuge in stilled serenity. He was looking across the audience chamber at her, his face pale, his eyes full of agony.

He knows what's going to happen too.

A companion in despair was little comfort.

She stared back at him. She realized there was more than dread in his expression. There was guilt.

He knows how to stop this.

"There will be no mercy for those who break their oaths," Akemi said.

"No," Doreni agreed. "No mercy at all." He rose to his feet.

"Wait!" Barako shouted. "Junji! You have learned something! You know how to stop the oni!"

The audience hall fell silent. The samurai turned to look at the monk. His face was an agony of indecision.

"You do!" Barako called out to him, pleading. "You do know!" *No more "not yet". Act now. Take your stand now. Now or never.* "Tell us! You must!"

"There is a way," Junji admitted. His whisper was low, mournful. The indecision on his face gave way to even greater agony.

Barako wondered what caused him such pain, but she could not grant him any relief now.

Doreni was not satisfied. "Another delay," he said, seeing his chance at the leadership of the castle slip away. "Another pointless delay to aid an unworthy leader."

"Has any of you ever known Junji to be swayed by political winds?" Barako asked.

Her words carried weight. No one had. Not even Doreni could make that claim.

"There is a cost," said Junji.

"There is always a cost," said Barako.

He looked around the audience hall, and Barako knew Junji was again seeing what she had. He was seeing the inevitable destruction if he did not act.

Junji nodded. "Very well," he said.

"This will be another failure," Doreni said.

"Let us try," Barako pleaded with him. "Junji has been searching for a way to fight the oni since this struggle began. He will know better than any of us what must be done."

"And if what must be done is to kill Haru?"

"Is it?" Barako asked Junji.

"No," said the monk. Then he added, "Not necessarily."

Triumph flashed over Doreni's face.

"Wait," Barako said again before he spoke. "Wait. Give us this chance. This one last chance. You cannot wish to kill Haru if he is innocent." Part of her did wish Haru dead for the harm he had caused. But she would not act on it. "You *are* a man of virtue, Lieutenant Doreni. Remember everything that means. Let Junji try."

"And if he fails?"

The question hung in a new silence. There was only one answer that Barako could give, only one answer that would satisfy Doreni and stop the tragedy before it happened.

There is a cost, Junji had said. Yes, there was a cost. There was a cost, right now, for the words she would speak. She asked herself if she was prepared to pay it.

She was not.

She also had no choice.

"If this attempt fails, then you will do with Haru as you see fit."

"*What?*" Akemi cried.

Barako advanced from the rear of the audience hall. She walked past them all, coming to the edge of the platform. She remained standing, the figure in spiked black steel supplanting the authority of the seated idol. "I swear before all the honored ancestors that I act with the sole purpose of preserving Striking Dawn Castle." No one contradicted her. She had a reputation, and it mattered. It made this difference. It made such a difference that Akemi cried out as if stabbed, because she knew what Barako's word was worth too. "I swear that my word to Hiruma Doreni is a true one," Barako said. "If Junji and I do not find and destroy the oni, then I will turn Kakeguchi Haru over to the lieutenant."

Only Akemi's moan broke the silence that followed. Junji rose and made his way toward the door at the far end of the audience hall. Doreni watched him, then faced Barako and nodded, satisfied for now.

Barako said no more. She turned on her heel and marched across the platform to the door. As she stepped into the corridor, she paid the cost she had known would come with those words.

"Traitor!" Akemi screamed after her. "*Traitor!*"

CHAPTER 23

Barako stopped at the threshold to the library. She watched Junji wander slowly around the room. He walked the length of the table, brushing the scrolls with his fingertips. He smiled softly at the delicate rustle of paper. He paused over a couple, picking them up and reading passages, his lips moving silently, taking pleasure over the grace of calligraphy and the shape of words.

He moved away from the table and circled the room, gazing up at the shelves, running his hands along them, a lover bidding farewell to the beloved. When he had completed the circuit, he returned to the center, beside the table, and turned around slowly, taking in the high-ceilinged chamber, and the rows upon rows of knowledge, thought and art. He closed his eyes. The peace Barako saw in him in that moment pierced her heart.

I have asked him to pay a price without knowing the cost.

She dreaded what she was about to discover.

Junji took a deep breath that shuddered only once. "Thank you for giving me this time, Lieutenant Barako. It means a great deal to me." He opened his eyes and gave her a sad smile as she approached.

"You don't need to thank me," said Barako.

"I do, though. I owe you deep thanks."

"For what?"

"For recalling me to my duty."

"Isn't that what I've been trying to do for as long as we've known each other?"

He laughed. Instead of making Barako feel better, his mirth squeezed her heart. "This time is different."

"The circumstances are different. I understand."

"I don't think you do." He began to touch the scrolls again, rearranging them on the table as though they were ornaments of a meditative garden. "You should know that it was not a lack of care that has kept me from taking the stands you have urged upon me so many times."

"You don't have to explain." Barako joined him at the table.

"Yes, I do. It's important that I do."

"Then I'm listening."

"Thank you." He took another long breath. "There is a reason why I have remained apart from the politics of the castle. I believe it is a good reason, or at least it *was*, at the beginning. I am a Kakeguchi, but we are Crab Clan first of all. Our foremost loyalty is to the defense of Rokugan. Don't you agree?"

"You know I do."

"Then you can understand how I see matters. The internal politics of Striking Dawn do not matter as long as it is defended. Akemi or Doreni, Kakeguchi or Hiruma, what does it change who holds the castle, as long as they are responsible leaders, and Striking Dawn is protected, and fulfills its functions?"

"I see," said Barako.

"You think that is the position of an equivocator."

"It is a position that has frustrated me in the past. Though after what I have said and done in the past hour, how can I judge you?" She wondered uneasily where Junji was going with this.

"If there is one person in this castle whose judgment I would accept, it is you," Junji said. "That is why it matters that you understand what I thought was right, and how I erred. I believed that I would best serve Striking Dawn through neutrality. I thought one of us, at least, should stay above the *petty squabbles* of governance." He cocked his head, twisting his smiled into a self-deprecating grimace. "Petty squabbles. That is what I considered them."

"No wonder my pleas fell on deaf ears."

Junji nodded. "There lies my sin of pride. We all fall short of the Code of Bushidō. I put so much stock in righteousness, I lacked the compassion to see past my own convictions. I became obsessed with neutrality for its own sake. I saw virtue in turning my face away when I was asked to stand with my kin. So. Now a reckoning has come, as is only right. But I wanted you to know that I see how I was wrong, and I am grateful to you." He was quiet for a moment. "I wonder," he said. "I wonder if you will have been my salvation."

Barako did not know how to deal with the pleading she saw in his eyes. "Please do not make me into more than what I am," she said.

"No. You're right. Of course I shouldn't. It was not my intent to add to your burdens. My hope was to do the opposite. Do you believe that I am grateful?" His eyes burned as he asked the question.

"I do."

"Good. Good." The diminutive monk reached up to clasp her shoulder. "Remember this, please. Remember this moment. Remember my gratitude."

"I'm sure I will, because you are starting to alarm me."

His laughter was hollow this time. "Yes. I suppose I am."

"What is going on?" Barako asked. *What price have I asked you to pay?* "What are we going to use against the oni? Why do you have to tell me all this?"

"Come with me."

Junji led her to the corner of the library farthest from the door. He knelt before the bottom shelf of a case. He pulled out the scrolls from the left-hand end of the shelf. There were no lanterns nearby, and the lighting in this spot was dim. Barako could barely make out what Junji was doing. She crouched beside him and peered into the shadow on the shelf. When he put his hand into the dark, she realized that the shelf was not as deep here as it was for the rest of its length. The cabinet had a false back here.

Junji pushed at the wood. There was a click, and a panel slid back. Junji pulled a small, dark oak chest from the compartment. He placed it on the floor between them and stared down at it. "There will need to be a decision about this box and what it contains."

"What is inside it?"

"Scrolls written in darkness. Foul scrolls. Ones I have only ever looked at once in my life, reading only the smallest fragments. Until today."

"What are they?" Barako whispered, as if the thing in the box might hear her. The shadows in the library seemed deeper and stronger.

"On them is written that which is forbidden to know. The wisdom of Jigoku. The rites they describe are used only by the mahō-tsukai."

Barako recoiled from the box, horrified that such an object resided in Striking Dawn. "Why do you have this?" she hissed, her mind conjuring images of corrupted sorcerers calling upon the oni to do their will.

"For many years, I forgot I *did* have it. Why keep it? It seemed too important to destroy. Perhaps fate whispered to me. Because I did not destroy these scrolls, we have them now, when we need them."

Barako's mouth dried suddenly with shock. What was Junji thinking? Wasn't the danger threatening the castle already bad enough? "You would not dare use the knowledge in those scrolls."

"I would not," said Junji. "Except for one thing. I have been reading them these last days. I turned to them in desperation. A few hours ago, I found a solution. But it is a terrible one. I could not contemplate it. Until you made me realize I must."

"No." Barako shook her head. "I would never ask you to do such a thing."

"You have not. But you recalled me to my duty. In order to save Striking Dawn, we must find the oni. If we do not, it will continue to kill until it has made us kill each other."

"It is very close to achieving that end," Barako muttered.

"Then we will find it."

"How?"

"By making it come to us." Junji pointed at the box. "There is a way of calling the oni."

"You would try to summon it?"

"No. It is here already. I am no shugenja, and I will not tamper with the might of the elements. There is another way." Shadows covered his face.

"How?" Barako asked, dreading the answer.

"By swearing fealty to it."

Barako's heart skipped a beat. Her throat closed in horror. It took her two attempts before she could speak again. "It cannot be that simple." She blinked at the awfulness of her words. There was nothing simple in this. A monstrous abyss had opened before them. They were standing at its edge, and Junji was preparing to leap. "The oni would know you were lying."

"It would," said Junji. "That is why I cannot be lying."

Barako stared. She could not speak at all now.

"I must go all the way. I must perform the rite of fealty." His breath shuddered, and he put a hand against the bookcase, holding himself upright. "I must corrupt myself," he whispered.

Barako could not move. She understood now. She understood what she had demanded in the audience hall. *There is a cost*, Junji had said. *There is always a cost*, she had answered. Such a glib, facile response, when she had told a man to cast away his soul.

"I cannot ask you to do this," she said. "I did not know, earlier. You must not. It is too much."

"No," he said. "It is exactly what I must do. It is how I will save the castle I told myself I was serving through all the years of considering myself above the currents of its life."

"You said I might be your salvation. This is damnation."

"With your help, I will have two salvations. How many of us can say they were so blessed?"

"With my help?"

"My first salvation was my return to duty. My second will come later, with the defeat of the oni."

Barako could not believe she would even contemplate agreeing to Junji's plan. It was as if someone else made her speak the next words. "I will share as much of your burden as I can. I will walk this path with you."

She still could not see his face, but he made a noise that sounded like a sob of gratitude. "You must promise me something," he said.

"Anything."

"You must swear it."

"I will," said Barako.

"Swear that you do not corrupt yourself. What we will have to do will bring you dangerously close to the line, but you must not cross it. Striking Dawn has too great a need of you. Without you, we will all be lost. So swear. Swear you will resist corruption."

"I swear it."

Junji sighed, and his body sagged with relief. He even smiled. Then he kneeled. He worked on the box. Tumblers clicked, and he opened the lid. He removed a scroll, closed the chest again, and put it back in its place of concealment.

Barako had to help him up. He held the scroll as if it were a scorpion. With a shudder, he hid it in his robes. "Let us begin," he said.

Junji took them first to the daimyō's quarters. Akemi was not there. She would be sleeping elsewhere. The hall was cold from the wind blowing in through the shattered door of the shrine. Two guards, a Kakeguchi and a Hiruma, had watch at the shrine.

"I must make a few more examinations of the body," Junji told them. "I will perform some rites of purification too. You may go and inform Lieutenant Doreni that he can make arrangements for the funeral. Return in a few minutes to take Mioko to her family."

When the guards had left, he and Barako entered the shrine.

Suspended by its arm, the corpse swung back and forth in the wind, a pendulum of flesh.

"Let me do this," Barako said to Junji.

He nodded. She was glad he did not thank her. There was nothing in what she was about to do that deserved thanks.

While Junji prepared a small porcelain container, Barako took out her knife and approached the body.

She cut off a lock of hair. She cut off a finger. The backwards flesh hung from the bone like a loose sock.

Then she took the body down. Junji performed the purity rite over the rest of the corpse, and they waited with it until the guards returned and took it away.

"Go back to the library," Barako said. "Make your preparations. I think what I have to do next will go better if I am alone."

She left Junji and made her way to the barracks where the Hiruma samurai were quartered. She hadn't been sure whether to hope Doreni was present or not. He was the last person she wanted to see at this moment, after what she had done, and because of what she had come for. He was also the one person who could make her task easier.

He was there, moving between small clusters of samurai. Less than half his complement was present. The others were on the outer wall or on patrol in the castle. Doreni might have been convinced that Haru was the oni, but he had not pulled his warriors out of the rotation. At the practical level, he was acknowledging the possibility he might be wrong.

Barako waited near the entrance for Doreni to notice her presence. When he saw her, he left the bushi with which he was speaking and approached her alone. "What do you want?" he asked. "Have you done it yet?"

"No. We're still preparing."

"Has Junji told you what he is going to attempt?"

She nodded. When he waited, expectant, she said, "If it succeeds, you'll know it has. If it fails, you'll know that too."

"You are not going to tell me what is going to happen."

"Be thankful I am not."

He read the look in her eyes and backed down. "Why are you here?" he asked.

"Have you performed the cremations of Tsuru and Nisobu yet?"

"No. We were preparing to do just that."

"Where are they?"

Doreni pointed. At the far end of the barracks, a tall screen had been set up, sectioning off a corner of the hall.

"I need to look at them."

Doreni frowned, then shrugged. "Very well." He began to lead the way.

"Alone," said Barako.

He stopped dead. "Why?" he asked slowly.

"It would be better."

"That is not an answer."

"It would be better if you accepted it as one."

Doreni did not move.

"If, after Junji has done what he means to do, and I am still alive, I will tell you what you want to know. It would be better if you never ask me, but I will tell you. For now, please listen to me. Take your warriors to the shrine of the kami. Prepare the pyre. Then come back and claim your dead. I will be gone by then. And soon you will know whether or not everything has been in vain."

Doreni regarded her for a long time. He kept opening his mouth to speak, then thinking better of it. His eyes narrowed in suspicion.

He's guessed. Good. If he's guessed, he'll realize he doesn't want to know.

Finally, Doreni walked away, back toward his warriors. Barako moved off to lean against a wall while Doreni gathered his samurai and left the barracks. Then she went behind the screen.

There were two coffins. She pulled the lids off and looked

down into a confused mass of piled flesh and jumbles of bone. What lay in each coffin was barely a memory of a human. They held the cast-offs of a butcher.

Do what must be done. Do not think about it.

Barako gathered the two skulls. She steeled herself, leaned in, and pushed the flesh around until she found the tufts of hair, still attached to the scalps. She cut the scalps free from the larger flaps of skin, murmuring apologies to the dead as she worked. Then she replaced the coffin lids and took her blasphemous prizes to Junji. He accepted them as sorrowfully as she had gathered them. Then it was time for the final preparations.

Barako went down to the basement level, to the prison that held Haru. Ten bushi guarded him. She ordered them to withdraw until they were out of earshot. She wanted to speak with Haru alone.

She looked through the small, barred window in the door to the cell. The heir to Striking Dawn looked as broken as he had in the shrine. He sat against the foundation wall, head slumped, arms around his knees.

"I would speak with you, Kakeguchi Haru," Barako said.

He raised his head with an effort. His eyes were dull, his face slack. He had the appearance of a man who had lost the last, tattered shreds of hope. "Why do you call me that?" he asked. "You don't believe that is my name."

"I don't know if it is or not." She kept her stance and her voice neutral. If she was speaking to Haru, she didn't want to give him false hope. If she was speaking to the oni, she didn't want to give it any information about how she was feeling.

As if even I know what I'm feeling.

"Why are you here?" Though Haru could no longer feel hope, he could still experience pain. He looked at her with heartbroken agony.

"I came to tell you that the truth is coming. In a short time, we will know who or what you are."

"I see." He showed no interest. "Are you hoping to taunt the oni?"

"If that is what you are, yes. If you are the oni, I swear to destroy you." She spoke without emotion, as if making a simple statement of fact.

"And if I'm not the oni?"

"I may not survive the next hours. In case I do not, I wanted to tell you something."

He was interested now. "What is it?" He pushed himself off the floor and stood.

Some of her anger crept into her voice. It was too strong. She could not hold it back. "I want to make sure you understand what your hunger for glory has caused. Because you were so concerned about your status in the castle, we have lost more than half a company so far. Lieutenant Doreni's family has been murdered. And Captain Ochiba remains lost in a slumber from which she may never awaken. You know all this. I wanted to remind you of the deaths your pride has caused. I wanted to tell you that the cost has not been worth it. If you are Haru, and if we survive this storm, then you should also know this: I will never forgive you. Even when and if you become daimyō, I will never forgive you. I will always serve Striking Dawn. But I will never forgive you."

Haru tried to press himself back into the wall. "I am so sorry," he said.

"I don't care."

She abandoned the prisoner. Oni or human, she hoped he suffered.

Barako went to the Hiruma barracks next. She gathered Sakimi and nine other samurai, along with rope and grappling hooks, and took them with her to the second floor. Junji was ready, and waiting at the broken window near the staircase.

"Junji and I are going to lay a trap for the oni," Barako explained to the bushi. "You are to wait here. If we succeed, it will be obvious. Climb up to the roof and help me destroy the oni." Barako had thought about having more than two squads, but there would not be room on the steep slope for more than this.

"Shouldn't we wait with you on the roof?" Sakimi asked.

"No." She would stand with Junji, and she would see the ritual he performed. She would not expose anyone else to the monk's voluntary corruption. "There are other risks we will be running before the oni arrives. There is no point in more of us than necessary running them. Do you understand your orders?"

They did. The samurai opened the window's repaired shutters, and those of the next window over. They set up ropes and grappling hooks.

All was ready. There was no reason to delay any further.

Barako and Junji climbed out into the dark howl of the storm and onto the roof. They pulled up three lanterns passed out by the waiting samurai. They spaced the lanterns out, creating an unbroken path of illumination from the edge of the roof to the glistening spiral on the wall. They walked up to the sigil.

From within the fold of his robes, Junji produced a jade dagger. He presented it to Barako. "I have been too proud," he said. "I have been proud where I should have been humble. But this is work of which I am proud, and it is right for me to be so, because it is good work. It is the last good work I will do, my last sanctified act before I damn myself."

Barako took the dagger. Its handle was ornately carved ivory, but the blade was simple, clean in its design. Its shape was direct and elegant, a rebuke to the contortions of the spiral on the wall.

"I have no descendants," said Junji. "My ancestry is a narrow line in the Kakeguchi family. This was passed down to me through generations, as was the chest of forbidden scrolls. It was important that something cursed be countered by something blessed. This dagger has been blessed, and blessed again, by every one of its possessors. Those scrolls are the most foul things I know, and this is the most holy. You are my hope of salvation. You are the hope of the oni's destruction. With this dagger, may you be the fulfillment of my hopes."

The dagger was perfectly balanced, yet it had a spiritual weight greater than any Barako had felt in a weapon before. Her hammer was a sanctified relic, and the creatures of the Shadowlands fell under its blows. But the dagger was jade. It was carved of the matter that destroyed the material forms of the oni. The dagger was blessed in its making and its substance.

"In the name of what this dagger represents," Barako said, "and in the name of the honor you do me now, I will see your hopes realized. My hand will save you. My hand will destroy the oni."

"Thank you," Junji said. "Thank you."

His gratitude filled her with shame. How could she live up to the sacrifice he was about to make? How could she be worthy of his example?

Junji closed his eyes. "Lord Hida, forgive me for what I will do. Great Kami, forgive me for what I will say."

He opened his eyes, his face set, determined. Then he kneeled before the oni's symbol, just to the side of the blood circulating in the snow. He opened the sack he carried and pulled out the components of the rite. He put the finger, the hair, the scalps and the skin in a grinding bowl, and crushed them together with a pestle. He stopped to spit on them three times. Then he took a knife and drew it along his palm. He squeezed his hand into a fist, dripping his blood over the ground pieces of the oni's victims.

"Here I make myself one with the damned," Junji intoned.

He took the skulls from the bag, and placed them on the blood in the snow, on opposite sides of the outer circumference of the spiral. "These are the witnesses of your might," he said.

He picked up the bowl and stood. He wavered in a shrieking gust of wind. "Barako," he said, "you will be my salvation. Swear you will be."

She wanted to tell him to stop. *How can I permit this to happen? How can I let him damn himself?* But they had no choice, and so she said, "I swear."

"Then let this be done." He moved sideways until he was sanding inches from the wall, and in the middle of the spiral. He raised the bowl. "These are your dead," he called out, "claimed by you forever. I am with them, I am of them, and so I am yours forever." He took something from the bowl and ate it. He swallowed convulsively. "I renounce the kami. I kneel before Fu Leng and the powers of Jigoku. I embrace your sign, great oni. I give you my body and my soul." He put down the bowl, stretched his arms out and pressed himself against the sign on the wall. The blood of the spiral ran up his body, making him part of the design. "Come for me!" Junji shouted in agony.

To the right of the symbol, snow and wood exploded upwards as a tremendous force punched a hole through the roof. Barako raised her hammer in readiness. *This time we have you. This time, the trap is ours.*

The oni shot up through the hole. A graceful leap took it high in the air, and it landed next to Junji. Still in its human form, it seized Junji by the shoulders. Then it saw Barako, and it paused. It released Junji, who slumped, gasping. It turned to Barako. It smiled at her.

No. Oh no. Oh no oh no oh no.

This could not be. This must not be.

The oni smiled at her.

Ochiba smiled at her.

Ochiba smiled, and her neck began to grow.

CHAPTER 24

"Time for the game to end." The oni's voice was a choir. It spoke with the voices of Ochiba, of the wind, and of the cracking of bones. It was dry and sibilant and intimate. It was the known, the beloved, twisted and braided with the uncanny, the inhuman, and the sickening. It was the sound Barako had prayed to hear again, and it was the sound of everything that made the human soul draw back in horror. It was honey of love, and it was breath of lies, and every syllable struck Barako with a blow so painful, death would have been a mercy.

The oni had no mercy to give. It was here for its own pleasure, and for the glory of a darker master yet. It was here for prey. It transformed as it spoke, and the emotional pain it inflicted on Barako was so profound, so precisely executed, it was as if words and sights alone would be enough to flay her as fully as Tsuru and Nisobu.

Ochiba was there, recognizable, even as the body changed from the human to monstrous, and even as the skull widened and elongated. Ochiba's smile widened until it was a terrible grimace. Her teeth shone in the light of the lanterns, a brilliant white and distressingly human, only there were far too many. The neck grew and grew and grew, until it was fifteen feet long. It whipped back and forth, bobbing the skull up and down with a gesture of idiot mockery.

The body grew broader, the arms becoming thicker and longer, their hands developing claws as long and wide as cleavers. Two other arms, thinner and more delicate, sprang out of the monster's chest. Their fingers were longer, with many articulations, and their claws finer. The great arms were the weapons of a butcher. The small arms had the grace of a torturer. The long arms incapacitated and killed. The smaller ones performed the more artful acts of skinning and replacing flesh.

The skin of the monster was moist and pale, silken as a moon-blooming petal, rippling like a corpse about to burst open under the pressure of maggots.

"*The castle is nearly mine,*" said the oni. "*Even your monk has given himself to me. I no longer have need of a disguise. Not when revelation will feed me so well.*" The Ochiba skull tilted to one side, contemplating Barako. Ochiba's skin swung to one side, lank and coated with the slime of deliquescing skin. "*Maybe I will take your face. Should I? I will not need long, though you will not be alive to have it returned. I would use it just until I had set the rest of the castle against itself. That will not be difficult.*" It slashed at Barako with one of its great arms. She ducked out of the way easily, then jerked back the other way, in time to meet the swipe of the other arm with her hammer. The oni snatched its arm back before the hammer struck. It danced a step away, bowed in satire, and laughed with a laugh that rang like Ochiba's and writhed with worms.

Unkei, one of Barako's samurai, appeared at the edge of the roof. Before he could finish his climb, the oni pounced upon him in a single leap. It decapitated him with a stroke of its huge claws, and sent his body tumbling to the courtyard below.

The oni came back to Barako, its movements a dance of glee. "*I will speak with you alone,*" it said.

"Stay back!" Barako shouted, hoping her voice carried over the storm to the samurai trying to obey her earlier orders. "Stay off the roof!"

She watched the edge of the roof, a barely visible line in the lantern light. She held her breath, waiting for a slaughter. But she must have been heard. No one else tried to climb up.

"*Very good,*" said the oni. "*I wish to savor this feast without interruption.*"

The oni and Barako circled each other, looking for an opening. Junji stayed where the oni had left him, pressing himself into the symbol on the wall.

"*Setting samurai against samurai is rewarding,*" the oni said. "*I revel in the spectacle of my enemies destroying one another. But it is so easy. There is other sport that is much better. The taste of its meat is much richer. The meat of your pain.*"

It jabbed at her with its claws, playfully, not really trying to hit her. Its attack was in its words, and in its presence, and in Ochiba's distorted visage. It did not want her to die too soon, and end its feast of pain. It wanted her tears, her screams, her rage, and she had not given them to the oni yet.

The oni was not concerned. Ochiba's tongue, a foot long, licked Ochiba's stretched lips, and left them moist, luscious as rot.

Barako lunged in, trying to throw the monster off its guard and give her the opening to strike it with the full force of her fate. If it wanted her pain, she would return the gift a hundredfold. But the oni parried her easily, almost absently.

She recognized the grace and speed of its movements. It had been her joy to witness them on the battlefield and in the dojo for year upon year. She stifled the moan of pain. There was too much of Ochiba in this horror. Too much of what she loved.

"*Shall I tell you what you are thinking?*" said the oni. "*You are thinking of all the things you said to Ochiba, and never will again. You are thinking of all the things you wish you had said, and now never will.*" The oni inhaled deeply. It parted its lips and released a thunderous sigh of ecstasy. "*AHHHHHHHHHHH!*" The storm-riven darkness filled with the smell of spring blossoms and abandoned slaughterhouses. "*Regret. Lovely, lovely regret. How often I have tasted its nectar, and I will never tire of it. The honor of samurai is so exquisite in the tortures it makes you inflict on yourselves, it must surely be an offering you have chosen to make to me. For why else would you so faithfully give yourself pain and thus pleasure to me? So much you should have said to Ochiba. All the things you should have said because you love her, and yet convinced yourself you must never say because you love her. The things she longed to hear but vowed to refuse! Glorious! Glorious! And now the regret! Why regret what you swore you would never say? You have kept your oath! And now it is here! The regret! The regret! The regret!"*

Barako charged the oni, fighting to keep her footing on the slope and in the deep snow. She swung hard, swung fast, unleashing a disciplined fury of strikes. She clenched her jaw tight as she attacked, clamping down on the screams of anger, and on the words of defiance that would have sounded too much like denial, too much like lies.

The worst part of the oni's taunts was that everything it said was true. She had to shut the truths out from her heart, or they would destroy her.

The oni blocked her attacks with slashes of its heavy arms. It did not counter-attack. It wanted only to keep her at bay until it finished its attack on her soul.

"Regret," the oni said again. The long neck dropped the head to within a few feet over Barako, just out of her reach. Ochiba's face sniffed appreciatively, then jerked away again. *"Regret and shame! Shame and guilt! Because you wonder how you never knew. You love her, yet you did not see that it was not her who returned with you from the City of Night's Hunger. You sat so close to me. You opened your heart to me. You sought comfort with me. You gave me the words you dreamed of giving to her. You searched for the imperfect disguise, when the simplest disguise of all, the sleeper, lay before you. I don't think you really did love her. You could not have. Your love was a lie."*

Barako screamed now. She could not contain the pain and the rage any longer. If she had, she would have proven the oni right beyond any doubt. But she could not. Ochiba was gone, and the love Barako had for her was the only thing that remained, and she would protect it to the end. She came at the oni like a hurricane. She struck with a blow to shatter stone.

The oni snarled, angered for the first time, and lashed out. It parried Barako's blow with such force that it hurled her back. She fell, sliding through the snow to the edge of the roof. She leapt to her feet and pressed the attack again. She feinted with the hammer this time, and when the oni blocked she dropped low. Her charge slammed her into the oni's torso, making it stumble, and she whipped her hammer into its flank.

The oni hissed. It moved like lightning made flesh. Barako did not even see what hit her. There was a blur, a crash and explosive pain, and she flew across the roof to crash against the wall. She slid down, armor cracked, body riven in pain.

She advanced on the oni again. It regarded her with amusement, yet it backed up, cautious now. It circled to her right, and she moved left, in the direction of the immobile Junji.

"*You could have revenge on your duty,*" the oni said. "*Give yourself to me, and you will burn the codes that enslaved you. Give yourself to me, and there will be an end to regrets. Blood will wash them away. Your monk knows. Follow his example. Or do you wish your love for Ochiba to end in meaninglessness?*"

"There will be meaning in your destruction," Barako hissed.

"*Seize her,*" said the oni.

Junji jerked into sudden action, and he burst away from the wall, grabbing Barako's arms and pinning them behind her. The jerk made her release the hammer with her right hand, and she held the shaft awkwardly with her left.

"*I will take your face*," the oni said. "*I shall put it over this one. You and Ochiba will be closer than you ever were in life. Does that not please you?*"

Barako spat her hatred at the oni. It came forward, its great limbs spread wide to embrace her, the thin arms stretched out, twitching in their eagerness to slice her face from her skull.

Junji's grip trembled. Tremors shook his entire body. Animal whines emerged from his throat.

Barako heaved herself forward and down. With a scream, Junji released her. He jumped over her, launching himself at the oni. The monster stopped, and Barako saw its surprise, saw that it had fallen into their trap. Junji had performed the rite of fealty. He had committed unforgivable acts of blasphemy. For the oni, his obedience was a given. Yet with the cries of a soul ripping itself apart, Junji attacked. He latched onto the oni's massive right arm. He held on as if he were clinging to life itself. The oni tilted, off balance.

Junji's grip and weight held the arm still for just a moment. It was all the time Barako needed. She pulled the jade knife out of its sheath at her belt. She came on like a battering ram behind Junji. She could wield her hammer well enough with her left hand, and she struck the oni's arm at the joint. The sanctified hammer crushed bone. The oni shrieked, its arm flopping loose at the elbow.

With her right hand, Barako plunged the jade knife

into the arm where her hammer had struck. The oni's flesh smoldered. Acrid smoke billowed out of the wound. Barako twisted the dagger. The matter of the oni's being split. It parted like rotten wood. She jerked the blade down, and the oni's forearm fell away.

The oni screamed. It howled, staggering away, the stump of its right arm flailing back and forth. Blood smoked and burned. Flames licked around the wound, and violent ripples washed over its form. The shape seemed to lose consistency. The oni passed in front of a lantern, and its silhouette was uncertain. The wound in its arm was spreading across its body, eating away at its material being.

Barako attacked again. The oni lashed out, savage in its pain, and as fast as ever. It sent her flying again, and she came to a halt with her legs dangling over the edge of the roof. The snow beneath her slid off as she tried to scramble up, and she slid further back.

The oni grabbed Junji. It pinned him to the ground with its remaining left arm. The two small ones ripped his chest open. The oni plunged its stump into his blood. Junji screamed, and sounded like he was his own echo, as if his voice had split and there were two separate screams at once. The oni's form became stable once more. The severed arm began to grow below the elbow.

And then there were two Junjis. A bright glow appeared, surrounding his body, and then began to separate from it. The light had no shape, yet Barako knew, with the same certainty she had known that the oni had been attacking her with the truth, that the light was as truly Junji as his body, his body that was becoming vague and soft in its form, and that the oni was feeding on both to restore its material form.

The oni rocked its head back. It growled in pleasure.

Junji cried out to Barako. He cried out twice. She heard his voice, weak and desperate and dying in the howl of the storm. She heard his soul, as desperate but its voice loud in her head. "Barako!" he pleaded. "Now! Oh, now! Be my salvation!"

His call to her was the last act of a man who had damned himself for the sake of Striking Dawn.

Barako dug her arms into the snow and pulled herself forward. Her boots found a purchase, and then she was on her feet again. She lurched up the roof. The oni and Junji were only a few yards away. It felt like miles. The oni was devouring Junji in spirit and body. Its hunger could be sated at Barako's next step, and Junji would be lost, his sacrifice for nothing as she fell too. The wind, caught up in the pain and the fury of the oni, tried to lift her from her feet. She held fast. She ran, and the oni was still feasting on Junji when she reached him and thrust the dagger into his heart.

Junji stilled. The light vanished. His body became solid again, its contours no longer draining into the matter of the oni. The agony on his face turned to peace, and for the briefest second, during the jade dagger's descent, his eyes had widened in triumph. Then he was gone, taking the feast of the oni with him.

The oni shrieked again. Its howls were even greater than before. It leapt away from Junji's body, escaping Barako's hammer by a hair's breadth. Blood and flame erupted from its incomplete, malformed arm. The face that had been Ochiba's screamed at the storm, and screamed at Barako. The oni's grace had abandoned it. The horror hurled itself back and forth, trying to escape the pain. The arm disintegrated, and rot spread onto the oni's shoulder, and down its chest. One of the torturer's arms withered to nothing, and then blew away, vanishing in the gusts of snow. Barako ran at the oni, dagger aimed at that grotesque, whiplashing neck. She would end it now, and she would no longer see this thing that was Ochiba remade into a nightmare that would never leave her.

The oni saw her coming. With a last scream that sounded far into the darkness, it jumped from the roof. It fled, vaulting over the outer wall. It vanished into the paroxysms of the storm.

Then the wind began to die.

Sharp as hope yet painful as truth, a ray of sun pierced the dark.

Barako moved to the spiral on the wall. The blood no longer circulated. What had been glistening was already turning dull and dark.

We have won, then. The thought gave her no comfort. She felt no sense of victory.

She found the bowl with its foul contents, and broke one of the lanterns over it, spilling burning oil over the remains. While the flesh burned, she gathered up the skulls. She would cremate them too as soon as she was able.

Now the wind was no more than a breeze from the north, and the snow fell gently. The sun forced the clouds apart, and their strength faded from black to gray. Day was returning to Striking Dawn Castle, reclaiming more of the land so quickly, Barako perceived the changes with every breath.

Sakimi climbed onto the roof. "Lieutenant?" she called.

"Help me with Junji," Barako said.

She kneeled over the monk, folding his torn robes and flayed flesh as best she could, trying to give his corpse a semblance of dignity. She kept the dagger at her belt.

With Sakimi's aid, she brought Junji back inside the castle. "Take him to the Shrine of the Kami of the Land," she told the samurai. "He will need the rites of special purification. But he will be cremated with honor. Junji has saved Striking Dawn. Let that be known. Let it be known that the oni has gone." She braced herself for the next words. "Let it be known that it had taken the form of Captain Ochiba."

Sakimi nodded. The sorrow with which she looked at Barako was profound. So was the pity. "Yes," she said. "We heard the oni's taunts."

"I'm glad," Barako said, surprised to find she was. "I would not want matters so important to me known only by the creatures of Jigoku."

The samurai carried Junji's body away. Barako leaned against a wall, then pushed away almost immediately. The mere suggestion of rest made her feel weak. She could not afford to give in to exhaustion yet. Her tasks were not finished. If she let herself fall now, she did not think she would ever rise again.

She started down the corridor. She was halfway to the intersection when Doreni came around the corner. They stopped a few paces away from each other.

"Have you heard?" Barako asked.

"I have."

They regarded each other in silence, united, for the moment, in the sorrow of loss. It was not a fellowship Barako desired. It was one that she needed.

"Is it over, then?" Doreni asked.

"No," said Barako. "It is not."

CHAPTER 25

Barako went down to the prison again. She dismissed the guards. "Haru is innocent," she told them. "It has been proven. Lieutenant Doreni will explain."

She waited until they had left, until she was alone, before she walked up to the cell, the keys to its lock in her hand.

Doreni had offered to release Haru. "He is there because of my insistence."

She declined. "You and he will have your peace to make with each other. What form it takes is of no concern to me. I have things to say to him as well. They have nothing to do with peace."

Doreni had given her the keys without another word.

Now she unlocked the cell door and threw it open with a crash. Haru jumped. He was sitting exactly as she had last seen him. It was as if he had not moved at all. He raised an arm in a defensive reflex, and lowered it slowly when he saw who was in the doorway of his prison.

"You have been exonerated," Barako said coldly.

Haru stood up, the first signs in days of animation

returning to his face. It was as if his hopes mirrored the state of the storm around Striking Dawn. The idea displeased Barako.

"Doreni doesn't believe I'm the oni?" Haru asked.

"He *knows* you aren't. We all do."

More light in his features. More hope. The way he looked at her made her grind her teeth. He started across the cell, then stopped when she did not move from the threshold.

"Is something wrong?" he asked.

"Aren't you curious how we know you are who you say you are?"

"Yes! I assumed you would tell me. Do we know who the oni is?"

"The oni has departed. It was Ochiba." She didn't raise her voice. She spoke with, she thought, admirable calm.

Haru stepped back as if she had raised her hammer to strike him. "Ochiba ..." he said. "I don't understand."

I don't understand. Her cheek twitched in anger. Such weak words from a weak man. Words to hide behind. If he did not understand, then he could not feel his share of the blame. That would not do. *I will tear that shield away from you. I will not let you find comfort in your ignorance. Not any longer.* "She never left the tower in the City of Night's Hunger," Barako said. She spoke in short, simple sentences. She would make him understand. This was the one expression of her anger that she would permit herself. It would give her little satisfaction. But it would be justice in a small way. And she would recognize the weight of Ochiba's sacrifice. "She went in to save you. The oni took her, and it stole her form. Then it brought you out of the tower."

Haru shuddered. "That's horrible."

"Yes it is. It is very horrible. The oni tricked us all. It tricked me. On that march back, I thought I was fighting to save the life of the person I love most in the world. Instead, it was already too late."

"Could Ochiba still be alive?"

"No." She thought of the horror the oni had inflicted on Junji at the end, of what it had been taking from him to reknit its form. "Ochiba is dead. She died because the oni used you as bait. Do you understand now? That is what you are good for. Bait. You were useful to the oni because of what you did. Ochiba died because you are a fool, her soul consumed by Jigoku. Am I speaking clearly? Do you comprehend what I am saying to you?"

Haru was the son of the daimyō. Barako was speaking to the son of the daimyō in the most deliberately insulting of ways. Doing so gave her no pleasure. It did give her a small taste of miserable satisfaction. If there were repercussions for what she said, she did not care. What mattered was that she completed the lesson she had begun here before the confrontation with the oni. Haru would know what he had done.

If he felt offense at her words, he did not show it. He winced again and again. He shuffled backwards, as if he would choose to remain in the cell, as if he no longer believed in his own innocence.

Good.

"I understand," Haru said.

"And you remember what I told you?"

"That there would be no forgiveness."

"There is not. There never will be. The fool with blood on his hands is as contemptible as the murderer. You are free of this cell. But this is the beginning of your sentence."

"I understand," he whispered.

Barako shook her head. The sight of him was disgusting. "Ochiba died for *you*," she hissed with all the venom of loss. "That makes her sacrifice *worthless*." Haru flinched as if struck. "That is what I have to live with. That is what I will think of every time I see your *worthless* face."

That was enough. She would never be able to express the full extent of her anger. There was no point in going on.

Barako walked back into the corridor outside the cells. She left the way open for Haru. "Go," she said.

"Barako," he began, "if I could only–"

"*Go!*"

He scuttled out of the cell, shrinking away from her, and then almost running down the hall. She watched him as she would watch a maggot.

Barako lingered in the dimness of the cells for a bit longer, and then she walked away, slowly making her way up to the second floor and to her chamber. There was a stone in her chest. It was the same one that she had seen bear Doreni to the ground. It grew larger as she walked. Its coldness and its painful contours filled her awareness. She passed people in the halls, and she did not acknowledge them. People tried to say things to her. They tried to *thank* her. She ignored them. Life was returning to Striking Dawn, life and the pageant of normality, and she resented it all. There were even sounds of *joy*, and how could that be possible? How could the world exist as before when she was carrying this huge and cold stone, this terrible and cold stone, this heavy, and crushing, and cold, cold, cold stone? The life, the gratitude, the *joy*, none of this was real. Not truly. It was a brittle veneer. It had nothing to do with her. It had nothing to do with the truth of things, because there was no room any longer for *joy* in the world. There was only room for the stone.

When Barako reached her chamber, the stone was so massive, she could barely walk. She sank to her knees on her sleeping mat. She doubled over, eyes screwed shut, mouth agape, and now, now, now, it was time for the stone to come out.

First there was a low moan, then a rasping gasp of indrawn breath, and then the moan again, a bit louder as the stone began to move in her chest, to demand its freedom, to force her to give the grief her voice, because without voice, it would surely kill her. The moan turned into a growl, a growl of hate for the world that would take Ochiba from her, take Ochiba for the most *stupid* and *unfair* and *pointless* of reasons. But Barako's greatest hate was not for the world, not for Haru.

It was for herself. Because everything the oni had said was true. The words had struck her, and she had been bleeding from the heart, but she had refused to let herself feel the wounds. She had turned her spirit from Ochiba as much as she had been able, or she could not have fought. She hated herself for that betrayal too. It was the least of them, though. It was insignificant compared to *why had she not seen through the disguise?* and *how could she mistake an oni for Ochiba?* and most of all, most grievously of all, *why had she never told Ochiba how she felt?* Because she had respected the promises Ochiba had made to her family, promises made to people disappointed over a loss of social standing, and this was where those obligations had brought her and Ochiba. Because of duty and respect and the crushing weight of her integrity, she had nothing but sacrifice and pain.

And the next breath was a great one, because the stone was going to come out all at once now, and it did, tearing her apart from the inside, shattering her heart to dust, wrenching her throat raw, and she was howling, giving the grief all her voice, howling to bring down the walls, howling to tear down the sky.

She howled until her voice was gone, and then she curled in on herself, tighter, and tighter, and tighter, her fists so tight her fingernails drew blood, her arms so tight they should have shattered her armor and broken her ribcage, tighter and tighter and tighter until, at last, when she had withdrawn deep into the darkness behind her eyes, she had turned into a stone.

But then.

Then. In the darkness, behind the walls of stone, inside the iron cell of grief, she heard an answer to her cry.

Barako.

The voice spoke her name without using words. It was not really a voice. It was reaching out across distance, and across death. It was a touch more than a voice, but she experienced it as a voice, because she knew it so well, so deeply, so truly.

"Ochiba," Barako whispered.

The voice answered her cry, because though the oni had spoken the truth, it had not spoken the most vital and profound of truths. It had used the bond that linked the two women in order to attack Barako's soul. It had used what it could not acknowledge.

But the bond was not broken. It endured. It prevailed. Barako felt Ochiba. She felt the link. It pierced night and pierced stone, and so she heard it. She heard the cry for help.

Haru had changed kimono. He had cleaned himself up. He wore his katana. He was worried his attempts to appear appropriately be read as arrogance. As the reduced, wounded council gathered, he did not know how to stand, or where to look, or whether he should speak, or whether he should be there at all.

No, that was not true. It was right that he be here. If his instinct was to hide in shame, then he should resist it. The one thing Barako had not accused him of being was a coward. There were faces he must encounter, Barako's not least among them. Staying away from council would be trying to escape his penance. What he did might not matter to anyone other than him. Very well. He had little self-respect left. What respect he had once had, he lost in the City of Night's Hunger. It could be that the only thing he had left was the ability to accept the personal consequences of his folly. If it was, then he would cling to that.

The council was diminished in more than numbers since he had last been part of it. Ochiba was gone. Junji was gone. Akemi sat on her chair as if it took a supreme effort not to collapse. She had aged to a terrifying degree. She looked thinner, too, her bones too close to the surface of her skin. She seemed closer to death than Haru had ever thought possible.

Number her among your victims too.

And Doreni too. He was still physically powerful. At the same time, he seemed hollow, scooped out. His face was gray, and he did not look at the other members of council with the intimidating air of calculation that Haru had come to think of as Doreni's natural mode of being. His gaze was duller now, blunted by pain.

Only Barako seemed as strong as ever, though her presence had become a harsh one. She wore her armor, and her helm. Unless she was facing a brazier or a lantern, her face was invisible inside the massive, horned helmet. It was as if she were only the armor, a walking mass of iron. She had been intimidating before in her skill and her strength, a figure to be emulated.

And loved. The thought flickered through his mind, then winked out, extinguished by shame.

Now Barako was frightening. She was judgment; hard and merciless. Her dark, ominous shape was too forbidding to look at, and too powerful to ignore.

Though Haru could not see Barako's eyes on him, he felt them. He felt their anger. He felt them passing sentence.

Before he could stop himself, Haru wondered how much more ferocious that anger would be if Barako knew the whole truth. Then he wondered if maybe she did, and his forehead burned with guilt. His obsessive quest for glory that she had rightly condemned him for was a result of Haru's desire to be worthy of her. Ochiba had died trying to save him, true enough. But Barako had lost Ochiba because Haru had imagined being able to win Barako.

When he thought about this, Haru's self-disgust was so great, he wished he was back in the cell again.

If only he could remember what had happened in the tower. His mind was a blank from the moment he had crossed the tower's threshold until he staggered out. Barako was right. The only thing he had been successful at was being bait.

"Lieutenant Barako," Akemi said, "the samurai of Striking Dawn Castle owe you a debt we cannot ever repay. I owe you an even greater one."

"It was my duty," Barako said. Her tone stopped short of insolence, but only just.

Akemi saw she should not pursue the matter. "Where do we stand, then? The storm has ended. We can see the sun again, and there have been no further attacks on our outer wall since its return. That seems like a victory to me."

"I injured the oni," Barako said. "I forced it to retreat. That is all. I did not destroy it. Our struggle has not ended."

"You think it might return?"

"Once it has rested and restored its being, yes."

"An outpost will have to be established at the entrance to the cave system that leads to Night's Hunger," Doreni mused. "And we should see about collapsing the entrance too."

"There must always be a sentinel at the gates to Night's Hunger," Akemi agreed.

"In the long run," said Barako. "We must win this war first, otherwise we are not really any better off than we were before the first attack by the snow skeletons. The oni knows the castle, it knows our weaknesses, and it knows *us*. It will return. Whose face will it wear this time? Whose *faces*? How do you stand guard against suspicion? The oni came very close to having us destroy each other for its amusement. It will not give up on the promise of that pleasure."

"We are forewarned now," Haru said, and immediately wished he hadn't. *What a stupid thing to say.*

"We were before," Barako said, speaking as she had in the cell, as if she were addressing a stupid child. "We knew there was an oni in the castle. We suspected it was disguised as one of us. We thought it might be you."

He shook his head. "I know," he said. "I know. I withdraw the remark. You are right. The oni must be sent back to Jigoku." *Fool.* He promised himself he would not say anything else at this meeting of the council.

"Our losses have already been terrible," said Akemi. "You are proposing another expedition to the City of Night's Hunger, Lieutenant Barako?"

"There isn't a choice," said Barako. She seemed to be having trouble believing Akemi's reluctance was genuine.

"Doing so would leave the castle vulnerable," the daimyō said.

"It is vulnerable now," said Barako. "We have no choice," she insisted.

"No, we don't," Akemi said very quietly.

You knew that all along, Haru thought. His mother's reluctance was not a reasoned stand. It was her exhaustion speaking. She had let herself express her wishful thinking that somehow the nightmare was really at an end.

"Another full company?" Akemi asked.

"Yes," said Barako.

"And if it is lost, what becomes of Striking Dawn?"

"It will not be lost. The bulk of the company will act as before, holding the gate to the city. I will take one squad inside, to the tower. I know the way."

Akemi did not look reassured. "You know the way to the tower," she said. "You do not know what is inside. That is the oni's stronghold."

"Yes," said Barako. "That is where the risks will be greatest. They are also necessary."

"What if the squad does not return?"

"Then the call must go out to the other castles. For aid. For an even greater force."

"What shall they be told?" Akemi asked.

"Not to make the same mistakes we have."

"Summoning more aid will take time."

"That is why we must act this way now," said Barako, "and pray to the ancestors for victory."

"There might be another way," Doreni said quietly. "Even if we defeat the oni, the City of Night's Hunger will always be a threat."

"Of course," said Barako, sounding puzzled.

"Then why not seal it off now?"

"Were you not listening? The oni *will* return."

"I was listening. Yes, it will return. Or it will try. And if its material form is destroyed, then something else will, sooner or later, emerge from that cursed place. I think we should treat Night's Hunger as we do the Shadowlands. We don't invade them in the hope of destroying all the evil they contain. We wall them off. Let us do that to the city."

"It may be better than risking an entire company or worse," said Akemi.

After a short silence, Barako said, "I believe we ignore that active threat at our peril, and the oni *is* an active threat. I do not believe a cave-in and an outpost are sufficient protection *now*. Lady Akemi, if you insist on going down this path, then at least let me take a single squad into the city to try to destroy the oni."

"Will you defy me if I say no?"

"I will go alone," said Barako.

They all stared at her. That was a degree of recklessness utterly unlike Barako.

"Why?" Akemi pleaded.

"Because Ochiba's soul is in torment there. I will not abandon her."

"How do you know this?" Doreni asked.

"She reached out to me."

"Have you considered that what you felt may be the work of the oni?"

"Yes. I do not believe it is, but yes. If the oni is luring me, then let it. Let it draw me to it. If it thinks it is not finished with me, it will learn that I am not finished with it."

A slow smile spread over Doreni's face. It was a sorrowful smile, but a genuine one too, and eager. "Yes," he said. "Yes. And I will go with you. The blood of my wife and my children cries out to be avenged." He shrugged, clearly aware that this decision had little of the political calculation he had always shown before. "I have no other legacy," he said quietly.

"I must go too," said Haru.

Akemi shuddered. Barako turned in his direction with a violent jerk. He could see her eyes behind her helm now. He thought he might burn in their hatred. He would have welcomed such a death. But he did not back down. "Please," he said. "I have no right to ask this of you, but I am asking. I must go. I must help."

"You," Barako said. "Help."

"I must try to make reparations for what I have done."

"That is impossible."

She was right, but he still had to try. He tried another tack. "If it is not the oni that is calling you, it will fight hard to keep you away."

"I expect that."

"It had me once. Don't you think it would please the oni to take me back again?"

Barako's glare became speculative. "Go on."

"The oni used me as bait. Now you should too."

"Haru," Akemi pleaded quietly.

"I will be the temptation. Don't you think the oni will be pleased by the thought of the victory it will achieve through my destruction? Bring me, and my presence will open the way to the tower."

Akemi had slumped in her chair, her head buried in her hands. Everything she had feared, and barely been spared, was coming for her again. Haru was sorry for her pain. He also knew his decision was as final and as fated as Barako's determination to save Ochiba's soul.

Doreni put a hand on Haru's shoulder. "You have arranged striking symmetry in your doom," he said. "You should have been a poet."

My fate has not been decided yet. It can't be decided by me.

Haru waited in silence for Barako to pass judgment. He waited for an age.

In the end, all she said was, "We leave at dawn."

CHAPTER 26

Once again, it was daylight when they reached the cave, and endless night when they emerged from the tunnel before the city. Barako did not pause at the first sight of the bowl. She kept moving, heading down the slope and starting the journey across the ridge. The City of Night's Hunger and the oni within it had not tried to stop her with another storm. If she and her party were to be made welcome in this place, then she would accept the invitation.

In the end, Akemi had sent a full company. "Someone must return," she had said. "Someone must tell us what has happened. And we must have a victory. We must have an end." Most of the company was made up of veterans from Ochiba's expedition. They knew what to expect, and they came for justice too. They came to avenge their captain. Two squads remained at the east entrance to the cave, to begin the process of engineering a collapse. The rest marched with Barako, Doreni and Haru, and none of them paused before the descent to the ridge, either.

The snow fell, and broke like glass. Lord Moon looked

down over the landscape without time. The wind snarled at the samurai and tried to pick them from the ridge. In the distance, past the gate, the great tower of the City of Night's Hunger looked down on its enemies with its impassive green stare.

As they closed in on the gate, Doreni asked, "Have you heard her again?"

"No," said Barako. She had tried to find Ochiba's voice again during the entire march. She had listened actively as she walked. When the company rested, she meditated, following the thread of her bond with Ochiba. She had found only emptiness. Where Ochiba had been, there was a void. It felt like bereavement. It felt like the shape of loss, the shape that sooner or later was the lot of pain that came to every mortal, yet was experienced as a terrible isolation, as the agony that no one else could ever share or know.

The loss was real. But there was the memory too. Not the memory of Ochiba as she had been alive. The new memory, the one that had come after her death. It changed the emptiness. It turned into something that, if it was not quite a lie, was not really true, either.

"The oni may be veiling her from me," Barako said.

"Or so it wishes you to believe."

Barako gave a short, grim, bark of laughter as she walked up to the gates. "Are you trying to tell me this may be a trap?"

Doreni's grin was as dark as her laughter. "There is no reason at all for me to think that, is there?"

"None. Including the state of these gates."

They were open. Just a bit, a gap easily widened by a push.

"You left these closed," said Doreni.

"We did. They acted as a barrier to the skeleton samurai. Now they are exactly as they were on our first journey here."

Doreni looked around and shuddered. The blurring effect of the spiral still disturbed her, but Doreni had not encountered it before on this scale. "You said time was suspended here. I had not really understood. I see now. And the gates are part of it, aren't they?"

"I think so. An eternal invitation."

"Not a trap at all."

"Not at all."

Barako looked through the gap in the gates. The streets were empty, except for the lurking, patient drifts of snow. She pointed at the drifts. "And there. Do you see what I mean?"

Doreni nodded. "They are too..." He searched for a word.

"Too liquid," said Haru.

He had hardly spoken on the march from Striking Dawn. Barako had not commanded he kept silent, though she had been glad he had chosen to do so. There was nothing she wanted to hear from him. But he was right about the shadows.

"Yes," Doreni said. "Liquid." He paused. "Are they moving?"

"They do when they wish to," said Barako. "Hungry ghosts travel within them." There was a furtive rippling at the edges of some of the drifts, like a pond in a wind, or a lake disturbed by the leap of a predator.

Barako glanced back at the company. The samurai had

drawn their weapons and stood ready for the enemy attack. They saluted her, ready to hold the gate once again.

"Let us see what form of trap awaits us this time," Barako said. She pushed the gates open. "Stay close," she said to Haru. He obeyed, and they entered the city together.

Nothing happened. She advanced, cautiously, moving a dozen yards away from the gate. The drifts stirred, hiding secrets and teeth. No attackers emerged from them. She listened for the rattle of bones from the army of skeleton samurai. All she could hear was the gentle, sharp tinkle and crack of the snowflakes.

"All is quiet," said Doreni, just inside the threshold to the city.

"The silence is not to be trusted," Barako said. "We are in the oni's domain. Whether it serves the ends of the city, or the city serves the oni, the deception is strategic. It waits to cause the most harm." She gazed toward the tower. She imagined that it and she were taking the measure of the other, planning the next placement of the game piece. "I think Haru and I should go alone," she said.

"No," said Doreni. "You are the savior of Striking Dawn Castle. Do not be quick to sacrifice yourself. You are needed still."

Barako wondered what had made him say that. She disliked flattery. He knew it. She had often made her feelings clear. Was he saying what he believed? Or was he looking ahead, once again, to the succession of the castle, and still wanting Barako as an ally? She wondered how much the politics of Striking Dawn had followed her here.

She decided she didn't care. She doubted she'd survive

to see the outcome of Doreni's machinations, if he was still thinking to the future.

Perhaps he wasn't. Perhaps he felt time was ending for him too.

"Shall we advance as a company?" Doreni asked. He had deferred to her judgment since the start of the march.

Go alone. Just you and Haru, and Doreni if he insists. If we die, what of it? Two warriors spent by grief and one who has never been of real use to anyone. But the whole company would be a grievous loss.

She stopped herself. She was thinking entirely in terms of endings and defeat. She had not come here to die. She had come to free Ochiba's soul, and to destroy the oni. She was here for war, and victory.

"An attack in force…" said Doreni. He did not have to finish the sentence.

"All right," Barako said, hands flexing tightly on the shaft of her hammer. "Bring them through. Leave two squads to guard the gates." She watched the darkness of the streets as the samurai began to cross into the City of Night's Hunger.

She began to move forward once half the company was through the gates. "Keep to the moonlight," she reminded the samurai. "Where there is no moonlight, run."

With Haru and Doreni half a step behind her, Barako advanced into the dark twists of the city's geography, making for the first of the secondary towers. The distorted pagodas and the shells and the ruined monuments leaned over the streets, the drifts deep at their base, and draped like curtains down their facades. The silence beneath the glittering snaps of the snowflakes was oppressive. It was taut with the promise of an unseen trap.

The company filed down the long stretch of the first road, staying in the cold light in the center. Barako felt that she should be running. The slow pace and the narrow line made her samurai too vulnerable. Speed was how she and Ochiba had reached the tower the first time.

The oni wanted us to reach it.

Speed was too dangerous with this many troops. An error would be inevitable.

If I haven't made one already.

There was no way to know until the blood flowed. She could not see what piece the oni would play. She could barely see the board.

She was almost at the first intersection when the blast of the tower's horn thundered over the city. The declaration of war had come. "The enemy is upon us!" she shouted with the echoes of the horn still rebounding off the walls, its tremors shuddering through her soul.

Still no rattle of bones. No wail of dead things.

Instead, the tide of ghosts came.

On both sides of the street, the snowdrifts rose, becoming angular white waves that stretched the full length of the road. They climbed high, towering twenty feet above the company. They paused at the top of their climbing, bulking up, as if the whiteness were savoring the moment of its feast. When the frozen waves rushed in, the path of moonlight would be gone.

The ghosts surged across the street. The samurai faced them, men and women with swords and hammers and polearms, ready to fight what could not be fought, but must be. Barako and Doreni stood back to back, Haru just behind them. Barako smashed her hammer into the wave, determined she would strike it before it tried to devour her. The whiteness recoiled from her weapon, its movements a silent scream as the spectral snow twisted into a vortex.

The company met the waves with a shout, and then the unholy white covered the street. The ghosts met in silence where the sea would have crashed, and the silence within the white was sinewy, as much a thing of substance as the snowdrifts themselves. It tried to grab Barako. It tried to press its smothering weight into her mouth and nose. She pulled the hammer back to her side, then swung wide, leaning into the momentum of its arc. She felt the whiteness cry out. She heard the silence come apart like tearing flesh.

She fought without seeing. She held her breath, keeping the touch of the shadows from her lungs. She struck at the whiteness until light erupted around her hammer, its sanctity burning the unholy. In another few moments, she broke the surface. The tide of ghosts, wounded, was withdrawing from her.

Doreni slashed his way out with his katana a moment later. Shreds of specters clung to him, dripping from his armor and then fading away. His eyes were wide with hate and horror.

The rest of the company too was forcing the ghosts back. Down the street, the tide receded, slashed at and battered by the bushi. Not all had survived. There were ragged screams as the ghosts swept samurai back with them, the ones who had breathed the whiteness in, and were caught in the grip of the night, and were taken to feed its hunger.

Haru was fighting too. No ghosts clung to him. Then Barako realized that none were approaching him. Wherever he moved, he was in an island of moonlight. The ghosts fled from him, unwilling to touch.

He is prey for something else.

The drifts pulled back to the walls, and then gathered again, higher this time, and higher. The tower horn sounded. The snow overhead whirled violently, and ghosts from across the city closed in, an ocean coming to drown the intruders.

"Back to the gates!" Barako shouted. "Haru and I must go alone! All of you, back!"

She dreaded for a moment that the samurai would resist her order. But they knew she did not demand cowardice of them. They ran back down the street, racing to reach the gates ahead of the tide of evil.

She grabbed Haru by the arm. "Stay close," she said. "The tower wants you, and so it must have me too."

"And me," said Doreni. He drew near, inside the small circle of moonlight around Haru.

"Now we run," Barako said.

They ran, Barako and Doreni on either side of Haru. The ghosts paced them. They flowed down the buildings of Night's Hunger like a heavy fog. The white current frothed with anger. Tendrils lashed out from the edges, snatching at the legs of Barako and Doreni. Behind them, the storm surge of whiteness was huge, and it came after them, a flood barely held at bay by the presence of the chosen prey.

"You were right," Doreni said to Haru. "The oni wants you back."

"Good," said Haru. He sounded pathetically grateful to be of use. It was, Barako thought, the first time she had been glad of his presence on the battlefield.

"The oni does insist on his return," she said. "It does not want the rest of us."

"You have given it reason to fear you."

"I have not finished its lesson yet."

Barako remembered each turn and intersection. Her journeys through Night's Hunger were impressed upon her mind in the smallest detail. When she had marked the route the first time, she had held to the memory, knowing that in the end, she would have to return.

She had just never imagined she would come back for this reason. She had never imagined not following Ochiba into battle. The thought would have been too painful.

The reality was worse.

Her stride was longer than Haru's. She misjudged a step, outpaced him by the slightest degree, and gave the shadows their chance. Her foot came down outside the moving circle of moonlight. A ropy tendril of snow whipped around her leg and pulled her down so hard the jolt knocked the hammer from her hands. The drift covered her in an instant. Ghosts clawed and bit. The coils of the snow squeezed. The fall had knocked the breath from her lungs. She denied herself the air she was desperate for, and pulled the jade dagger from her belt. She stabbed upwards, ripping through the snow. The dagger blazed with purifying light when it touched the ghosts. The heat was intense, and the snow whipped away, smoldering at the edges.

Barako jumped to her feet. Haru and Doreni had stopped

immediately, and Doreni had recovered her hammer. She rejoined them in the light.

"When you fell, you vanished at once beneath the snow," Doreni said. "We didn't know where to look."

"Then I will not fall again," Barako said, accepting the hammer again. "You must be vigilant too."

"I am."

The ghosts had been snapping at his flanks too. He cut at them with the katana, as if hacking through tall reeds. As they ran on, the ghosts snatched and bit at Doreni with increasing ferocity. He held close to the light around Haru, and scythed at the specters with his blade.

"I will see the killer of my family," Doreni swore. "I will see it, and it will see its reckoning." He slashed at the dark, and when the tower sounded the horn again, he looked up, teeth baring in pain and defiance as he braved the blast. "*I will see you!*"

"You will," Barako told him. "We are nearly there." His need was strong like hers. And she, at least, had confronted the oni and enacted a prelude to justice. For Doreni, the monster that had stolen everything from him was still a thing of shadows, less real to him than the ghosts that assailed him now. He had thought he had found the destroyer wearing Haru's face. He had been wrong. An invisible thing had shattered his life. He was owed the reckoning. He was owed the parting of shadows, and the truth revealed in light.

Green light. Green light shot through searing black. The light that flashed and pulsed inside the tower, visible from the open doorway of the tower. The flanking, wing-like rock formations, which had fallen during the flight, stood as if nothing had happened. The ghosts paced the three samurai as they came before the tower. The snowdrifts fell from the heights like a cataract, filling the square, moved to storm by the tower's rage. The ghosts clawed for Barako and Doreni. This close to their goal, they were even more careful to match Haru's pace. His face shone with the hope of redemption, a hope he did not utter, and that care tempered Barako's contempt.

No guardians awaited the bushi. There was only the tempest-tossed darkness. They ran for the entrance, the archway outlined in spikes like teeth.

They were quivering. The maw was eager to snap shut.

"You see the teeth," she said. They were twenty yards from the doorway.

"Yes," the other two said.

"We go through at exactly the same time."

Barako and Doreni matched their steps with Haru's. He ran at a steady, unwavering pace. They closed on the doorway like a single entity.

Three yards from the threshold. Two. One. They crossed.

The ghosts lashed out.

A clawed hand clutched at Barako's foot at the moment it left the ground. The hand missed, and she passed through the doorway with Haru.

Another ghost caught at Doreni's heel. It could not grab hold and drag him back. It did make him stumble. He fell behind. Less than a heartbeat slower.

The maw slammed shut.

Barako and Haru whirled around.

Doreni's upper chest and arms extended from the sealed doorway. Interlocking spiked teeth crushed the rest. His mouth was open in the shock of pain. His eyes were frozen in the ache of failure, of an oath unfulfilled.

Struck by a blade of sorrow again, Barako knelt beside him. Will there never be an end to loss? How much more will I be made to bear? "I will avenge you too," she said. "You and your family."

She stood, and once more denied herself the need to grieve. Then she advanced with Haru into the architecture of darkness, to meet the sound of the oni's laughter.

CHAPTER 27

The tower was carved from hunger. It was built of stone made of white death, of white death made of stone. The interior was hollow, its entire height filled with the model and source of the spiral design. The ramps of shadowstone circled up from the floor, rising to the peak. The engravings that had tortured Barako's eyes were the palest imitation of the original. Its complexities spun around each other. Web-like strands linked the great lines of the spiral, and the whole immensity seized the eye and the mind and carried them up, up, up. At the peak was a continuous explosion of blinding darkness. A corona of corrupting green surrounded it. The black light, with the green entwined around it like a vine, blasted down in a pillar through the center of the spiral, striking the floor with an endless roar, spreading the pounding flashes throughout the space of the tower. And then the spiral seized the eye again to carry it up and resume the cycle.

There was another light at the center of the black storm. It was bright, golden, standing against the shadowlight and tortured by it. There was suffering there.

Ochiba was there.

Barako felt her again, felt the bond that held fast beyond death. Inside the tower, the oni could not conceal the presence of Ochiba's soul.

She is too strong for you, monster, Barako thought. The exultation was as painful as sorrow.

The oni perched halfway up the spiral. It looked down at her, directly at her. Its laughter was aimed at her, not Doreni.

The oni had all its limbs again. A nimbus of green light surrounded it, turning its pale flesh into the color of rotting death. A flickering beam extended from the golden center of the dark and reached the oni's renewed palm. It was feeding on Ochiba. It used her soul to heal.

The oni had not concealed Ochiba from Barako. It had forced her to cry out.

"*You have come at last!*" the oni boomed in triumph.

The instant that he crossed the threshold, Haru remembered. He was in the scene of his torment once again, and it all came back. He remembered being grabbed by hands with claws as long as his forearm. He remembered the play of light. The oni had plunged him into the violent green, the corrosive green. He had found himself in a limbo between life and death. The black light was the final void. Had the oni thrown him in there, he would have died. Instead, he had he been caught between the states, held by the timelessness of the city. Time had ceased, yet eternity stretched before him, one single, agonizing moment after another.

He had screamed. He had screamed for help, and then for mercy, and then for death. He had screamed forever, and then suddenly Ochiba had been pulling him out.

But he had been the bait.

The oni had seized Ochiba and hurled her much deeper into the light, into the blackness. It had kept her body for itself, and her soul as a prisoner for its amusement.

He remembered all of it now, and his gorge rose in terror at the thought of why the oni had let him return.

Ahead of him, the massive armored figure of Barako set foot on the shadowstone spiral, and began to climb. He followed.

The oni watched them, its Ochiba-face twisted in amusement. "*Are you coming of your own accord?*" It laughed again and leapt from one arc of the spiral to another. "*That is the bravery of ignorance, I think. This city was my prison. Now it will be yours, as it has become for so many of your kind before you. I can no longer remember what summoned me here. I was kept for an age of ages. Time enough to make Night's Hunger my own. The city answers to me. That you challenge us means your ignorance is wed to arrogance.*" The serpentine neck lunged in Barako's direction. "*I have not forgotten the debt of pain I owe you.*" It flexed its palm. Then its head weaved across the space to gaze at Haru. "*Welcome back, Kakeguchi Haru. It is time to return to your rightful place. It disappointed me to release you, but it was for an end that I will yet achieve, and your usefulness is at an end.*" It looked back at Barako. "*And you. You. Thank you for bringing me your face.*"

Barako burst into a sprinting charge, leaving Haru behind as she closed with the oni.

The oni fought silently. It rained attacks on Barako, its huge claws trying to smash the hammer from her grasp. She parried and lunged, driving the oni back, higher and higher on the spiral. The webbed confusion of the structure stabbed into the corner of her eyes and tried to seize her attention. It wanted her to lose her awareness in the contemplation of the endless twists. It was fighting her alongside the oni. She resisted. She kept her focus on the oni. Her passion for its destruction was absolute. The soul of her beloved was visible before her, and the path of her justice was unwavering.

The oni's silence made her think she was pressing it harder than it had expected. Then she blocked a biting lunge from the head, and saw that the monster was still grinning. She was so concentrated on blocking the next blow, and they were coming so fast, that it was only now she realized that the oni was attacking with only three of its arms. The fourth, the new one, reached over and over into the column of light. The hand plunged into the green blaze, and whenever it did, a blast of green shot back up the sorcerous chain that connected the oni to the soul of Ochiba. With every blast, the golden light spasmed in transcendent pain.

The oni saw the look on her face. "*Yes,*" it said. "*Now you see. Our duel means nothing to me here except amusement. I will strike you down and torture Ochiba at the same time. Now you have seen, and you are tortured in your turn. Around and around, the cycle of suffering, pain breeding pain. This is the hunger of the night, forever consuming, forever craving.*

Time you knelt before it."

Barako took a few quick steps back. She saw, but she pushed the understanding away. To understand was to bleed, and come closer to the edge of destruction.

But she saw all, and chose to focus only on what might be useful. When the oni reached into the light, it never reached far. Its hand never touched the dark light. Only the green.

The oni stalked toward her, and she backed up quickly again, out of the range of its attacks. She retreated a dozen more steps, resisting the squirm of the shadowstone beneath her feet. Then she stopped. She held herself motionless.

The oni snarled and lunged.

Barako was ready. The few seconds of rest had given her the chance to center herself, and to open herself to the void. The oni and its city embraced the death of time. Barako embraced the future in all its formless fluidity. The oni attacked as it had been attacking. It fell too easily into the patterns of repetition, because that was all there was in the City of Night's Hunger. Its blows were rapid and powerful. They could smash stone and strip away flesh. They encountered Barako's defense, and the defense was a lie. She deflected the worst of the blows, accepted the pain of the rest, and her parry was the first beginning of her attack. She struck as the void, flowing out of the present into the possibilities of the future, possibilities that coalesced into the certain moment of the hammer smashing into the oni's right shoulder. The unnatural flesh burned. The stolen bones beneath crumbled. The oni howled, its arm swung loose, and the connection between it and Ochiba flickered out.

The oni snarled. The jaw that had been Ochiba's dropped low and the monster roared its anger. Then it charged, hurling its full mass against Barako. She leaned into the attack, but it was like trying to stop a rockslide. The oni carried them both off the edge of the spiral. They plunged to the floor of the tower.

Before he could reach them, Barako and the oni fell past Haru. Barako struck the ground with a crash of heavy armor. She tried to rise, but the oni landed on its feet and attacked first. She had kept her hammer, and fought off the blows, but she could not rise.

The oni screamed in anger and triumph. It would not tire. She would.

Haru started down. He stopped after two steps. He saw what would happen. The oni's defeat of Barako was inevitable. Then his end would come. He knew how much help he would be.

Make the right decision. For once, choose the right path.

The only other path was up. Where Ochiba's soul writhed in torment.

Her agony is your fault. Her death is your fault. She died for nothing.

He saw the promise of redemption.

Haru sprinted up the spiral. He glanced down once at the struggle below. He needed time. If Barako fell in the next few seconds, all of them were lost. She was holding the oni off, though, and the horror was beginning to laugh again. It had its prey at bay, and was savoring her slow defeat.

So Haru ran. He threw himself into the embrace of the spiral, and it welcomed him. It flexed, and he rose higher, for it was built of the night and was hungry, and it hurried him to its center, where all was revealed and all was ended. Haru ran, and he laughed now. He laughed with joy. He saw the pattern of fate, and how it must be drawn, and how he would complete the pattern.

He reached the top, and sprinted ecstatically, with no hesitation, to where the spiral ended, at the horizon of the explosions of black light nestled within green, and the golden soul trapped within the black. As he reached the end and leapt, time stretched. The moments of the end multiplied. He had time to know and understand, and he laughed, now, finally, with gratitude. He leapt across the green limbo that waited to make him a prisoner again, crossed it because he had leapt for the finality of the black light. He did so of his own accord, with joy, because he did it out of love, for the sake of another love. He did it with joy, because he acted with true selflessness, for the family, for the clan, and for Rokugan. He did it with joy, because he knew he was acting with honor.

And in the multiplicity of fragments that hovered uncertainly between time and its absence, when he was of the world and touching the next one, Ochiba grasped him from inside the dark.

They became one.

The living samurai in his last moment of life, and the dead one crossing back through him to use the same final moment.

And strike.

• • •

Golden light blazed from above. Its bolt slammed into the back of the oni, and the creature of the Jigoku let out a scream of surprise and pain so huge that the shadowstone spiral trembled. It staggered away from Barako, off balance, and weaved backwards toward the column of light.

Barako rose. *Ochiba*, she thought. *Ochiba. Ochiba. Ochiba.* The name was her purpose and a blessing. "Lord Hida," she cried out, "grant her justice!" She burned with anger and sorrow and love, and she attacked with that fire. She struck as fire, her hammer hitting the oni from left and right, breaking its arms.

The oni hissed, and the monstrous distortion of Ochiba's head descended, teeth bared for Barako's throat.

Only she knew it was not Ochiba. The mockery could not work any longer, because Ochiba had been there with her, fought at her side one more time, been the lightning that precedes the thunder.

And Barako thrust the jade dagger into the oni's neck.

Purifying flames erupted from the wound. They consumed the flesh. They ate into the oni's material form. It flailed its broken limbs and tried to smash the dagger out of its body. It looked up from pain, and as Barako charged into it, ramming the oni with all her force, she saw fear in those inhuman eyes.

Finally. Finally. Fear.

She carried the oni backwards, and with the strength gathered to express the full immensity of her loss, she hurled the monster into the column of light. The oni fell through the green limbo, and into the black light of ending.

Its material flesh plunged into the dark energy of death.

Was it an explosion that blinded Barako? There was light, searing light that filled the world. But there was no sound, unless the concussion was so vast it could not be heard. Barako closed her eyes against the light, and she could still see it. The light banished time. She was suspended in the instant of destruction or creation. She did not know which.

The light did not fade. It simply ceased to be. She could see nothing, hear nothing, know nothing except the intensity. And then she was standing on the floor of the tower again. The pillar of light was gone. The oni was gone. Barako looked up. All the power that had filled the tower had vanished.

Ochiba was gone.

Barako could see because daylight was streaming in through the open doorway of the tower.

She blinked. She wavered, unsteady on her feet.

It is finished. The war is over.

All the emotions she had locked away now strained at their prison. She had to keep moving, or they would burst through all at once.

Haru lay in the center of the floor. He must have fallen the full height of the tower. His body was smashed, a limp bag of shattered bones. She crouched beside him, and looked at the joy on his face.

"I forgive you …" she started to say. She stopped, unsure whose forgiveness was needed.

In the open doorway, Doreni's body lay cut in two. "I hope you have found peace," she said. "We have brought justice to Night's Hunger. Striking Dawn is safe. And you fought well."

The words were weak, insufficient.

Barako walked out of the tower and into the awakened city.

It was late afternoon, as it should be. The eternal, immobile moon was gone. The clouds had parted, and no snow fell. The sun shone in the cold air over ruins that were just ruins now. They were dark, tainted, but they were no longer predators.

The only shadows were her own.

In the distance came the sound of human voices raised in rejoicing. Her company. The samurai would be on their way.

She would stand here and wait for them. She would have until then to keep the fellowship of loss.

ACKNOWLEDGMENTS

Writing this book has been an exciting pleasure for me, and I would like to say a few words of thanks to the people who made this such a great experience. So, thank you to Marc Gascoigne, Lottie Llewelyn-Wells, Nick Tyler, Anjuli Smith, and everyone at Aconyte Books for welcoming me into the fold. My goodness, this has been fun, and I can't wait for the next escapade. Special thanks to Lottie for having invited me to join the Aconyte party in the first place, and for her superb editorial stewardship of *Curse of Honor* from conception to final draft. It's a privilege to work with her, and to learn from her.

Thank you to Fantasy Flight Games for their guidance and for letting me play in their marvelous universe. In particular, thank you to Katrina Ostrander for her invaluable guidance and feedback.

And turning to home, thank you to my stepchildren, Kelan and Veronica. You keep me honest, keep me laughing, and keep me joyous.

Finally, thank you, always, *always*, to my wife and

partner, Margaux Watt. The happiness I have in imaginary worlds finds its source in the happiness we have in our joint adventure through the real one.

DISCOVER MORE NEW WORLDS

A brave few fight against the nightmarish, ancient evils striving to force their way into our realm, their only desire to consume the bright life of our world...
Welcome to Arkham Horror.

Explore a planet of infinite variety – wild science fantasy adventures on an impossible patch-work world of everything known (and unknown) in the universe, in the first explosive and hilarious KeyForge anthology.